SINGLE SPARK

N.Z. Komninos

COPYRIGHT

This is a work of fiction. Names, characters, places, and incidents are either the product of the author's imagination or are used fictitiously. Any resemblance to actual persons, living or dead, events, or locales is entirely coincidental.

For Niki, Ellie, & Marina

"The eyes of all future generations are upon you. And if you choose to fail us, I say – we will never forgive you."

Greta Thunberg
UN Climate Summit, New York, 23 September 2019

PROLOGUE

The outbreak took place in September 2022, somewhere in the Middle East. No one could trace it back to Patient Zero, and experts were stumped as to how the disease had appeared concurrently in several countries across the region.

At first, only a handful of people were infected. However, it was clear from the very beginning that the disease was nasty, and it immediately drew the attention of the World Health Organization. Two of its investigators scrambled to Geneva Airport to board a flight to Muscat in Oman where a patient was in the early stages of the disease. By the time they landed at their destination 11 hours later, the patient had expired. Though he wasn't the first, they called him Patient A.

They interviewed the grieving relatives and quickly discovered that two more members of the family were in urgent need of hospitalization. Meanwhile, a nurse who had attended to Patient A was coming down with the flu and everyone was afraid of the worst.

Within two weeks, more than half of the people who had come into contact with Patient A were sick, and within three weeks, twenty-three people had died from the virus in Muscat, thirty-five in Amman, twelve in Damascus, five in Doha, fourteen in Kuwait City and two in Riyadh. In total, fewer than one hundred people had died of the disease in early October, but the WHO was taking no chances.

Dr. Tarek Khoury, head of the WHO Middle East division, called an emergency summit to assess the situation. The data was still sketchy, but if confirmed, it was scary indeed.

First, about 50% of all the people who had been in contact with the affected were infected themselves. This could mean only one thing: that the virus was airborne.

Second, the disease was fatal in more than 15% of its cases, which was high enough, given the large number of people who contracted the disease.

Third, the incubation period was relatively long, about two weeks, which meant that the carriers of the virus could infect others without even knowing it. This was the most troubling fact because it meant that there were possibly hundreds, maybe even thousands of people who were already unknowingly infecting others.

The fourth characteristic that made this disease unique was the speed with which it killed the unlucky patients when it eventually broke. In extreme cases, death occurred within an hour of the first symptoms appearing.

By mid-October, the virus itself had been identified. It was the H7N9 mutation of the bird flu of 2009. During the previous outbreak of H1N1, the WHO had been heavily criticized for overreacting and, this time, they needed more proof that the situation was serious.

The Middle East was a very strange place for the virus to appear, and this prompted conspiracy theorists to suggest that it had been manufactured and spread by the West to finally put an end to the problems in the Middle East that had dominated global politics for years. This theory gained some ground, despite the West's frantic attempts to stop the virus from spreading in order to avoid a repeat of the 2020 pandemic.

By early November, the fatalities had reached over a thousand, and the WHO rushed to issue a global travel warning ahead of the 2022

Qatar Football World Cup, which was due to start that month. But it was too late. Millions of fans had booked their flights to Qatar, and there was no stopping them from flying out to support their teams.

Then, on November 7, the WHO pleaded with FIFA to cancel the games or move them elsewhere. Neither was possible. As the first World Cup ever to take place in the northern hemisphere winter, most other alternative venues, like those in Russia, the 2018 hosts, were ruled out due to the weather. There was not enough time and too much money at stake to cancel the games. FIFA had managed to keep the tournament in Qatar despite claims of corruption and construction worker abuse; they were not about to cancel due to some odd virus that the WHO was overreacting to, especially after the financial disaster brought about by the Euro 2020 postponement.

Failing to convince FIFA, the WHO turned to the governments of the participating countries. But they had already lost too much credibility after it had advised governments to spend billions on H1N1 vaccinations in 2008, which had later been deemed largely unnecessary. Plus, no government could take, let alone implement, this kind of decision at such a late stage.

Dr. Khoury flew to Washington to meet with the UN Secretary-General. In a rare joint appearance, they made a direct emotional appeal begging people not to fly to Qatar.

"Unfortunately, so soon after the coronavirus, we have another disease that we know so little about, growing as fast, and threatening the lives of so many. Please, do not ignore this," pleaded Dr. Khoury.

Following the plea, would-be travelling fans got into fights with their worried spouses and parents, and, as a result, many people cancelled their trip. The tickets went onto eBay and were quickly sold to bolder individuals who did not believe the WHO "propaganda". Dr. Khoury's plea that people should boycott the games altogether was missed by both buyers and sellers, who, for a hundred-odd dollars, sent their neighbors in their place to bring the virus back home.

So, when the World Cup started, the stadia were full. Perhaps not with the people who had originally bought tickets, but full nonetheless. The concept that abstaining was for the benefit of the World Health did not resonate with team fanatics. They would risk anything to be close to their national teams, from street fights with rival fans to mysterious Middle Eastern diseases.

To be fair, the number of infected individuals in Qatar at the start of the games was not large. But the constant movement of fans from one city to another, and from one venue to the next could only help the explosive spread of the virus.

In the first two weeks of the games, you could hardly find anyone showing any symptoms of the disease, and the media were already slamming the WHO for overreacting once again. But by the start of the quarter finals, several hundred fans were rushed to the local hospitals, complaining of flu-like symptoms. By that time, the teams that had not made it through the group stages were already on their way home, as were hundreds of thousands of their disappointed supporters. When the symptoms started, it was already too late. Their fellow airplane travelers, neighbors, family, friends were already exposed, faced with the odds of a 50% infection rate.

Despite the unfolding global crisis, the games were allowed to go on, and the situation went from bad to worse when some of the top players also got sick. Germany's star striker was rushed to the hospital, shortly followed by one of Italy's iconic players. At that point, the media frenzy changed direction, now slamming the WHO for not making greater efforts to stop this. FIFA was also blamed. Still, the semifinals had just ended, and FIFA decided that the final game should take place within closed doors and without fans.

The final, between England and Mexico, was on December 18, 2022. Both teams had surprised the bookies by making it to the final. Billions of people gathered around TV sets around the world to watch the final game, unexpectedly the most infamous football game ever to be played.

Then, in the twenty-seventh minute, the unthinkable happened. After being dominated by England, the Mexicans were finally on the attack. Ernesto Souza, the best Mexican forward who was leading the World Cup scoreboard, unleashed a powerful long-range shot from outside the penalty area, and England's goalie Hugh Knowles jumped into the top left corner to make an unbelievable save. He dropped to the ground, ball in hands, but never got up. Paramedics rushed in, and before long an ambulance drove onto the pitch. The cause of death was later known to be the H7N9 influenza strand.

Several English players dropped to the field, shocked, while the Mexicans were in disarray. The officials, not knowing how to handle the crisis, insisted that the game should continue, but neither side could summon the will to play with any enthusiasm, not in an empty stadium. So the game ended goalless, and so did extra time. When it got to penalties, the substitute English goalie remained motionless as one Mexican player after the next sent the ball deliberately wide, in protest. The English players did the same. After thirty penalties had been kicked but no goals scored, the referee consulted with the fourth official and stopped the game.

Eventually, both teams were disqualified, and third place Germany were once again crowned World Cup champions. In the meantime, the FIFA President and management team resigned. But none of this mattered. A billion people were watching a man, later known to have been infected with influenza, play for 27 minutes before collapsing and dying live on TV. The behavior of the England and Mexico teams following the incident only increased the impact of the story which remained the headline news of every newspaper, website and news bulletin around the world for several days.

Expert doctors appeared on every news channel across the globe, and tried to make sense of the mess. Quarantines were now being established in Qatar, but the virus had already travelled to thirty-two countries and from there to another fifty-five. This was the fastest ever outbreak of a major fatal disease, faster even than Covid-19, and while the numbers of the infected were still in the low thousands, the media spotlight on the World Cup created a worldwide frenzy. People cancelled travel plans and some refused to go to work or visit the supermarket. Christmas family reunions were called off, holiday sales stalled, companies revised quarterly earnings projections – frankly, the world was falling apart.

The WHO, now in full-blown panic itself, advised people to stay at home and not to get in contact with others. The goal was to reduce the probability of infecting others.

But people had jobs to go to, so the WHO was again ignored. People had grasped the severity of the situation, but each individual on their own was failing to take the personal responsibility needed to ensure that the outbreak was controlled. The difficulty in controlling the outbreak was a case study on the failure of the human race to think of and decide upon a collective action for the common good. A worldwide session of the UN General Assembly took place via a video link on Christmas Day so as to examine a possible military curfew, but no decision was reached. The world's politicians were similarly failing to deal with the speed of the developing crisis.

By the end of the year, the outbreak reached what experts identified as the point of no return. While the number of infected was still small, relatively speaking, and of the dead even smaller, the projections - now based on accurate data - showed that at least 1 billion people would be infected, and more than 150 million would die from the virus in 2023. The only hope was for a medical solution.

CHAPTER ONE
THE RECRUITMENT

3 years earlier

Cecilia stepped out of the elevator on the 77th floor, directly into her penthouse apartment, complete with an astonishing view of Central Park and the Midtown skyline. The Metropolitan Tower was over 30 years old and the 49th tallest building in New York. There were newer and probably more luxurious buildings that perhaps would have been more fitting for a young, nouveau riche entrepreneur. But Cecilia was not nouveau riche, and money, fame, and the 'good life' had never been her goals. She had never known poverty. She was the only child of an ultra-rich investment banker father whom she'd rarely seen growing up. She had never met her mother. She had no brothers or sisters or other family she knew of.

She grew up on the Upper East Side, and the penthouse suite she was now entering was not the result of her entrepreneurial success, but rather a gift from her father given to her when she had secured venture capital funding for her company. He had offered to invest in her firm directly, an offer which she had declined, determined to make it on her own. Instead, he bought her this apartment. Of course, a couple of million dollars of investment in her company then would now be worth

1

hundreds of millions, but David Stein was in no real need of more money. Plus, New York's real estate was not doing too badly either.

Cecilia sat in her favorite love seat, which was ideally positioned to provide the best possible view out of her floor to ceiling windows. She glanced over at the coffee table and saw her own face on the cover of Forbes magazine. She picked it up and flipped through, as she had done a few times in the past month. OK, fame was perhaps something she did care about, certainly more than money or the good life.

The Forbes story was as much about her, as it was about her business. Of course, you can't put a business on the cover, you need a face, especially if that face is a beautiful one, even if in a non-descript kind of way. Cecilia was neither tall nor short. She was not blonde, nor brunette; her straight hair was a natural light brown color. Perhaps her most intriguing feature was her eyes. She had green-gray eyes that tended to change color depending on the light, or even the clothes she wore. But what was most impressive about her eyes was her stare. You could tell immediately just from looking at her eyes that behind them was a seriously intelligent woman. She had an IQ of 185, and was a graduate of the MIT School of Engineering, breaking the trend of young, successful entrepreneurs being college dropouts. At just 33 years of age, Cecilia was one of only a few billionaire entrepreneurs to emerge from New York and not Silicon Valley.

Cecilia read the Forbes article again. A true depiction of her business, but missing the point entirely. Mindalikes was a social network that did more than just connect people. It brought them together in ways that were not previously possible. Using artificial intelligence and natural language recognition, the software behind Mindalikes recognized trends in the topics, language, tone, and words of its users, and intelligently brought people together to build like-minded communities. Unlike other social networks, Mindalikes charged a subscription fee, and millions of people paid for their chance to connect with other human beings just like them. Of course, as revenues grew, so did the interest of venture capitalists, who in the end achieved their goal of shifting focus to profits and away from Cecilia's vision.

Cecilia set the magazine back on the coffee table. Today was a good day, she thought. Today was the day that she had sold the company she founded just 7 years ago. Today was the first day of the rest of her life, and she was again free to do whatever she wanted. And, she had more than a billion dollars to do it with - 2.2 billion, according to Forbes magazine.

***

He was jogging alongside the Schuylkill River, having already covered a distance of some 8 miles, when he climbed the stairs onto the Walnut Street Bridge. As he turned to face downtown, the sun began to set behind him, casting the Philadelphia skyline in gold.

His first name was John, last name Walker. This always sparked conversations and jokes when he met new people, who tended to call him Johnny and ask if he was "Scotch". For him, it was a joke that had lost its humor many years ago, and he was never happy to hear it repeated. At one time, he considered changing his name altogether.

He ran all the way to Rittenhouse Square and entered a bar on the other side of the square. He was wearing shorts and a $10 GAP t-shirt. Heading straight to the restroom, he threw some water over his face, took a glance at the mirror, and then walked out toward the rear of the bar. He found his way to the back terrace where she was waiting for him.

"Hey, Sandy, sorry I'm late," he said, looking at his smartwatch.

"No problem. I kind of gathered you would be late, so I only just arrived myself. Beer?"

"Sure, hon," he said, picking up her beer and sipping it rather than ordering his own.

"How many miles did you run this time?" she asked. Taking a look at the training app on his Smartphone, he said, "8 miles, 753 yards."

"In kilometers?" she asked in her southern European accent.

"About 15km."

"That's quite far for a casual run."

"Yep," he said, taking another sip of beer.

They sat there in silence for a while. He caught his breath, and she ordered another beer. Sandy was a petite girl, aged 21, Swedish-Greek, raised in Athens and currently studying at the University of Pennsylvania. She had straight long blonde hair, which she usually wore in braids. She was wearing a summery dress that exposed her slender legs.

John was also a student at the university, a postgrad studying nanotechnology. He was not tall either, with dark hair and a perpetual tan. They had been flirting for a few weeks, but nothing had happened yet.

"So, how was your day?" she asked.

"Great! We had a breakthrough in our project."

"Awesome. What sort of breakthrough?"

"Well, it's difficult to explain. You wouldn't understand."

"Try me," she said, a little annoyed.

"OK. Well, you know how nanotechnology is all about making things smaller, right? Mobile phones, PCs, laptops, etc. Well, things are now becoming so small that we can barely see them. Even with microscopes. So, this is why, at the school, they've built this nanotechnology building where we can run experiments and see what we've built through special microscopes."

"I know all that," Sandy said, visibly impatient and beginning to feel sorry that she'd asked. John had a tendency to talk for hours about his research, and when he did, her thoughts would wander to other things they could be doing together…

"Anyway," he continued, "what we are trying to create is a device that is much smaller than a human cell that can track brain cancer cells and destroy them."

"I've read about that method of curing cancer. Sounds promising," she said looking away, and not really interested.

"Hey, babe, that's not the breakthrough. Today, we managed to attach our nano device to a brain cell."

"To a neuron? Really?" She asked, suddenly more interested.

"Exactly, yes," he said, excited and somewhat impressed by her question.

"So, does it attach itself to the neuron or the synapsis?" she asked, referring to the cable-like interfaces that allow brain cells, or neurons, to communicate with each other.

"Actually to the synapsis," he said, now very definitely impressed. He reminded himself that as a decision sciences student, Sandy, of course, had a base understanding of neuroscience. "We have reached a point where we can program a nano device to search, find, and attach itself to the synapsis of a neuron. We can even read the electrical signals."

"Sounds great, but scary at the same time," she replied.

"Great, yes, scary, no. Please don't tell me you're one of those gals who think the end of the world will come out of some new technological advancement?"

"Actually, I believe that the right technology in the wrong hands could be devastating. But I also think that's no reason to stop advancing," she added quickly when she saw in her mind all the wrong directions this conversation could be heading towards.

***

It was dark now and the view was even more magnificent. It had been a glorious day in more ways than one and she was growing restless, keen to set herself up for the day after. She sat down at her desk, a wooden antique type that felt out of place in this ultra-modern apartment. But it had been her father's desk and it was a personal gift from him. The fact that she had kept it for several years since his death showed that she was sentimental about some things … but not many.

She woke up her hibernating laptop, and immediately her screen displayed her Mindalikes page. Well, it wasn't exactly her page. She had created the page, alright, but under an alias, Charles Stern. She had chosen a male alias because what she wanted to get out of this page was something that throughout history had been dominated by men.

Having written a fair bit of the code for Mindalikes herself, she also knew how to manipulate it in order to achieve exactly what she needed. It had occurred to her that the day after would depend so much on the day before. But such was life, moving in circles and building from one experience to the next.

She quickly moved from the basic information page to the advanced settings and started typing in her keywords. She had them written down in a notebook but she didn't need it; she remembered them all by heart. After all, they had been all she had thought about for the past 6 months.

Mindalikes used keywords to identify patterns in posts in order to connect users with other people with the same interests. The more specific the keywords, the better the match. "Don't type 'music', type 'country music, Johnny Cash' to connect with people with the same passions," the 'how to' page of the website said.

And that was just what she did, entering keywords that were related only in her own mind: life, death, environment, sustainability, artificial intelligence, bio engineering, religion, and many more specific themes.

She sat back, looked at her screen, and pressed enter. The initial list would take hours to create and could be too large, including thousands of names filtered out of the 200 million Mindalikes users. She may have to do this in two steps, perhaps more.

Satisfied with her work, she shut down the laptop and went to bed.

***

She opened her eyes. It was still dark outside. She checked her alarm clock: 3:45. Too early! But she could not sleep anymore. She knew that 4 hours had already passed since she'd entered her keywords. More importantly, she knew that some of the queries she was depending on were scheduled to run between 3am and 4am EST, so they would be over in 15 minutes. That meant that in just a few minutes, the next stage of her plan was due to begin. In just 15 minutes, several people whom she had never met, had not even heard of before today, would have their lives changed forever. In just a few minutes, humankind would change its course.

***

Sandy was eager to finish her class today. Not because the class was boring, anything but. Psychology of Decisions was her favorite class. It was also not because she was due to meet (and flirt) with John afterwards. Actually, John had been away for a few days, on a trip to San Francisco to join some like-minded scholars from Stanford University.

Today was exciting for Sandy because she was due to meet a man with interests so close to her own. When the class finally ended, she exited the Annenberg Building and turned left toward the center of the campus. She walked briskly down Locust Walk, turned right and entered Houston Hall, a favorite student hangout. To the east side of the building was the Hall of Flags, a tall room with two floors, the upper one a balcony overlooking the lower. It was to this balcony that Sandy made her way, expecting to see her mystery friend.

She hadn't yet met him. They had exchanged a few messages online and arranged this meeting. So that she would recognize him, he had promised to leave a red rose on his table. She found that romantic, further fueling her excitement to meet this guy.

She looked around the hall; there were only a few people there. A group of loud students and a couple of loners at the far end, but both were women. Then she noticed that in one corner, there was a man. Even from a distance, she could see his sinister face. He did not look like he could be her friend, Charles. As she walked towards him, she noticed something strange about his face: a visible scar on his cheek, making him appear even more menacing. He looked more like a bouncer or a security guard than a man who was passionately interested in decisions and morality. She paused for a second, unsure how to proceed, and then noticed that the red rose that should have been on his table was actually set on that of one of the lone women. She looked vaguely familiar, but Sandy could not think of where they might have met. She walked towards her, and the woman turned to face Sandy with green-gray eyes and a strong, confident stare.

"Is this some kind of joke?" Sandy asked, affronted.

"Sandy, please, sit down," Cecilia said, her stare leaving no room for objections.

"Where's Charles?" Sandy asked, though she obeyed the stare and sat down.

"Charles isn't coming. In fact, Charles doesn't exist. He's just a figment of my imagination."

Sandy just looked at her, unable to think of anything to say. There was something very intriguing about the woman that sat in front of her, something she couldn't quite place her finger on. So, she just sat there, hoping for an explanation.

Cecilia pushed on: "Also, Johnny is not coming back", she said, clearly amused by the disbelieving reaction of her new acquaintance.

Shocked, Sandy managed to ask, "How do you know John? And, if you do know him, you must know he doesn't like to be called 'Johnny'".

Cecilia laughed an awkward laugh that did not help break any ice or remove any tension. "I do know," she said, "but now that he is one of mine, I can call him whatever I want." She spoke in a manner that sent chills down Sandy's backbone. "Johnny is now part of my team, a team of scientists gathered together to change the world."

Sandy was having trouble digesting what this woman was telling her. She needed more information, but Cecilia was not in any hurry. Sandy was the fifth person she had spoken to about this, and she knew by now to pace herself.

**

The first person Cecilia had approached had been a sustainability professor turned philosopher. She had not found Dr. Richard Bale through Mindalikes. She had known about him for many years; in fact, part of her current plan had been inspired by his ideas. Dr. Bale had inadvertently changed the course of history – no, he had saved humanity – and when she had met him the previous winter at the café overlooking the ice rink at the Natural History Museum in London, he hadn't even been aware of it.

Dr. Bale was British, a Cambridge professor in Environmental Science. He was pushing 60 and, unlike her other recruits, he was married with two children and a dog. Normally, she would consider parenthood a recruitment blocker, but with Dr. Bale it was different; she absolutely had to recruit him. He was essential to her plan, not so much to help implement it, but rather to inspire the rest of her recruits. For Dr. Bale had developed the theory, and it was her one purpose in life to put that theory into practice.

Unlike Sandy, Dr. Bale had been expecting to meet Cecilia Stein, and not her alias, Charles. In fact, she had needed the intrigue of her name, fortune, and success to persuade him to meet with her, as he was normally a private person. It had been his choice to meet her in a public place, and the Natural History Museum, a shrine to the theory of evolution, had seemed befitting of the conversation they were to have.

It had been Christmas time, and London was beautifully decorated as always. Children were ice skating below them, overtaken by the magic of the season. Dr. Bale had already been sitting at a table when she'd arrived. He had grey hair and had been wearing a mismatched ensemble of navy trousers, a white shirt, a brown jacket, and a cream bow tie.

"It's a huge pleasure to finally meet you, Dr. Bale," she'd said as she sat down. "I've read all of your work, and I'm a huge fan of your theory."

"It's always nice to meet a fan, Ms. Stein. I am, though, at a loss as to the urgency of this meeting," he had said.

"I understand. I'm going to tell you something that only a handful of people know. In the next three to four months, I plan to withdraw myself from Mindalikes. I would appreciate it if you could keep this information confidential."

"Of course, but now I am even more confused as to why we are meeting. I had assumed you wanted me to be some sort of advisor to your business."

"No, Dr. Bale, that's not it. But out of curiosity, would you have agreed to be an advisor if I had proposed it?" Cecilia asked, pleased to be able to employ the trick question that would determine the outcome of this meeting so early on in their conversation.

Dr. Bale had paused and, for a moment, Cecilia had wondered if he was going to give the wrong answer. But he hadn't. "No" he'd said, "I am not interested in taking on a position in the private sector. My only goal is to push forward with my ideas on sustainability."

She had smiled. Dr. Bale was everything she had expected, and more. It was not just what he said; it was how he said it, in a smooth, deep voice, though he spoke softly, so much so that she had to lean forward to hear him. Perhaps it was also his British accent, or the fact that he'd not once broken eye contact, but he spoke with conviction, and had come across as a man who knew what he wanted. It was just what she needed from him. The difficult part had been convincing him.

"Dr. Bale, I am looking to gather together a team of scientists to work on the implementation of your sustainability ideas," she'd said, watching carefully for his reaction.

Dr. Bale hadn't blinked, hadn't broken eye contact, and hadn't smiled. He'd been impossible to read. But the prospect of putting into practice his life's work had evidently been too tempting to dismiss her proposal. "What do you need me to do?" he'd asked.

CHAPTER TWO

THE TEAM

The first meeting was held at her apartment in New York. It was important to her to be in a private location and one that exuded power because what they were about to commence was the ultimate power game, though none of the participants knew this yet.

There were seven of them in total. Cecilia, Dr. Richard Bale, John(ny) Walker and Sandy Papas. Then there was Frank Connors, an artificial intelligence wizkid from Caltech, and Amir Levy, the robotics chief engineer hired out of ADS Systems, the leading Israeli drone manufacturer. Amir was already working in one of the most dynamic fields out there when Cecilia had approached him and offered twice his salary to join her. Amir had been her forth recruit and had caused her to break her rule of paying someone exorbitant amounts to join the team. She needed believers, not mercenaries, but she also needed the world's top talent, and the combination of keywords she'd entered into Mindalikes had made them hard to find.

After Cecilia, the most well-known and wealthy participant, and her final recruit, was Dr. Wayne Ross. In the first decade of the new millennium Dr. Ross had founded Curia, a biotech firm that soon became infamous for developing simple methodologies for cloning living creatures. A little younger than Dr. Bale, Wayne was still older than the rest of the group, but he did not look his age. This was perhaps down to his daily yoga, his pescatarian diet, or perhaps his long black hair tied in a ponytail, and black pearl earring. It could also be that he was single, with no kids.

Whatever it was, his looks showed no hint of his business or medical background. But he was leading his generation in both fields, and he'd made good money in 2013 when he'd sold Curia to a larger biotech company. He had been locked-in for another five years, but since 2018 he had been free to pursue new things, or to just relax and spend some of his millions. Yet, there he was, sitting here in Cecilia's living room, alert, and sizing up the other participants.

***

Cecilia was ready to begin her performance. And it really was a performance practiced many times in front of the mirror. The little intro she was about to give was meant to provide everyone with a small glimpse of her plan. Not her real plan, of course, no one else knew that one, but the initial phase, meant to bring everyone on board.

Sandy was sitting on the couch next to John. As one of the first recruits, John was already privy to some of the information he was about to hear. John had been amazed to be included in such an important group, and was visibly shivering in anticipation of Cecilia's speech. Wayne was sitting on the arm of the sofa, and wizkid Frank had crashed into Cecilia's favored love seat. Amir had turned a chair from the 12-seater dining table around to face Cecilia. And to her left, a couple of steps behind her, was Dr. Bale, in full English attire complete with a bowtie.

"Thank you all for joining me," Cecilia began. "I think you have all met each other now. I have taken great care and expended great effort building this team. Each of you has been hand-selected. You do not know this yet, but you all share much more than just a passion for your particular scientific field. You like the same music, support similar political ideologies, you all prefer flexible hours in your work and studies, but still, these tend to eat up all the hours in your day."

Everyone laughed. The ice had been broken. Just as she had planned.

"I'm not going to talk too much today. We'll be getting to know each other in the coming days and months. I want to now let Dr. Bale explain to you why we're here."

***

Dr. Bale was definitely the best dressed among the group. He too had practiced his speech, the last time in front of Cecilia. It had seemed to him like overkill for a renowned professor to practice a speech for an audience of six, but Cecilia had suggested it and he wasn't inclined to fight her on it.

"The planet will not survive another generation of human intervention."

It was not the first time Dr. Bale had made this bold statement. But it was the first time that it had elicited no reaction from the audience. Usually, even in groups of this size, there were climate change deniers, or just people who believed in the ills to come but not in the speed at which they would arrive. But not this group. In this instant, Bale understood the power of Mindalikes.

"Actually, Dr. Bale, with all due respect, the planet will still be here. It's just that life – certainly human life – may not exist."

"Quite right, Mr. Ross. If we want to be even more specific, both the planet and human life will exist in 25 years. My argument is not that the planet will not survive. Nor that all human life will vanish within a generation. What I am saying is that the next 25 years will determine whether human life, or indeed any form of life, will be possible on Earth for the next thousand years."

"Dr. Bale, I hear what you're saying, and I agree with your statement. But there are people who would consider it controversial, even a down-right lie. What do you say to them?" asked John, carefully. Everyone was being overly polite at the start of their new relationship.

"I meet deniers all the time," said Bale. "They will die alongside the rest of us."

Bale knew that this conversation was disturbing. He knew that their natural desire would be to believe that he was wrong. After all, were humans capable of having such a destructive effect on their planet?

So, he pressed on. "I would like to hear what you chaps think is the single biggest obstacle to sustainability?"

In this group of high-performers, there was no shortage of opinion.

Frank, eager to contribute, jumped in first and said, "Overconsumption of non-recyclable materials."

Dr. Bale nodded in a way that encouraged more ideas.

Wayne said, "The economics of things. Capitalism forces pricing to be set by demand and supply with no regard to sustainability."

It was a point with which everyone in the room visibly agreed, and Cecilia hid a secret smile.

"Very true," concurred Dr. Bale, but still he looked around for more ideas.

"Overpopulation," said Amir.

"Quite right. In what sense, Mr. Levy?"

"More people consume more," came the laconic reply. Amir did not look like someone who talked more than was necessary.

Bale nodded and looked around again. For a moment there was silence and it seemed nobody else was ready to offer another opinion. Dr. Bale cleared his throat, preparing to give his own view when Sandy jumped forward:

"The number of people is a huge problem, but the main problem is people's mindsets, their frame of mind, the way they think and make decisions," she said, leaning forward on the couch, totally engaged in the conversation.

Dr. Bale examined her closely. No one had known about his involvement before tonight, so no one could have done their research ahead of time. In fact, apart from John and Sandy, and of course Cecilia, no one had met before that evening.

What was this algorithm that had enabled Cecilia to find such smart recruits?

With this thought circling in his mind, Dr. Bale took a second to reply, during which time Sandy shrank back a bit, clearly doubting herself.

Then Dr. Bale smiled, and Sandy's relief was apparent.

"That is exactly right. Exactly right. Human beings are 'programmed' to make decisions that are mathematically guaranteed to lead to their own extinction." He paused for effect.

"They procreate in a world that is overpopulated. They over-consume when resources are depleted. They use fossil fuels, even though they have the technology to harness solar and wind power. Yes, some of them recycle, but that's more to make them feel better about themselves than a serious attempt to seriously tackle the problem of sustainability."

The initial pleasure that had shown on Sandy's face in response to being right quickly faded as Bale spoke, the grim reality wiping the smile off her face.

"The desire path!" interjected wizkid Frank. His eyes were electrified and Bale raised an eyebrow. Frank had a surprisingly deep voice that did not match his tall and super-slender frame. He didn't appear to eat much. And his unfortunate acne made him look no older than 19, which was OK, because he was actually no older than 19 years old. He was a senior already at Caltech, having skipped a couple of years in school.

Frank had used the name "wizkid" during his hacker days, back when he was 14 and a child prodigy. He had managed to expose a security gap in Google and for a brief moment, every query entered into Google from around the world would return the words "Wizkid rocks" as the result. This shocked everyone at Google, but not as much as it had shocked Frank, who quickly disabled his hack, sure he was heading for juvenile court. However, instead of pressing charges, Google had hired him for an internship and sponsored his studies at Caltech. This had been good news for Frank, who did not come from a privileged background. Indeed, his parents had separated years ago and he had been raised by his alcoholic father, who could not hold down a job for more than a few months at a time. When Cecilia met Frank, two months before, he was looking for ways to escape his sponsorship obligations. Google had already become too corporate for his liking, and Frank was still eager to change the world. He also needed some $100k to repay Google for his sponsorship. Cecilia had provided both.

Bale was impressed that Frank had made the connection to the 'desire path', let alone that a 19-year-old was even familiar with the concept. He let Frank elaborate.

"Depending on where you come from and where you want to go, it could be faster to just walk across a nice lawn, rather than around it," Frank continued. "If one person does this, it's OK. But if hundreds of people do this every day, they will eventually ruin the lawn, therefore creating what is known as the 'desire path'. Each decision made does not on its own have the ability to affect the quality of the lawn. It is the accumulation of all the decisions made by hundreds and thousands of people that make the difference. Unfortunately, we humans do not have what is called a collective intelligence. Each of us acts on our own."

"Isn't this why we have rules, regulations, and laws? So that we can fix this exact problem?" asked John.

Frank looked at John dismissively, as one college student to another.

"So you never break any rules or bend any laws?"

Bale let these thoughts sink in for a moment. Cecilia was watching him carefully.

"So," he said finally, "the problem of sustainability lies in the fact that humans make trillions of small decisions every day, not fully realizing that they are contributing as a whole to the destruction of the planet. Or, the problem is that perhaps, there are no rules and regulations to prevent them from making these decisions. But even if there were such laws, these trillions of decisions are totally unconnected, each one with such a miniscule impact on the environment that any intelligent human will be tempted to bend the rules for convenience."

No one spoke, and he continued, with a line taken directly from his rehearsed speech: "So if humans are incapable of changing their behavior and decisions, there is only one viable path toward sustainability."

Everybody was now hanging onto his every word, even Cecilia, who knew the answer.

***

The evening was coming to a close, and Cecilia stood up to make a closing statement.

"Before we try to find a way to protect our planet, before we find a way to create a more sustainable future for all of us, we need to agree on one thing. This quest – this project – will provide a unique and unparalleled sense of purpose for each and every member of this team. I invite you all to join me in changing the world – no, *saving* the world. I have the means to make this happen. And with Bale here, I know the way. All I need is the team. You have all been carefully selected. If you think you can contribute, I can promise a life of purpose, the very highest purpose in human history.

If you think you can buy into this vision, can trust me and your fellow chosen ones, then I invite you to take a week off and follow me on a global induction tour."

Cecilia paused and gauged the reactions. Sandy and John exchanged looks of excitement. Amir just sat there, expressionless. Wayne rolled his eyes.

"What exactly is the purpose of this tour?" he asked.

"We will make several stops to witness first-hand some of the world's great miseries, and visit some of the sites where the worst atrocities against humanity and the planet have occurred. We will also visit some places that have brought out the best in humans, and observe some of mankind's best efforts to reverse the current environmental trends. But the purpose of the trip is not to see things that we already know. We will travel together to get to know each other and bond."

But Wayne pressed on, "Do we need to take this trip to make that happen? Could we not achieve the same thing here?"

"The trip is a prerequisite to joining the team. And joining the team is a prerequisite to joining the cause. However, if at the end of this trip, you are still not convinced, then you can drop out. On the other hand, if in your heart you are fully on board, then I will make it worthwhile for you to drop whatever you are doing to join the cause. Fair?" she asked, looking at Wayne, who reluctantly nodded.

She privately wondered if Mindalikes had made a mistake with him.

***

Wayne let the matter lie, but he was worried that the trip would be a huge waste of time, and he didn't appreciate Cecilia's mystique. He wanted to know where he was going, and why. On the other hand, he could see that the younger of his new buddies were excited at the prospect of a round the world trip, except perhaps that Israeli fellow, who was difficult to read. Wayne did not have too much else to do these days so, what the hell, he thought, let's try it out.

"I can only tell you that during the next eight or so days, we will analyze the causes of the great miseries of the world, and make projections regarding the future of the planet," concluded Cecilia.

He couldn't stop himself. "Are we qualified to make this assessment," Wayne asked. "Should we not have a political scientist or an economist on board to support the discussions?"

"A political scientist can only identify the problems. An economist can only analyze the current situation using current paradigms. We are here to find a solution," Cecilia replied shortly, her tone final.

CHAPTER THREE

THE INDUCTION

They met the following afternoon at Teterboro Airport. Everyone was there. On the tarmac was Cecilia's own brand-new Gulfstream G650 private jet. As Sandy and Johnny walked towards the plane, excited for their first-ever private flight, Sandy whispered into his ear: "I could really get used to this."

As they sat on the bunk seats, glasses of champagne in hand, wizkid Frank checked out the plane on his smartphone.

"The Gulfstream G650 is the latest private jet plane and fits 18 passengers - though I can see we have the executive version, with just 10 seats. More space for us. Plus, we can turn the seats in any direction we like, forward, backward, sideways," he said, while trying the feature out.

Cecilia walked onto the plane and announced that everyone would need to surrender their cell phones. There was some grumbling as, one by one, the team switched off their phones and handed them to Cecilia. As they had been warned, no one declined. Cecilia took the bag of cell phones and entered the cockpit. She emerged five minutes later, a look of satisfaction on her face.

"This is the most important part of your induction. After this trip, you will either be 100% converted to our cause, or I will give you an incentive to quit early," she said, glancing briefly toward Amir, who looked away. He had certainly been convinced by the money, but by now he was also intrigued to find out more. At 35, he was bald and slightly chubby, not what you'd typically consider good-looking. An introvert by nature, he did not win people over with his personality either. But what he lacked in looks and charm, he certainly made up for in intelligence, though he occasionally came across as arrogant.

Before talking off, Sandy went to the back of the airplane to visit the restroom. When she opened the door, she came face to face with a man she thought she had seen before. He was at least six-foot tall, well-built, and had a rough face with a big scar running down his cheek. "Excuse me ma'am," he said in an accent that immediately revealed his Slavic background to the Greek girl.

As she returned to her seat, Sandy thought about this brief encounter. Most likely, the Slav had travelled with them in the cockpit. Perhaps he was their pilot, she thought, intrigued.

***

Sandy had drifted into a troubled slumber when she was woken with a start as the plane touched down. She looked out of her window and it was still dark. The mystery Slav was disembarking. She considered the events of the last few days that had led her to be here on this private trip. She still could not believe it. How had she got here? Where were they now? Where was she going?

Sandy was an orphan. Her young Swedish mother had met her middle-aged father in the nineties at a bar in Mykonos. They fell in love and, soon enough, Sandy's mother fell pregnant. They never did marry, and her mother had died while giving birth to her. An aggressive form of pancreatic cancer had taken her father's life just a year later. Her mother's family disowned her, as if it were her fault that her mother had died. Her father had no family to take care of her, so she had been taken into the care of a charity foundation. There, she met one of its most wealthy contributors, who took her under her wing.

Nelly Roussakis was the daughter and heir of the largest commercial shipping empire in the world, but she spent more time working with charities than running the business, which was her brother's job. She hadn't exactly adopted Sandy, but she'd made sure she was taken care of. With Nelly's support, Sandy had gone on to attend a great private school, where she was an exceptional student and hence won a scholarship to attend any US university she chose. She applied to seven and was accepted by three. Of the three, Penn was the only Ivy League, and by far the most prestigious, so that was where she chose to go. With her scholarship, she no longer needed the financial support of her guardian, and when she turned eighteen, she was able to sell a piece of property she had inherited from her father. She was now financially independent, and was only loosely in touch with her benefactor.

This meant that taking a year off from college would be entirely her own decision. She hadn't expected that she would do so but as the trip unfolded, she felt it was becoming more and more likely.

The mystery Slav man re-boarded the plane and entered the cockpit. The plane had just refueled, and then took off again with its destination still unknown. She would never know where they had landed. She closed her eyes and went back to sleep.

***

When Wayne woke up, they were still in the air, and he had no idea what time of the day it was. But breakfast was served and the sun was up, so it must have been morning. Cecilia was standing up, getting ready to present what looked like a slide show. A 55-inch LED screen had materialized out of nowhere and was now separating them from the cockpit. It seemed unlikely that they were about to watch a movie – it wasn't that type of flight. But it wasn't a slide show either. As the image came onto the screen, they saw the big blue ocean and some sort of manmade structure. The image had clearly been taken from above. An oil platform? Wayne wondered. Visiting an oil platform, or maybe even an oil spill, would certainly seem to fit the pattern of the trip.

Cecilia then said, "This plane has been fitted with military-grade cameras, the type used by drones. We are flying directly over the image that you see at the moment."

"But what is it?" asked Amir.

"An oil platform, no doubt," replied Wayne, now totally convinced.

"Not really," was Cecilia's surprising reply.

They stared at the image a little longer. Cecilia pressed a button on a remote control and zoomed out. The 'platform' grew smaller and, further away, they now began to see what looked like giant white pipes, creating a rectangular shape stretching several miles around the platform.

"Where are we?" asked Frank.

"We are midway between California and Hawaii."

"I know what this is. It's the Great Pacific Garbage Patch," Frank said. "Apparently all kinds of plastic collect here due to the currents."

"Do you see any garbage?" asked Sandy.

"You won't see any garbage here," replied Cecilia. "But Frank is right, all types of marine garbage and plastic gather around here, trapped by the currents of the North Pacific Gyre. By some estimates, 5 trillion pieces of plastic currently litter the ocean. Plastic photodegrades, which means that it disintegrates into smaller and smaller pieces without changing its composition. In the process, some plastics release toxic chemicals."

"So, what are we looking at?" asked Sandy. The image on the screen had once again zoomed into the platform.

"This is the largest ocean cleanup project in the world," came Cecilia's cheerful reply. "Fellow entrepreneurs started this project years ago, and they approached me for funding and support. The concept is that you can use the ocean's currents to gather small plastic particles if you position your 'net', so to speak, in the right place. This is their pilot project."

"This is awesome," said John. "You see, no matter how much damage we do in the world, there is always hope for a technological solution that can reverse things."

"That's not true," said Bale, in a professor-like tone. "We can use technology to minimize the impact of destruction. But we cannot reverse the human impact as we are now way past that tipping point.

"Then governments need to regulate against pollution," said Amir.

"Solving this will require much more than government intervention," Sandy said, jumping in. She paused, saw that everyone was expecting her to continue, and so she did. "The source of this waste is not one person, or even a group of people. This debris is coming from billions of sources, and it is caused by negligence, among other things," Sandy finished.

"So, governments need to ban plastic. This is already happening," replied Amir.

"But that's just not a realistic enough solution. Banning all plastic is simply not possible," retorted Wayne, a pragmatist, thinking of all the medical applications of polymer.

"I don't care how impossible a solution sounds," declared Cecilia. "This problem needs a solution. Ocean acidification and waste alone could destroy the earth, even before CO_2 and climate change take their toll. If the solution is to ban plastic, we must find a way to impose it. If it is to convince people to be more careful, to recycle, for example, then that's what we need to do."

Looking at the screen, Wayne couldn't ignore the irony that on this carbon-fuelled trip, they were contributing to the very problem they were trying to solve. But the feeling of flying directly overhead an ocean garbage dump was certainly having an effect; it was much more intense and impactful than seeing the same images on video from home.

"But how?" asked Wayne, beginning to worry that Cecilia was nothing more than a tree-hugging idealist who thought that the world could be changed with words. "I agree with Sandy," he continued. "Plastic pollution in the ocean is a different problem to, for example, deforestation. They have different root causes, and will need different solutions."

"No, we need to find one solution for it all," came Cecilia's cryptic reply.

***

When they started their descent, there was no land to be seen anywhere. A second before they touched down, a runway appeared as if from nowhere beneath them and out of their windows they could see paradise.

Tropical sands. Light blue seas. Underdeveloped.

The door opened and warm air flooded the airplane, filling the team with cheerful enthusiasm. Only Wayne was skeptical. After spending a couple of days with Cecilia, he knew there had to be a catch. She would not have brought them here for a tropical holiday. Then it dawned on him.

"Is this the Bikini Island?"

"It most certainly is," Sandy replied, laughing, thinking Wayne was joking.

"Bikini atoll to be precise," Cecilia confirmed, her tone more serious.

"What's Bikini atoll?" Frank asked, half hoping it was a place with many girls wearing Bikinis.

"After the Second World War, the US conducted dozens of nuclear tests on this island," Wayne explained.

"Twenty-three tests between 1946 and 1958, to be exact," Cecilia explained. "Some 42 mega tons of nuclear explosive have been detonated on the ground, in the air, underground, and underwater. This is 10 times the total explosives used during WWII."

"So, what are we doing in this place? Let's get out of here," said Frank, and some of the others, looking slightly unnerved, appeared to share his feelings.

"Relax. We're only here to do some deep-diving," Cecilia said, smiling.

***

They disembarked and were met by Ed, who Cecilia explained was one of six people currently living on the atoll. Ed was old, though it was tough to tell just how old, as he looked 75 but he moved like he was 55. Ed's job was to help the U.S. Department of Energy with soil monitoring, testing cleanup methods, and mapping the wrecks in the coral reef.

They walked to a small pier where Ed showed them 'The Nuke', a small submergible vehicle, the kind used for deep-water explorations.

"You gotta be kiddin' me," said John when he saw the small tin can and understood that he was supposed to get inside. The Nuke could fit six people plus the driver, so Sandy sat on John's lap. As they went underwater, the team began to relax.

"Water is a great insulator of radiation," Ed explained. "In fact, they use water in nuclear power stations." They were in deep water now, drifting alongside an impressive coral reef.

"Great," said John, "but what are we supposed to be looking at?" not seeing any signs of a huge explosion. In fact, he was surprised to see some astonishing underwater life, full of colors. A shark suddenly appeared out of nowhere, and for a moment, he was concerned that he would soon be part of a scene from the '80s movie 'Jaws'. In a split second, the shark disappeared.

"What do you see, John?" Dr. Bale asked

"I see... life. Not what I expected."

"Remember, the tests stopped in 1958, so nature has had plenty of time to recover. But the point is, it hasn't recovered fully. It will never truly recover."

"Why would anyone choose this paradise to test the deadliest devices ever created by man? Who would endanger such a beautiful ecosystem?" asked Wayne, mesmerized by the astonishing underwater life that he saw, rich in color and texture.

"We can't judge them, sir," said Ed in a deep southern accent. "They had only just escaped the chaos of the Second World War. Them Russians were developing their own nukes. Damn things needed to be tested somewhere."

"Of course we can judge them, Ed," Cecilia replied. "These decisions were taken by politicians in the name of ordinary Americans. They didn't even tell us."

The conversation had taken over, and they were no longer paying close attention to the scenery outside the windows. Suddenly there was a jolt, as if the submergible had hit a rock. Instinctively, they all turned to face the outside. Through the large rectangular windows, a large manmade structure appeared before them.

"What the fuck," said John, struggling to see ahead from behind Sandy.

"Yep," concurred Ed. "Now you can see the kind of damage these motherfuckers can do."

Sitting upright on the ocean floor was a large ship. As they moved closer, they could see that this was no ordinary ship.

"It's a bloody aircraft carrier!" exclaimed Bale.

"Meet USS Saratoga," said Ed. "It sunk as a result of the blast from the Baker nuclear test, a 23-kiloton bomb named Helen of Bikini. The Americans intentionally placed the carrier in the lagoon, close to the blast, to see the effect the bomb had on the fleet. Two more ships and four submarines were also destroyed. One of them, the LSM-60 amphibious, was never found, presumably vaporized by the nuclear blast."

"Why would they do this?" asked Sandy.

"The tests took place in 1946, just a few years after Pearl Harbor. The Americans wanted to see what would happen if a nuke was dropped in the harbor, presumably in World War III," Ed replied in a matter of fact way.

"Did they really have any doubts?" asked Frank.

"Well, they certainly didn't after this," joked John.

They were now moving parallel to the flight deck of the aircraft carrier. Cecilia glanced back and was visibly pleased to see the awestruck looks on the team's faces.

Ed continued his tour. "When the blast hit, the Saratoga was some 400 yards away. Legend has it that it was lifted from the sea before landing again on water and sinking. Think about it. This ship weighs some 37,000 tons. And the blast lifted its whole length – that's 900 feet," he said in a well-rehearsed speech he'd probably repeated before to the rare visitors to the atoll.

"Unbelievable," was all Amir was able to say.

They reached the end of the flight deck, and the nuke dove deeper and swerved around so that they could all take in the massive upright bow of the ship. On the ocean floor, they came across a couple of fighter planes.

"Helldivers," said Ed, "the Curtiss SB2C dive bomber that the US produced during World War II. They were probably knocked off the flight deck during the blast. The name 'Helldiver' certainly takes on a different meaning from this perspective," he joked, but no one in the team was much in the mood for laughter.

***

They were all thankful to be back above water, this time on the main island of the atoll. They were all famished, and Ed had promised them a barbeque. Wayne once again noted the irony of having a barbeque atop an atoll where forty plus megatons of fire had been unleashed some fifty years ago. He also knew that most probably, some of the residual radiation would contaminate their meal. As a doctor, he wasn't worried –

he knew that only long-term exposure to small doses would damage one's health.

As he prepared the charcoal fire, Ed told them about his life on the atoll. It hosted only five other people on the atoll, and they got along well. Their circumstances did not allow otherwise. They needed to work together, on separate tasks, making sure each played their part. Of course, if things got tough, especially during storms, they could count on the other Marshall Islands for support, but most days of the year, they were completely on their own. There was Ed's younger sister, Elsa, and her 20-something son, Freddie. Elsa's husband George had passed away some years ago. Cancer, most likely caused by radiation, but they couldn't be sure. Fred wasn't going to stick around the island much longer, Ed thought. It was no place for young people. The other three residents were an old couple from the capital of the Marshall Islands, Majuro, who, surprisingly, had decided to retire on Bikini Atoll, and Ed's oldest friend, Sam, who had just joined them to help with the cooking.

Ed told them how most mornings Sam went fishing, and that the sea was their main source of food. They were worried about long-term exposure to radiation working its way through the food chain, "But at least we're not breathing in all those emissions from cars, in the cities you live in," Ed reasoned.

Lunch was charcoal-grilled shark fillet. Shark fishing was actually illegal in the Marshall Islands, which was home to the world's largest shark sanctuary, established in 2012. Apparently, Ed thought that these laws did not apply to the inhabitants of Bikini Atoll. There was also some perfectly legal tuna sashimi, but most of the team stayed clear of it, mistakenly thinking that cooked food was less likely to retain radiation.

"We don't get many visitors around here." Ed continued to chat away, clearly delighted to host guests. "Sometimes we get scuba divers, wanting to dive where them atom bombs were detonated. Once a year, a scientist from the US government is sent here to gather data and make sure I'm doing my job right, but we've never had a bunch like y'all come to stay for less than a day. Why are you here?" he asked.

"We're looking for a solution to the problem of humanity," Cecilia told him, bluntly.

***

After lunch, they had some free time. Cecilia pulled out her laptop and immediately started typing. Bale found a hammock and closed his eyes. Wayne, Frank and Amir decided to go skinny dipping on the south side of the island. Sandy preferred to stay above water. After eating shark for lunch, she preferred not to expose herself in case any of its buddies harbored vengeful tendencies.

Instead, John and Sandy strolled across the atoll, taking in the breathtaking beauty, the turquoise waters, and the distant horizon. They reached a beach on the north side, far away from the others. There was a 30-foot drop from the edge of the atoll to the beach, creating a feeling of seclusion. They were literally in the middle of nowhere, a godforsaken place. But for the first time in her life, Sandy felt that she was exactly where she ought to be.

She was seeing new places, learning new things, interacting with ultra-intelligent people. For a moment, she had wondered what she was doing being part of this group but she quickly dismissed the self-doubts in order to seize the moment.

She let a scream out and the echo returned from the surrounding cliffs before it was drowned by the sound of the waves hitting the shoreline. She started running and John followed her before they both fell onto the sand, side by side, laughing. John then rolled over her and gave her that long-overdue kiss. They looked around and there was no soul in sight.

So, they continued kissing, and were soon pulling off each other's clothes. They were both burning with desire. Within seconds, they were rolling around in the sand, making passionate love. It didn't last long, as they were both super excited. Perhaps it was the fact that they were in the middle of nowhere or the feeling that they might just change the world. Whatever it was, Sandy could not remember ever having a sexual experience as intense.

***

They remained on the island until a little after sunset. As the sky turned dark orange, they reluctantly boarded the plane for the next leg of their trip. Cecilia told them it would only take four hours to get to their next destination – it seemed impossible that anything could be that close.

By now, they had completely messed up their sleeping clocks.

Cecilia told them that they would be sleeping in a hotel tonight, which was a big relief to all of them. Knowing that they would picture a 5-star hotel, Cecilia smiled inwardly.

CHAPTER FOUR

SHARING

For the first time on the trip, the plane encountered some severe turbulence on their descent. No one was scared of flying, but apart from Cecilia, no one had experienced turbulence in a Gulfstream before. It was not a pleasant experience.

Amir, in particular, was caught off guard. He wondered if anyone in Israel would ever find out if one of its citizens died in a private plane crash on the other side of the world. Not that anyone would really miss him. Of course, there would be those who would wonder how he'd disappeared, but Amir did not have any close friends. Assuming that they survived the trip, this group of people, this team, could be his salvation.

Suddenly there was a loud thump, and the plane touched down. Everyone looked out the windows, but it was pouring with rain and the view was obscured. The rain was heavy. Really heavy.

Cecilia had still not disclosed where they were. They ran from the plane to a Hyundai van parked about 10 feet away and still got soaked. They were all looking forward to arriving at the hotel and a nice bed.

As the van drove through the streets, they could see that they were in a very poor country. The road was not well paved and there were holes in the ground, now filled with water.

"So anyone wanna guess where we are?" asked Cecilia.

"North Korea?" joked John, though he could not dismiss the possibility.

But Cecilia laughed and everybody relaxed. "I wish," she said. "NK would have been a great destination for this trip, but even I couldn't pull that off."

"So, where are we?" asked Bale.

"Papua New Guinea," Cecilia replied. "We are here to witness what happens when people refuse to share."

***

The ride to their hotel took almost an hour, and with each passing minute, their hopes of arriving at a 5-star hotel were fading away. This was no tourist destination. You could tell from the tiny airport, the lack of commercial airlines, the roads, the complete absence of any restaurants. The rain made it all more miserable and collectively they thought about Bikini Atoll and how they would rather have spent the night there.

But this was not their trip. This was Cecilia's trip. They were just following her, lured by the promise of a renewed sense of purpose, with each step falling deeper into the trap she had so masterfully set to get them to buy into her vision.

The Seeadler Hotel was certainly not a five-star hotel. Had it been in the USA, it would have been at best a non-rated highway motel off an interstate somewhere. Each room had its own door leading directly to the road in front.

Sandy thought that her room was surprisingly decent considering the horrific exterior of the hotel. She had half expected to sleep with cockroaches or to share a filthy bathroom, but this was thankfully not the case. Still, the rain and the shabby environment made her feel uneasy in this strange place.

*****

The rain continued through the night and at times it became a thunderstorm. The team was exhausted, having spent many hours on the plane, and all of them slept through the night. Only Cecilia suffered from her usual insomnia. At two in the morning, she got up, picked up her mobile phone and made a call. Fifty minutes later, there was a muted knock on her door. She opened it and let the man into her room. "Sometimes, we just need to succumb to our programming," she said, as she unbuttoned the shirt of the man with the scar.

*****

In the morning, the Slav man was nowhere to be seen. The rain had died down and the sun was shining. It was a pleasant 25 degrees, apparently a bit cold for this time of year. After breakfast, the group walked to the beach, which they were surprised to discover was only a couple of hundred yards from the hotel. But today, they weren't going swimming or diving. The 200-horsepower engine propelled their speedboat to 50knots, cruising them to their next destination.

*****

The Manus Island Detention Center was an Australian run operation. In 2012, Australia opted to pay Papua New Guinea to host refugees that had been turned away on their journey towards the new continent. In 2017, following public outcry, the center was closed.

The speed boat approached the center, slowed down, and reached a small dock. They disembarked and took a walk amidst the temporary structures in the form of old containers – the type carried on container ships – which were stacked into two-storey buildings, each one making a separate apartment. Makeshift metal stairs had been built to reach the 'apartments' on the upper floor.

Barbed wire surrounding the camp had prevented the refugees from fleeing, not that they had any desire to do so, as Papua New Guinea was not exactly the land of promise they had been seeking. Cecilia told the team that about one thousand people had once been held in this detention center, and most of them had been there for more than three years. What had been meant to be a temporary arrangement until governments found a longer-term solution for these people had in reality become permanent incarceration. Yet the average Australian had just been happy that these people were not on Australian soil. Thankfully, sense had finally prevailed.

They climbed up a set of stairs towards one of the upper floor homes. The strong smell was the first thing that Bale noticed as he entered what had been a home that once hosted who knows how many people. It had been abandoned for 2 years and it was filthy, but he could still feel the presence of the people who had spent a good chunk of their lives here, as they were attempting to find their way towards a better life.

As he walked towards the back of the two by ten structure, he saw something underneath one of the makeshift beds. He knelt, reached in, and pulled out a stuffed toy. Bale did not consider himself an overly sentimental guy. But you had to be absolutely heartless not to be overcome with emotion at the sight of this toy, the evidence that a family had once lived here, this toy bringing joy and comfort to a child being raised in a world that Bale did not recognize and did not want to be associated with.

*****

They returned to their luxurious speedboat and moved about 100 yards out to sea before stopping to observe the center from a distance. Then John said, "I don't get it. Australia is, by land, probably the largest country in the world. And by population, they are – what – 15, 20 million? Smaller than New York City. Why would so few people with so much land not share some of it with these poor refugees? Instead they've chosen to pay another, poorer country to host them?"

Bale picked up on this point. "The global refugee crisis is a clear example of people's reluctance to share. Unfortunately, it's only going to get worse when climate change disasters displace millions of people."

"On the other hand, though," Amir countered, "I do understand that you can't just open the doors for all these people to come in, because then hundreds of thousands, maybe millions will make their way to your land." He had unconsciously emphasized the word 'your'.

For Amir, the argument was clear. You want controlled immigration so that you're able to assimilate the incoming population, give them jobs, and give them the opportunity to build their lives. But the more you take in, the less likely it is that you'd be able to provide for them, and the more likely it is that they would become criminals, even terrorists, demanding from you what is rightfully yours.

"There is always a security risk," said Sandy.

Wayne was immediately dismissive, "Oh please, let's not re-hash the same old argument that jihadists are mixed in with Syrian refugees. So, what's the solution? Let two million women and children die in order to protect ourselves from a handful of extremists?"

"Of course not!" Sandy exclaimed, defensive, "but it is a concern that Australians might have had. I know Israel is worried about it."

"If you want my opinion, Israel is overreacting," said Wayne.

There was a brief moment of silence as everyone looked toward Amir, who was now flushed with anger. "That's easy for you to say. You didn't have someone close to you killed."

"So, you know someone who knows someone who knows a guy who was killed in a random terrorist act. More people die in the USA from psycho mass shootings. Tell me, who was it?" Wayne asked, challenging Amir.

"My parents," Amir was tempted to say, but didn't. Two suicide bombers had taken the lives of Amir's parents at the 2003 central bus station massacre in Tel Aviv. He had been 20 at the time, still a student at the University. But he did not want to bring his personal story into this conversation, not now. He would have stood up and left, had they not been surrounded by shark-infested waters.

Bale had also noticed that the boat was a restricted space for a conversation like this. No one could storm out of the room, banging the door behind them. It was impeccable planning by Cecilia, who'd clearly left nothing to chance.

***

Cecilia noticed the tension and decided to step in. "Guys, we set out to solve problems and this is a particularly difficult one. It's part of human nature to care first for your own kind, and then for humankind, or nature. Any attempts to achieve sustainability will need to take this simple fact into account."

"So," John said, "The challenge is, how do we change human nature so that we are less selfish and able to share more? I guess you could try to do it over a generation, by teaching your kids different values than your own?"

"The planet will not survive another generation," Bale reminded them.

Cecilia threw an encouraging look at Bale, prompting him to carry the fight forward.

"So, on the issue of sharing, how is our group any different from the average Australian? Here we are, top of our fields, ambitious to reach ever greater heights, taking a carbon-heavy trip in the company of a billionaire, claiming to be searching for solutions to mankind's most fundamental problems. Who are we to judge others?"

He paused for effect. No one dared to speak. Cecilia, interestingly, did not look the least bit annoyed. Bale had just stabbed everyone in the belly, and he was about to start twisting the knife in all directions, to make the wound all the more painful.

"Tell us, Wayne, did you discover any drugs capable of curing third world diseases? And did you offer that medication to those in need but without any means to pay for it? And you, Johnny, you are playing with technology that could destroy us all, depending on how it's used. Hiding behind the claim that it's not the technology itself but the way it's used that could have dire consequences, like the US politician claiming that it's not the guns that are the problem, but the 'psychos' who use them to kill others. Amir, you're building drones that you know are being used for military purposes so that humans can send machines to kill other humans. How do you justify that?" Frank and Sandy were looking at the beautiful sea around them, hoping that Bale would skip over them, but had no such luck.

"Frank, we know that your involvement in Anonymous, the group of cyber terrorists, has never been proven. But we also know it to be true." Frank suppressed a smile. "Did you hack those systems out of curiosity? Was your aim to do something good? And Sandy, you might think you're more righteous, but here you are, travelling with the rest of us around the world, not believing your own luck, when refugees like these are being held in your country in even more atrocious conditions, right this moment.

Sandy looked up, incredulous at this attack. Unlike the others, she objected. "What am I supposed to do?" she asked, "fix all the world's problems? Feel guilty for looking after my own well-being? How about you, Cecilia. You made billions from your business and, unlike other entrepreneurs, I haven't heard you committing any part of your fortune to good causes. Instead, here we are, happily spending that fortune on a self-indulgent, unproductive holiday," she blurted out, and then sat back down, half expecting to be immediately expelled from this group and sent back home for having the audacity to challenge the host and her sidekick.

But it wasn't that type of group. There was no James Bond style 'eject' button that could be pressed to throw her to the sharks. Instead, and surprisingly, Cecilia seemed quite happy that the conversation had turned back to her.

She spoke softly, looking directly at Sandy. "You're right. I haven't committed any funds yet to try and solve any one particular problem, for exactly the same reason that you're not sitting at home trying to save a handful of refugees off the beaches of Lesbos. I don't want to cure the symptoms. I have committed to spend my fortune trying to find and implement a solution to the overriding problem of our world. The mother of all problems."

CHAPTER FIVE

HUMAN NATURE

The plane took off and within minutes they were able to see the early afternoon sun again. Everyone was happy to be out of Papua New Guinea, a place most of them would rather not visit again. They were reaching the point of exhaustion and Cecilia was worried. She needed to keep their minds focused on the task at hand.

A few hours into their flight, the plane started its descent. One by one, all the members of the team woke up at the smell of freshly brewed coffee.

Sandy looked out of the window and saw that they were flying low, right above a forest. She immediately realized that they were not preparing for landing but rather another session on the environment.

Bale was leading this session. "One of three major rainforests in the world is here, beneath us, in Sumatra, Indonesia. And this had the fastest rate of deforestation," he stated, pointing towards the windows. "Palm oil is the cheapest vegetable oil in the world. It's used in everything from potato chips to detergents. Its only benefit over other kinds of oil is that it's cheaper."

"Demand for palm oil is growing internationally, and here in Indonesia, the locals are destroying one of the last remaining rainforests worldwide to cultivate it," Bale proclaimed.

At that moment, the plane took a sharp left turn and started flying over the deforestation line. On the left side, it was the green color that dominated their view, while from the right windows, they could see endless planes of deforested land.

"How do we solve this problem?" asked Bale.

"Indonesia needs to regulate against deforestation," said Amir.

"We can't rely on some foreign, probably corrupt government to do the right thing," Wayne shot back.

"Plus, this is a poor country, where palm oil creates employment and revenue for the locals," said Sandy, eager to contribute.

"Okay, Wayne and Sandy, that's true, but we want to solve this, right? How?" Bale persisted.

It was Frank who picked up the conversation. "This is bullshit, man, the companies who use these products need to pay a bit more to buy a less destructive alternative. Period. Problem solved."

"Hey, 'man', but do you expect some white-collar yuppie working for a snacks company to put his neck on the line and reduce his employer's profitability? I'd say that's pretty unlikely. Man," said Wayne sarcastically.

They were still flying beyond the deforestation line, over the vast palm tree plantations. Bale directed their attention to the windows, and also to prevent the little skirmish from escalating. "Everything you see here used to be a rainforest," he said.

"There has to be a way to stop this," said John.

"It's the same as the plastics problem in the ocean," Sandy reasoned. "It's not up to any government, nor a corporation, to solve this. Each one of us is fueling this demand, every time we buy a product that contains palm oil."

Cecilia eyed her closely. She was impressed. More than once during this trip, Sandy had helped steer the conversation in the direction Cecilia was hoping for. Not everyone shared Sandy's view, though.

"C'mon, Sandy, what you're suggesting is utopic. We can't hope to affect the buying decisions of every redneck in the US, or whatever the equivalent is in other countries," replied Wayne, ever the pragmatist, in too aggressive a tone.

Wayne had not shared with the others that he had once taken a trip to this rainforest, together with his college sweetheart, Amy, a beautiful pre-med student with an ambition to cure the world's diseases. She had just taken a class on the medicine that had been discovered in the rainforest and was keen to get there. She literally dragged Wayne on the trip.

It hadn't been clear to either of them exactly what they should be looking for when they got there. They spent their days trekking through the rainforest, smoking weed, making love – certainly not looking for any new medicine.

Yet, the tropical forest of Indonesia had had a profound impact on Wayne's life. It was the first time that he had felt truly connected with nature. A city boy from San Francisco, he had never really visited any woods other than the Yosemite Park once, on a school trip. But the rainforest was different. So different. Amy was right; there was something really special about that place. Amy and Wayne had discussed the destruction of the rainforest even back then, 30 years ago. They had bonded in more ways than one in the rainforest.

As soon as they had returned stateside, Wayne had bought the largest ring he could afford, which back then was not very large. He had proposed, she'd said yes, and then, in a whirlwind, Amy was gone, a misdiagnosed case of malaria resulting in severe respiratory distress which, combined with her chronic asthma, took her life within just a month of their return.

Amy's death still infuriated Wayne. Even though he admired the rainforest, he had long decided that it would not provide cures, only diseases. Wayne became a pragmatist, the hard way. He began working on and contributing to big pharma research, initially looking for better diagnostic tools and treatments for malaria, before diversifying his research and eventually starting his own company.

Wayne had been in relationships since, but he had never found a connection that came close to what he'd had with Amy. She had been his soul mate, and as far as he was concerned, you only ever find one of those.

***

They landed at Krabi airport, and before long they had arrived at the 5-star Rayavadee Resort, a Thai paradise: White sand, light green-blue waters, long-tail boats coming and going from the edge of the beach and a 200-foot tall mushroom-shaped island rock dressed in local plants, floating in the middle of the water.

After a good night's sleep, the group gathered for some more speed-boating. Their destination was about an hour away from Krabi. The Phi Phi Islands are a collection of small Thai islands, and a popular destination for tourists. The smaller Ko Phi Phi Lee is uninhabited and had until recently been a day trip destination for the tourists who opted to stay on the larger Phi Phi Don. Every day, they had packed into fishing boats of questionable seaworthiness to go visit the magnificent Maya beach that had been the set of the popular Hollywood movie, *The Beach*. Then in 2018, Thailand abruptly closed Maya beach to allow the magnificent environment recover from the tourist activity. This ban apparently did not apply to Cecilia's team who arrived at Ko Phi Phi Lee in the early morning. They circled around the island until the boat entered a large hidden cove, which could easily have been as big as four Olympic-sized pools. The surrounding hills were tall and vertical, 200-foot high, all dressed with local plants. The sea was a fluorescent turquoise. The water was so clear that the boat appeared as if it were hovering in the air. From where the boat had stopped, you couldn't see the exit of the cove. There was no one else around.

Sandy sat at the edge of the speedboat, mesmerized by what she saw. As a Greek, she was no stranger to magical sights. But this was beyond anything she had ever witnessed before. Her mind raced thinking about how this part of the trip could be connected to their previous stops. What did Cecilia have planned?

She turned to face Cecilia and was shocked to see that she was standing at the edge of the boat, entirely naked. In a split second, she jumped and disturbed the calm waters. Seasoned skinny-dippers Frank, Amir and Wayne didn't wait for an invitation. They removed their clothing and jumped in.

Sandy turned to look at John, shrugged and removed her blouse revealing a laced bra. She put her hands behind her back and removed it, then completely undressed. Her body could have been the inspiration for a nude ancient Greek statue. Soon she too was in the water, releasing a scream as she jumped in. John followed right behind her.

The speedboat driver showed no interest in all of this. Bale was the only one still on the boat, very much dressed and looking embarrassed, the reserved Englishman. Wayne, then Frank, then John, prompted him to make the jump. Then Cecilia shouted across the water, her voice echoing eerily off the walls of the cove, "Come on, Bale, this is part of the initiation."

Bale slowly undressed to his boxer shorts. Then, after a moment of hesitation, he removed them and swiftly jumped. The water was surprisingly warm. Cecilia invited them to form a circle, the first of many to come. The sea was too deep for them to stand up, so they were all treading water to keep afloat, creating a semi-transparent veil covering their nude bodies.

Cecilia then moved into the center of the circle and spoke. "When we remove our clothes, we are all the same. We are children of Mother Nature, and just look at the beauty of Mother Nature all around us." It was cliché, no doubt, but it resonated with the others as they swam naked in paradise. As Cecilia spoke, in a loud but soothing voice, she turned around herself to face each individual in turn. It seemed as if she was dancing in the water. Her intense stare moved from one member of the team to the next, locking eye contact with one after the other.

"This is my favorite place in the whole world. But the world has so many incredible places. I am bewildered that we dismiss this beauty and seem bent on destroying it. We are not alone in the world, and we need nature to survive. This need must transcend all nations. It must transcend religion and race. We need to act as one human race, as naked as we are now. We are human beings. That which connects us is so much more than that which separates us."

Their circle was in the middle of the cove and as Cecilia spoke, her voice echoed off the walls of nature. Sandy could not help but think that this experience felt deeply spiritual. Sandy was a Greek Orthodox Christian by birth, but not much of a believer. Indeed, she thought that religion had brought more harm to the world than good, a belief that was shared by the whole group, though she did not know this.

But as a decision scientist in training, Sandy also knew that religion was just a deep belief in something. She knew that people needed to believe that their existence was meaningful. She had never believed in an afterlife, but she did have faith in herself, and believed that she could make a significant difference in the world. She was too young not to.

This spiritual experience in the turquoise waters of Thailand, on the other side of the world from New York, did more to bind the group than any other part of the trip so far. Here they were, in the middle of nowhere, in a place of exceptional beauty, swimming naked as they had been when they were brought into the world, and vowing to save the world. They did not yet know how they would do this, and they didn't need to know, not just yet. They were nearly at the end of their trip, and at the beginning of a very long journey. All Cecilia needed, for now, was their agreement that something needed to be done, their unconditional commitment to do it, and their trust that it was she who could make it happen. With their help.

This should give them more meaning and direction in their lives than any religion ever could.

***

They had lunch on the larger Phi Phi Don, the tourist epicenter of Thailand that had been completely destroyed by the tsunami of 2004.

Unlike Amir and Wayne, who chose to keep their personal stories private, Cecilia started revealing her own traumatic experience. "I was here when the tsunami hit on December 26, 2004," she said to everyone's surprise. "I was in my freshman year in college and was doing really well, so my father decided to buy me a holiday as a gift for my birthday. I brought a friend with me, my dear Adam," she said, and paused. She wasn't making eye contact anymore.

"Adam and I were high-school sweethearts. Adam was smart, attentive and truly loving. He was strong and athletic. He used to wake me up each morning to go for a morning run along the Charles River in Boston.

"Since my father was paying, he booked us into the best hotel on the island. As it happens, it was the only building that survived. And I survived with it. Adam didn't." The team looked at her, shocked. No one dared speak.

"He had woken up early that morning; jet-lagged, and tried to get me out of bed for a morning swim. I rolled over and he went anyway. I wish I could have opened my eyes, just to look at him one last time." She was speaking in the coldly detached voice of someone describing a deeply painful experience that they have learned to live with.

"Anyway, after the tsunami hit, once things became quiet again and it seemed safe, some of us survivors in the hotel, tourists from several countries and locals, formed a team and went out to look for survivors. We were risking our own lives, but we never once questioned what we needed to do. Of course, I was deeply worried and desperate to find my love. But I also knew that other people's fathers, sons, daughters, sweethearts were also missing and they needed my help.

This team, made up of people of different nationalities, race and religions came together and saved many of those who'd fallen victim. We found people in the rubble, badly hurt, and unable to move. Our first aid stopped the massive bleeding and stabilized people suffering from immense trauma. I don't know how many people we saved, but they were many. Our little team, with no leader, no authority, knew exactly what we needed to do, and we got it done.

It was here in Thailand that I realized that we human beings are inherently good. We lose touch with our good side. We become competitive. We like to win, but it is in the face of grave loss that we unite with each other. It's a paradox that so much good could happen in the world if people tended to act during good times like they are programmed to react in the face of disaster."

At this point, Cecilia stopped and looked around. No one had touched their jumbo shrimp. "But enough about me," she said. "Let's eat," but none of the group had any appetite left.

"What happened to Adam," Sandy asked, unable to suppress her curiosity. "He was never found," Cecilia replied. "I stayed here for over a month, helping out with relief efforts, searching for news about him. His spirit is here. I don't know where his body is."

***

The following morning, their Gulfstream took off from Krabi airport and turned west. When the plane reached cruising speed, Cecilia got up to speak. At her request, all the passengers adjusted their seats to face inward. Cecilia moved up and down the aisle, and for the first time, her speech was not interactive. She was lecturing and explaining. She spoke loudly and confidently, making eye contact with each member of the team. None of the pain they'd witnessed the day before was visible on her face now.

"On this trip, we have seen the beauty of nature. And we have witnessed its destruction at the hands of mankind. We are now almost past the point of no return, meaning that unless things change radically, and immediately, there will be no turning back.

But things will not change radically on their own. They won't, not in the Darwinian way, anyway. We human beings are incapable of working with each other to even acknowledge the problem, let alone agree on a common solution. Through millennia of self-governance, we have failed to find a system that strikes a balance between ensuring our short- and long-term well-being. Our basic survival instincts kick in, and we pursue short-term satisfaction. For every virtuous path some of us choose, there will be those who oppose it, those who put obstacles along the way.

We tear the environment apart for pure profit, driven by greed. Our actions put our own self-interest over and above the collective good. In our struggles to survive, we destroy the environment. Even when our intentions are noble, sheer negligence does the damage for us. Whatever way you look at it, this is not a problem that can be solved by democracy or dictatorship, by capitalism or socialism.

We have to acknowledge it. Humanity is not equipped to deal with a problem as complex and urgent as the one we now face.

Unless disaster hits. When disaster hits, we are programmed to work together in ways that transcend our nationality, religion, race, and sex. But, when it comes to the environment, disaster rarely hits the people who created the problem."

Cecilia paused for effect. No one seemed to disagree.

"There is wide consensus in people who share our belief that this planet is doomed. Humans will destroy it. But show me one individual who is doing anything to stop it. Yeah, sure, you have the billionaires of this world funding clean energy, ocean cleanups and the like. But that's not enough. We should be screaming our lungs out to stop the madness now before it's too late. But we don't. We just hope for the best. A technological solution that will reverse things," she said mockingly, looking directly at John, who couldn't hold her gaze.

"So, before we go on to discuss what we can do about this, we're going to make one last stop. There we will discuss what humans do to each other when resources run low. Where do you think that should be?"

She handed out Post-it notes to everyone asking them to write down destinations to choose from. Even Bale got one.

Amir reluctantly took control of the conversation. "We are flying west from southeast Asia. So our path could take us through India, former Soviet countries, the Middle East, Africa, and Europe. Half the world is in our path. Let's first think of places and times in history where natural resources were scarce," he said.

"Wow. Where do we start," John smiled, picking up a pack of Post-its and writing a country on each. Within seconds, he had a piece of paper for Afghanistan, Iran, Iraq, Yemen and Israel.

"How about Africa?" Sandy suggested. "The civil war in Rwanda, the apartheid in South Africa, the blood diamonds of the Congo and Sierra Leone," she paused for a second, then picked up a pack of Post-its and started writing down the names of the countries she'd listed.

"What about the Holodomor," said Bale, referring to the man-inflicted famine in Soviet-held Ukraine that had killed millions of Ukrainians in the mid-1930s.

"Well, as long as we're in Europe, how about Nazi Germany?" Frank asked. "What, too obvious?" he said, looking around at the faces of doubt around the table.

"The reason for the Holocaust was the redistribution of wealth, masked behind some racial cause," Wayne objected.

"Money is the ultimate scarce resource," said Bale, again taking his professorial tone. "Wars start when social cohesion breaks down. When the poor stop accepting the status quo and revolt against the privileged few. War is, indeed, the most effective way to redistribute wealth and resources."

"Unless, we decide that sharing is a better option," said Cecilia.

Everyone accepted that conflict and war was part of human nature and that atrocities had happened and still happened all across the world. Whether they were purely due to a lack of resources, natural or otherwise, was beside the point. When your own survival was under threat, history had shown that you could – would – kill another in order to survive.

"Perhaps war and genocide are nature's way to control population growth," said Bale, in a damn right provocative statement.

"Well, if it is, we need to find a way to work together, rather than against each other," said Cecilia as she sat down. "So, which of these lovely places would you like to visit?" she asked. Sandy picked up a random sticky note from the table and turned it around. It read "Nazi Germany."

So the plane adjusted its course toward the site of one of the greatest atrocities ever committed by man: Auschwitz.

***

On the eighth and final day of their trip, the plane took off from Krakow in Poland and headed toward New York. There was silence on the plane. The group had just visited the camp where one million people had been exterminated, gassed to death with a cyanide-based pesticide as if they were ants.

The usually vocal group had toured the compound in near silence, and listened intently to their Polish guide on this cloudy day. It was only seven decades since people had arrived there, in trains, disembarked, were made to undress, shoved into a building, and were gassed to death before their bodies were withdrawn, their gold teeth removed, and their corpses burned.

And this hadn't been carried out by Islamic State radicals. It had taken place in Europe, under the orders and supervision of German Christians.

Even though everyone had heard of Auschwitz and knew the history, visiting the camp was entirely different. It was even more different in light of what they had seen and discussed in the past few days. Cecilia's words took on a new meaning.

"If humans were prepared to exterminate millions of people for whatever reason, there is no hope for humanity when the problem of overpopulation meets the challenge of diminishing resources caused by natural destruction. Unless we are prepared to share," Bale had said during their visit.

Even though it was not explicitly discussed on the plane, what had most moved this group of scientists and academics was the precision and coldblooded methodology that was used and it made the extent of this atrocity feasible. Nazi scientists had discovered and applied the most efficient way to exterminate humans. Even though it had happened during the Second World War, it'd had almost nothing to do with the war itself. In fact, if Hitler's soldiers had not been preoccupied with carrying out mass exterminations, Germany might have had a better chance of winning the war.

While ethnic cleansing and mass genocides had occurred numerous times in history, all over the world, the scale of the Nazi exterminations was only made possible by the efficiency of the German killing machine. This was what set the Holocaust apart from all the other acts of genocide throughout history, written on the post-it notes still scattered throughout the plane, despicable as they also were.

Everything, from the numbering of human individuals as if they were sheep, to the process of making them remove their own clothes to ensure more efficient disposal, was carefully planned and orchestrated so that 7,000 soldiers could oversee the deaths of millions of ordinary people. Could someone like John, Frank, Amir or Wayne have devised such an efficient and deadly process? Without a doubt they could. They were leading their fields, and they could solve any challenge if they put their minds to it.

But would they have? Of course, it was easy to claim that you would not act in the same way as these atrocious Nazis of the past century. But the whole team knew that this was an overly simplistic answer.

There was definitely something poisonous in human nature. Their visit to Auschwitz had sealed this for this team. Had they really needed the trip to acknowledge this? Perhaps not. But with the trip, Cecilia had convinced them that something needed to be done. They weren't yet sure what, but they were happy that Cecilia had decided to take things into her own hands. They were, for the most part, elated to be part of the team that would venture into the unknown, looking for and implementing a cure for human nature, and saving their natural habitat.

There was just one member of the team who was still not sure if he wanted any part of this.

CHAPTER SIX

THE PLAN

The evening Manhattan skyline view was as breathtaking as it was just 10 days ago when the team first met here. Cecilia handed out a 12-page document written by Dr. Bale, on sustainability.

Everyone in the room was relaxed, with a drink in hand and quietly reading the document. Wayne seemed to complete the pages first. He let a sigh, downed the rest of his beer, and walked over to the fridge to pop another one open. Then, he sat down by the dining table and examined carefully everyone in the room.

Cecilia was not in the living room. Perhaps she was resting. More likely, she was quietly monitoring everyone's reactions through a hidden camera in her apartment, Wayne thought, looking around to see if he could spot it. Dr. Bale could be heard talking on the phone in a different room.

His mind wandered back to what he had just read. It was utopic bullshit if you asked him, but out of respect, he didn't voice his opinion until everyone had finished the document. Bale was referring to 'collectivism', a political philosophy where decisions were made for the benefit of the group versus the individual.

Dr. Bale had pointed out that human beings lack a sense of collective reasoning. As they had witnessed first-hand, this was at least partly true. Sometimes, human beings did act as groups, as they had following the tsunami at Phi Phi Islands in Thailand. But this seemed to require an immediate threat to survival, and clearly there was no such sense of urgency when it came to solving the problems of overpopulation, climate change, and ocean acidification. Indeed, it was next to impossible to even witness the destruction of the environment. There was no way to take photos of global warming, or shoot videos of the ocean acidification. Environmental problems would not be depicted like, for example, world hunger, even if they often have been its cause. The current political systems and governments were evidently also incapable of rising to the challenge.

There was a glimmer of hope in the emergence of social networks. According to Bale's thesis, 'Horizontal Collectivism' could be achieved using tools like Facebook, Mindalikes, LinkedIn and the like. Mindalikes had taken this a step further by creating groups based on shared values and ideas. The social networks emerging within the Mindalikes platform were not based on the randomness of acquaintances.

There could be no future for the human race, or Planet Earth, unless people utilized social networking technology to fill in the void of the absent collective conscience, Dr. Bale argued in his thesis. Perhaps this might be true, but it's theoretical, thought Wayne. How could you apply it in practice? Well, he supposed, here they were, a group of people including a professor of sustainability philosophy and the world's foremost social networking entrepreneur aiming to turn theory into practice.

This would be an interesting discussion indeed.

***

Cecilia walked back into the room, stopped, glanced around, and poured a glass of Malbec. So far, everything was going according to plan. She was quite happy with the team, the way they were bonding, the quality of the discussions - even the ones fraught with tension - their stamina, and especially their engagement.

But no matter what had happened thus far, it all would come down to tonight. She had laid out the problem, and, for the most part, she had their agreement on that. Both in terms of the causes, and the dire consequences. Now, she had to talk about the solution. There was no way to know how they would react. Tonight was crucial.

***

The discussion began right after dinner. They each pulled out a dining room chair and sat in a circle with nothing in the middle. Wayne looked around and saw that everyone was fully engaged and ready for the conversation to start.

For a moment no one spoke. They looked at each other, relaxed, some of them smiling at the awkwardness of the moment. Others expected Cecilia or Bale to speak first. In the end, it was Wayne who broke the silence, summarizing the 12 pages in one sentence:

"So, a social network designed to install a social, collective conscience in everyone occupying this planet. Interesting, though perhaps utopic," he said, and the others nodded their heads in agreement. Even Bale looked tempted to do so.

Wayne eyed Cecilia who was smiling and silent. He noticed that all of the coldness of her demeanor had evaporated tonight.

Wizkid Frank was sitting directly across from Cecilia, and she gazed directly into his eyes, her intense stare prompting him to speak next.

"I think technology can be used to influence micro-human decisions so that they are guided by the pursuit of collective good rather than individual good," he confirmed.

"What a load of bullshit" thought Wayne but Cecilia seemed to encourage the thought as she turned her stare – and her smile - to Sandy, who as the group's specialist in decisions was compelled to speak next. "I wonder if we can enhance the moral conscience of each and every one of us so that the decisions we take are more likely to be for the common good."

"We cannot solve this by enhancing anyone's moral compass. We need to give people incentives to change their behavior now. People believe the environmental destruction is not imminent, that it will not affect them during their own lifetime," Bale countered, "Of course, one way to solve this is to find a way to extend life. As long as we are leaving the issue of feasibility off the table for now, this could be a solution."

Sandy let out a small laugh, but Cecilia wiped the smile off her face by saying, "I agree with you, Richard. An extension of life, or even eternal life, could be a way around this problem."

"Regarding sustainability, eternal life would certainly compel us to make smarter decisions," said Bale. "We would not want to live on a dying planet in 100 years' time. On the other hand, there is the issue of overpopulation. We are biologically pre-programmed to want to have children, and the one sustainability problem that we as a species have never had to face is the recycling of human beings. So, eternal life cannot solve the issue of sustainability, unless we stop breeding altogether, which will be the most selfish thing humanity has ever done."

As a medical doctor and former owner of a major pharma company, Wayne had spent his life trying to extend life. He had never realized that by doing so, he had inadvertently contributed to overpopulation with the related environmental consequences. The conversation had just taken an interesting turn and it was about to get even better.

Cecilia stood up and went to the center of the circle. She turned around a couple of times, smiling, as if dancing to the soft lounge music playing in the background. Her knee-length freefall dress pulled up as she turned, revealing her slender thighs.

Cecilia stopped circling around and looked directly at Wayne, who, as if on cue, said "You could probably extend life by curing all disease and developing artificial body parts. While this does not guarantee eternal life, it does make the stakes higher."

Cecilia, still standing up, turned left and right to face each person as they spoke. As the conversation became more animated, her moves got faster. She raised her hands, smiling, and pointed to Frank, like a conductor giving a saxophone player their cue.

"I think that eternal life is not the solution we're looking for, as humans would probably value their current self-interest over their future self-interest."

Cecilia pointed to John next, who says, "We need to build on human nature rather than go against it."

And then to Sandy, "We need to activate the human trait that forces us to come together at times of crisis."

Amir next, "We need to influence human conscience for the benefit of everyone."

Cecilia, quite literally dancing at the moment, points to Bale, "We need a social network that helps us to make collective decisions," he said and then Cecilia points to Wayne who says, "Exactly, but how?" and the dancing stops.

***

Sandy raised the ethical repercussions of this first. "Assuming we could find a way to ensure people made collective decisions, it would implicitly involve limiting our ability to make individual choices? This is definitely problematic: we would be limiting individual free will."

"We wouldn't be the first to try and do that, dear," was John's retort. "At least this is for a noble cause."

"And hey our free will is restricted from our first day of school," Frank added.

"We don't need no education, we don't need no thought control," John agreed, quoting the famous Pink Floyd song.

"But thought control has led to some of the world's most atrocious crimes. The atrocities committed at Auschwitz, to name just one," argued Sandy.

Bale cut her off. "In the western world, we do have free will. We are allowed to buy what we want, spend our time as we choose, travel as we please, marry who we love. And the world is becoming freer. We have free will, within boundaries; we need money to exercise it, and we are not allowed to break the law."

Bale continued, "The problem is how we use, and waste, our free will. We spend our money buying a fancy car because our neighbor has. We are passive citizens when it comes to voting. The majority of human beings end up wasting their free will. We are not pursuing happiness at all because we are not programmed to pursue happiness. We are programmed to strive for survival. In the western world, where for the longest time in human history, survival has barely been an issue for the majority of people, people are looking for new ways to achieve satisfaction. They work hard to attain more material 'goods', they overconsume, and their ever more elusive satisfaction comes from comparing themselves with their neighbors and coming out on top. Bored, they then seek out extreme experiences, from bungee jumping to sexual deviance. It's the same feeling our ancestors had when they found food and knew they would survive another day. It's the only feeling humans acknowledge."

Sandy felt deep respect and admiration for the professor in front of her. But she also knew that many of the bad things that had ever happened in this world had started with a noble cause. She was determined not to let this pass.

So she pressed on, "The fact that people waste their free will does not mean that we have the moral right to influence it, even if it's for their own good. I mean, where do we draw the line?"

But Cecilia had clearly had enough of discussing morality, and changed the subject, returning to her normal ice-cold demeanor. "We will revisit the ethics of our proposed solution after we have talked about how we can make it happen," she said, effectively confirming that limiting individual choices was at the heart of her environmental solution.

***

During the next break, Wayne approached Cecilia for a quiet word.

Having been a successful entrepreneur himself, Wayne identified with her arrogance. However, he was worried that it would lead her down paths unknown and that she would take him with her. He did not need this. Yes, he wanted to help save the world as much as the next guy, but he was also fifty years old, filthy rich, and with no kids. He didn't need to worry too much about posterity. He could retire on a Caribbean island and spend his hopefully many remaining years happy and cheerful.

But, out of respect for what Cecilia was trying to do, he didn't want to voice his reluctance in front of the others. He wanted to have this conversation man to woman, millionaire to billionaire.

Cecilia was expecting it, especially from Wayne, though she hadn't been expecting it so soon. Wayne was an integral part of her plan, if not the most important part. Wayne would be the delivery mechanism, and she had to keep him onboard.

They left the living room and entered the study, a room Wayne had not entered before. Cecilia sat behind her father's desk and Wayne made himself comfortable on a Chesterfield leather chair on the other side of the desk. The hierarchy between Wayne Ross and Cecilia Stein was clear: the 50-year-old reporting to the 33-year-old; the self-made millionaire to the Forbes-cover billionaire. Was this intentional, Wayne wondered? Of course it was. He had come to believe that nothing that occurred in the presence of Cecilia Stein was accidental.

"So," asked Cecilia, "What's on your mind?" Her mood seemed different. She was less arrogant now, more relaxed, the manager was ready to coach and reassure the associate. Her mood swings worried Wayne. At the moment, he was asking for an easy way out, but he was intimidated by the impressive force of will sitting across from him.

"Listen, Cecilia, the past ten days or so have been an intense and eye-opening experience for me and I thank you for that. But I don't think there is any practical way to make it work. The moment it becomes clear that a social medium is taking sides on any particular issue, its power to influence its members will quickly subside," he said. "Plus, what we are discussing here is beyond my ambitions for the next fifty years."

"I want out," Wayne said, simply.

Cecilia stared him in the eyes, smiled, and said, "Wayne, tell me a bit about Curia. How did it start?"

Wayne relaxed a bit. "I was a research fellow at New York University Medical School and we were making good progress towards discovering a cure for AIDS. I got some funding, quit academia, and founded Curia," he said. "Our goal back then was to be responsible for the largest medical discovery since penicillin."

"So, your goal was to become rich selling AIDS vaccines?" Cecilia asked, provocatively.

"No, no," Wayne responded, animatedly. "Our goal was to get the vaccine tested and save millions of lives."

"American lives?" Cecilia was smiling, enjoying the moment.

"No, not just American lives," Wayne stressed, falling deeper into her trap. "We would have saved an entire continent: Africa."

"And did you accomplish that?" Cecilia, who of course, already knew the answer.

"No, we couldn't solve a significant problem related to the AIDS cure, but we did discover a vaccine delivery mechanism that was far more effective than anything that had gone before. We found a way to store and transport vaccines at room temperature. It was a turning point for us. We got some more funding, and the rest is history."

"So, you did save lives in the end, right?"

"I guess, though, more likely, we saved tons of cash for the pharma industry. We were able to provide our solution at a fraction of what it cost them to have refrigerated storage and distribution, and most vaccines now utilize our mechanism."

"And this made you a millionaire, correct?"

"Yes, it did. And now it's my time to enjoy some of that money."

"So, I suppose you succeeded in your original goal: to become a millionaire."

"Yes," said Wayne, and then "No. I see what you're saying, but we did make a difference. Who knows, maybe the millions we saved the big pharma were reinvested in research and a new miracle drug is now in circulation because of that. It's just how capitalism works."

"True, but have you achieved your life's dream? Of saving millions of lives?" Cecilia asked, no longer smiling, no longer cordial, almost scolding Wayne for his failure.

It was clear to Wayne now that he had fallen into a trap. Every entrepreneur out there, bootstrapping to build their own company shares the same dream: to make a difference in the world, to have a lasting impact, and to make a nice buck out of it. Entrepreneurs care about glory as much as they do about money. Perhaps more so. Wayne had certainly been more interested in glory when he started Curia. And he was even more interested in it now that money was no longer a problem.

But he wasn't ready to admit defeat to this impressive, arrogant woman who thought she was his boss. "What about you Cecilia. Couldn't you have used Mindalikes to influence people to do the right thing?" he asked. "I mean, the whole idea of Mindalikes was to bring together people with common interests and common ideas. You could almost build a virtual nation of environmentally conscious people."

Cecilia looked at Wayne and replied sarcastically, "You would think so, wouldn't you? They did not let me, that's why I left. I am staying true to my goals, to my vision".

"You're right, Cecilia, I haven't achieved my life's ambition, and I am now a 50-year-old millionaire with plenty of time on my hands to do whatever I want with the rest of my life."

"And what you want, Wayne, is to save millions of lives. You said so yourself," said Cecilia, with a firm tone of voice. "It's a bug, and it doesn't go away just because you earned a buck. Trust me, I know. And I am giving you the opportunity of a lifetime, a second chance to achieve what was not accomplished on your first attempt."

She paused for effect, and then softened her tone of voice a little, though her stare was still intense. She smiled and said, "You have to stay. I need a pragmatist on the team." Wayne, staring back at her, caved.

***

Back in the living room, Sandy had joined Frank, Amir and John by the window. A fog was settling in over Manhattan and several of the high-rise buildings now seemed to be emerging out of the cloud. It was really quite eerie. Also eerie was the conversation she had joined.

John had been arguing with Amir and Frank, who agreed with Cecilia and Bale that freewill was being wasted by human beings. John had made his way to the University of Pennsylvania and had chosen to study nanotechnology, a field that had fascinated him since he had been ten years old. He could not agree that he was wasting his free will.

It had not been easy for John; he had this much in common with Amir and Frank. His parents had divorced when he was five and, after winning the custody battle, his mother gave him up to his father just a year later. A good man, his father made ends meet by working double shifts at a nuclear plant near Pittsburg.

It had been clear early on that John was special, and his father had given him every possible opportunity to shine before passing away the year before John went to Penn. A financial aid program and a huge student loan had enabled John to pursue his dream, which he did also to honor his father who had given everything he had for him. In his first meeting with Cecilia, she had agreed to pay off his loan if he agreed to join her. But that wasn't the reason he was here. John believed he was special, one of a rare breed of people who was brought into the world to make a difference. It was a cocky and arrogant belief, but it had served him well so far.

Amir and Frank, on the other hand, argued that as a species, humans have a tendency to control each other. Slavery, human trafficking, wars, organized crime, and police brutality were just some of the examples of human beings exerting power over others for their own benefit they'd cited to support their view. Frank was adamant that capitalism was at fault. Though no communist, he was appalled by the fact that everything in the modern world could be measured in dollars. The life of a young girl, sold as a sex slave on the black market. The price of crude oil, set based on current supply and demand, as opposed to future availability and sustainability. Capitalism, according to Frank, had failed to solve the world's great problems.

Amir was less inclined to blame capitalism, and more inclined to blame politics. Anti-establishment politicians were on the rise around the world and they were feeding lies to the 'common' people to earn votes based on false hopes. It was another example of one group of people trying to assume power over others, shrouded by the legitimacy of democracy.

John noticed that the conversation was going all over the place, lacking any coherence. It seemed to him that they would not agree on everything, not here, and not tonight. He underestimated the persuasive powers of Cecilia Stein.

***

Once they had returned to their seats, Cecilia once again stood and took center stage.

"The question we have to answer, lady and gentlemen," she said, smiling at Sandy, "is whether there is a fundamental human flaw. Why is it that human beings tend to inflict so much harm on other humans, on animals, and on nature?"

No one spoke; it was clear that this wasn't to be an interactive session. Cecilia was once again circling around, her stare jumping from one member of the team to the next, each mesmerized by her captivating performance.

Not that she expected anyone to argue with her at this point anyway. They had seen and discussed enough over the past ten days to make them despise their own nature. As much as they wanted to believe that they were different from the masses, the enlightened ones, so to speak, they could not in all honesty swear that they might not have made the same selfish choices in different circumstances. This, above all else, was what united the group of Mindalikes recruits, which of course, Cecilia knew, as it was what she had specifically searched for.

Cecilia knew that Wayne would once again embark on a course to save the world in Amy's name and that John was on a lifetime mission to make his father proud by doing good through his nanotechnology research. Amir, right after his parents' death, would have been capable of strapping an explosive to himself and bombing a square full of people.

Even though he had not disclosed the fact to her, she knew that he had felt that much rage, but that he had also been looking for an opportunity to do good, rather than harm others. For Bale, to put his theories to practice was a prospect he could not pass. A hacker by birth, Frank would relish the opportunity to mess with the human brain for the benefit of humanity. And Sandy, young and idealistic who reminded of herself at that age, was a positive force in keeping the team in line, but she was also someone Cecilia could control when she started to design the core of their program.

Cecilia continued her speech by pointing out that everyone in the group was a staunch environmentalist. But were they fanatic recyclers? No. Were they appalled by the methods the food and farming industry had stooped to? They were. Were they vegans? No. They recognized the problems, but they did not address them. They could not address them. No matter how much each of them did, the problems of the world would not be solved.

"In the past 10 days, we have been to places where human nature has manifested at its worst and at its best," she said, partly repeating herself. There is a dark side to each of us. Whether it is evolutionary, based on survival instincts, or our inability to pursue happiness, as Dr. Bale says, we all have traits that allow us to become cruel, nasty, hurtful and shortsighted."

"We claim to love our children, but the world they are inheriting is in intensive care and full of evil. Is this the fault of capitalism? Of democracy? I don't know. I no longer care. Since the beginning of time, humans have failed to organize themselves in an efficient way that entails respect for others."

"We will never achieve this. Never! The planet will die, and we will die with it. Not all life will disappear. Whatever is not taken by nature, will be reaped by disease, violence, and nuclear warheads. The human race is doomed." Cecilia's tone was strict and scolding.

"The time is now. The need to do something is overwhelming. It has never been more urgent. We are no different from the tsunami victims of Phi Phi Islands. The human race needs to take the next evolutionary step. And this is not going to happen the Darwinian way. Not in time, anyway. We need to intervene. Fortunately, the technology we need is here," she said looking in turn at John, Amir and Frank.

"It will be humanity's finest hour. We will do this not to become heroes. Not to attract fame. We will tell no one. History books will not write my name, nor yours."

"We will not limit free will any more than it is already limited by governments, religion, the media, and the ruling classes. And we will not limit it for our own personal advancement. At the end of this, each of us will have a feeling of accomplishment unlike anything we have ever experienced. This will be your reward. This and whatever material resources you need to live the rest of your life in comfort."

Her voice was steady and confident. At times she spoke louder and used her hands to make a point more strongly. It was beautifully choreographed. Some of it had been practiced before, but most of it was pure instinct. For Cecilia Stein was indeed special. A one of a kind leader, exerting power over her people through words, not weapons, not lies, not money.

Of course, money would be needed in the coming months, as her plan unfolded and began to be implemented. Without money, none of what she had in mind could ever get off the ground. But money alone could not bring this group of believers together. She had chosen well and she needed them to make their own decision. She needed their unconditional buy-in. And now she had it.

CHAPTER SEVEN

THE DEVELOPMENT

The project needed to be developed quietly, under the radar. But they still needed a corporate vehicle in order to hire the appropriate staff. So, Cecilia founded Uniocom Inc., a company incorporated in Wyoming, a state in which company owners could still hide behind bearer shares. She didn't want some nosy reporter to find out about what she was up to. She assigned Wayne Ross to head Uniocom.

A biotech company, Uniocom was physically located across the Hudson in New Jersey. Its official purpose was to discover and develop new generation vaccines for common diseases, with a particular focus on AIDS. Wayne was once again on a mission to save the world. If Cecilia's plan failed, perhaps Uniocom would still be successful. It was a win-win for him.

John's research had been a breakthrough even before Cecilia had approached him. Her original plan had actually been more complicated, but his research gave her more options and more opportunities than she had previously imagined would be possible. John had unwittingly discovered a non-intrusive way to insert neural implants into a human brain. Or rather, the brains of mice, for these 'brain implants' had thus far only been inserted in mice during John's early experiments at Penn.

The research into brain implants had begun in the 1970s, way before John was born, and its main purpose had been to enable what was called sensory substitution, which involved implanting technological shortcuts that could bypass areas of the brain that were dysfunctional due to a tumor, stroke or accident. Early on, the concept of brain control had been discussed as an ethical complication of such implants, but the insertion procedure had turned out to be so difficult, and had such varying degrees of success, that even if brain control were theoretically possible, even achieved, it could only be on an insignificant scale.

John's research had demolished that barrier. So huge was his discovery that even he could not fathom the full scope of its potential practical implications until the team had sat with him one evening in Philadelphia, not long after they had met in New York following their trip.

They had just spent the day visiting the Department of Nanotechnology and talking to the Dean of the School of Engineering about a possible large donation. It was all part of a plan to convince the school to offer a research position to John Walker, who was due to obtain his Ph.D. within this year.

They had discussed that perhaps Cecilia should not visit the school in person, for fear of being recognized. They did not want her to be associated in any way with John. But there was no keeping her away from the tour, so she'd pulled her hair back in a ponytail, wore a baseball cap, and applied tons of makeup, which usually she rarely wore. For even greater safety, she wore fake glasses. She looked remarkably different, quite beautiful and carefree.

Wayne Ross, CEO of Uniocom, and his scientific team, Mr. and the much younger "Mrs. Bale", accompanied John Walker into the new nanotechnology building. As they walked in, Cecilia was impressed by the architectural marvel which looked as if a spaceship had landed in West Philly. It was built as an origami structure, where there was no main structure securing the building from the foundation to the top floor. Each floor was literally built on top of the floor below, and the front façade was all glass to ensure that no passerby could miss this stunning fact.

The team walked up a long set of stairs and arrived at the impressive main board room, which Cecilia noticed was hovering above the ground, several yards away from the main building. It looked to Cecilia as if Starship Enterprise had just docked.

While it was the above ground structure that gave the impression of an extra-terrestrial presence, it was the hardware underground that could really have been from outer space. Cecilia already knew that Penn's Nanotechnology Department had equipment that could produce electronic devices that were too small for the human eye to see. The researchers used electronic microscopes to see what they had created. Penn was the first university to possess such capabilities.

She found it interesting that the building was situated on a large cement plate that absorbed the slightest vibrations, whether from earthquakes or passing cars. When you make such small things, the last thing you need is for the production to go wrong because the Walnut Street bus happened to be passing by.

Wayne, Bale and Cecilia followed John and Anders, the Dean of the School. As they walked by the main lobby of the ground floor of the building, making their way towards the basement, Anders told them that it had been built with materials produced using nanotechnology, in order to "walk the talk," as he put it. "For example, the windows are made of glass stronger than steel," he told them proudly, pointing to the glass façade. "All of the bleeding edge technology is in the underground floors of the building." They took a staircase that led to two double doors, beyond which was the main basement. They then followed a corridor that seemed to circle around the center of the building. "Do you want to see the clean room?" asked Anders.

Of course, they did. Ascending a ramp that led to what must have been the center of the building, they found themselves in a steel foyer with metal air vents on all sides. Cecilia noticed that the entire room was one giant metal vent. Before she knew it, a loud humming sound surrounded them and they felt themselves being lightly pulled in all directions.

"This will remove all dust from you," said Anders, smiling at their bewildered faces. Once the humming stopped, Anders pressed a couple of buttons on the far wall, unlocking the entrance to the clean room, a steel door that looked like the door to the Gulfstream, complete with the small round window at eye level. Once inside the clean room, they all put on white lab coats and surgical face masks.

"We can't afford to have even the smallest particle of dust enter this room," said Anders.

"It could stick to the microstructures we are building with these machines," John explained.

Wayne felt his ears pop. "Do you have differential air pressure in this room?" he asked.

"Well observed. Yes, we do," John replied. "The air pressure is twice as high in this room as it is outside. Another way to keep the dust out."

They were shown the production floor, they asked questions about production capacity, and looked through the electronic microscopes to observe John's tiny invention. On a large plasma screen, they witnessed first-hand how it could attach itself to a brain cell taken from a mouse. This was the research that Uniocom wanted to fund.

As Cecilia watched the nano device, it reminded her of a small living organism. "Microbe," she whispered. "Excuse me?" Anders asked, and Cecilia, aware of the negative connotations of her word, quickly gathered herself, cleared her throat and said, more loudly "Microbees". Hence, the tiny technological devices due to change the world were given a name. And a meaning - though this would not become clear for many years to come.

***

That evening at John's apartment, Bale, Wayne and Cecilia explained to John just why his research was so important to the project. Frank, Amir and Sandy were there, but were silent for the most part, just trying to keep pace with the conversation. Darko, the Slav with the scar, who was Cecilia's private security guard, as they had found out, was stationed outside the apartment.

Wayne, whose mind had been racing all day long, spoke first, talking so rapidly that for a second, John thought he might be on drugs. It was still early days, and while the team had been through a lot together and their bonds had grown stronger, they did not yet know too much about one another. Wayne certainly looked to John like someone who may have done some heavy drugs in his younger days. But today, Wayne was excited at the possibilities and just couldn't control his enthusiasm.

Wayne said, "Listen John, this discovery is awesome. What's awesome about it is that the Microbee actually finds the cell and attaches itself to it. Do you think we can control a Microbee, directing it towards specific cells to attach to?"

"Yes, I think we can. The Microbee – love the name by the way," John said, smiling at Cecilia, "has both input and output sensors, so we can direct it to find and attach to specific cells."

"So, if we asked the Microbee to find a vision cell, a photoreceptor cell in the retina of the eye, we could?" Cecilia asked, clearly with something specific in mind.

"Yes," John replied, "theoretically we could program the Microbee to attach itself only to those types of cells. And what's great is that these particular neurons are common across all humans, regardless of race, age, sex, and so on."

"And what happens if the Microbee approaches a cell to which another Microbee is already attached?" Bale asked.

"Just like a bee, it will move on to the next cell. We can program the Microbees to search for the right type of cell until it finds it. And we can program it to quit looking after a few hours, at which point it will be expelled by the living organism through natural methods."

At this point Wayne stepped back into the conversation, seeming a little annoyed that he wasn't being allowed to lead. "All these questions are great. The main question though is: can the Microbee read the cell's electrical signals?"

"That's the beauty of it," answered John. "Indeed, we can get input from the brain cells. Neurons attach to each other using what looks like a collection of cables, called a synapse, effectively 'plugging into' each other. The Microbee attaches itself to this synapse and can read the electrical signals. Think about it. We are all just collections of trillions of cells – actually I think 37 trillion is the average. But do we look at ourselves as trillions of cells? No, we think of us as 'human beings'. The essence of life is that each of these 37 trillion cells has been built to perform a specific function, but more importantly, they need to communicate with each other in order for the whole to be more than the sum of its parts."

"That's exactly right," said Wayne, "but can we decode the electrical signal?"

"Not yet," said John. "We can discriminate between the different types of electrical signals that the cells transmit, but we are missing the Enigma machine, so to speak, to decode what those messages mean."

"When the Microbee attaches itself to the synapse, does it interfere with the neuron communication?"

"Excellent question, Wayne" said John, who was impressed with Wayne's intellectual ability to drill down to the essential components of the most difficult problems. "It doesn't. It just sits there and receives information. It's like the NSA. Do they interfere with your phone calls? No, they're just there, listening in to your conversations without you ever knowing."

"Speaking of which," interrupted Cecilia, "from now on, our cell phones will always be stowed away while we have these discussions," and she stood up and confiscated all seven cell phones, walked to the refrigerator and stowed them away, starting a ritual that would continue for years to come.

When she returned, she asked, "Can you change the signal? Can you interfere if you want?"

"Yes, theoretically you can." John said, hesitantly. "We don't know how to do it yet, and we don't know how to test it. We need the Enigma. Then we can work miracles. I have one question for Wayne, though. How do we know that these signals will be the same for different cultures and languages? Would we need a different decoder for each culture?"

Wayne had been involved in Parkinson's and Alzheimer's research in the past, and he had a deep knowledge of neurology. He considered the question for a while and then said, "I've not seen any scientific evidence to suggest that the signals in our neural network differ based on culture, race or language. On the contrary, most research suggests that neural network signals are very simple, that we are like computers, just a collection of switches, and zeroes and ones. This is why neurological diseases show exactly the same symptoms across cultures."

"And now for the trillion-dollar question," said Cecilia. "If there are 37 trillion cells in a human being, do we need to insert trillions of Microbees into a single human body?"

John smiled; he'd expected this question. "My knowledge of neurology is developing, and I understand that a human has 100 billion neurons, not 37 trillion. And then you can split the neurons into four categories. There are the neurons which interact with the external world, for example, the light receptors you mentioned before. Then, there are those that transmit the information, the cables, if you like. And then there are the receiving neurons, which make decisions. And finally, there are the memory cells. We only need to be in one end of the cable to affect behavior. So we only need maybe a billion or so Microbees to really affect behavior. That's how many transistors your iPhone has."

Wayne pondered this and asked, "If we are at one end of the cable, as you put it, how is it that we can affect behavior?"

"Well, for one, we can change the signals. In theory, of course; we're not ready to do this yet," John explained.

Frank who had been silent and visibly struggling to keep up with the conversation suddenly had an epiphany. "Fuck, are we talking about hacking the human brain?" he asked, finally realizing his own role in this project.

"Hell, yeah!" smiled Wayne. "So, you would use the brain's existing neuron network to communicate signals, but you would interfere with the signal as it leaves the transmitter cell. Like me talking on the phone, but the person on the end receiving a different message. Interesting; that's not how I'd do it," Wayne said, not sounding convinced.

"How would you do it, Wayne?" urged Cecilia.

"I would short circuit the communication line. I would take over the cable itself."

"And how would you do that?" John asked, interested.

"I would create a different mechanism for the Microbees to communicate with each other. Something like Wi-Fi."

"But that would increase the size and cost of the Microbee too much," John argued, putting that idea to bed.

"So then, how would the Microbees communicate with each other?" asked Bale, who was struggling to keep up, but understood the importance of communication.

"We'll use the brain's own neural network," explained John.

Sandy then pitched in, "Sorry, I may just be the dumb blonde here, but don't these Microbees need batteries?"

"Not a dumb question, babe," said John affectionately. "The Microbees we've developed last for a couple of hours before they need recharging. It's one of our biggest challenges."

At this point, Cecilia looked towards Amir and everyone's eyes followed hers, somehow making everyone turn towards him, which was strange because he had not said a word yet.

"There may be something I can do about that," he said carefully. "Technologies that have been developed for a different scale could perhaps be adapted for the Microbees."

"That's great," said Cecilia, wrapping the conversation up. "So, we know that human biology is consistent. We have the Microbees, which can attach to any cell we want them to, but we still need to research how to direct them to where we want them to go. We also need to figure out how to power them. We must decode the messages that neurons send each other. We will then need to intervene to replace these messages with our own. We have to do this for a specific type of decision because we only want to influence decisions that relate to environmental responsibility and sustainability. And, at the end of this, we need to somehow fund a billion Microbees on average per person, so if each Microbee costs 1 cent, we need, what, 10 million dollars per living person?"

"Yes," Wayne replied, confirming the calculation. The team exchanged shocked looks. "Surely there are cheaper, easier ways to fund sustainability. You could pay people to recycle. You could even pay governments to pass and enforce laws. You could eradicate world hunger, cure all diseases with that much money," Wayne said. "But," Cecilia interjected, "what would be the point if we all survived disease to deplete the natural resources that sustain life?" she said, too casually given the gravity of the choice she would need to make if that dilemma ever arose.

John, who was enjoying the moment, said, "The cost of the Microbee at full production will not be one cent. It won't even be one-thousandth of a cent. And we may need fewer than a billion Microbees for each human being," he said hurriedly, not wanting this plan to fall at the first hurdle.

There was no chance of that. If John could build the hardware, Wayne the decoder, Amir the recharging mechanism, and Frank the hacking algorithms, Cecilia would find a way to fund it.

And so, the foundations of what was to follow were laid that evening in Philadelphia. They stayed up well into the early hours drafting the roadmap for the R&D. At this point, all ethical considerations were set aside in the interest of furthering the greater cause.

No one dared to ask the question of how they would get billions of people to agree to have Microbees inserted into their bodies. Everyone assumed that Cecilia had a plan. And indeed she did.

***

It was one of the world's largest-ever acts of corporate and academic espionage. In the months after that evening in Philadelphia, John, Amir, Wayne, Frank and Sandy returned to work and school with clear orders: to steal any research and plans that they could bring together to complete the jigsaw puzzle of Cecilia Stein's project. The team Cecilia had assembled were all top of their field scientists. Still, they were missing large pieces of the puzzle, and there was no time to rediscover the wheel. A lot of the research they were after was being conducted at universities and corporations, and they needed to get hold of it, fast.

In the process, each broke several federal and state laws. What they did was unethical by most contemporary measures. But they were driven by a sense of purpose that Cecilia had instilled in them. They felt privileged and grateful to have been objectively selected from millions of people to take part in this mission. They were handsomely compensated, but money was not their main drive. They aggressively went after what they wanted, what they needed, because they were on a mission to save the world. As each team member sought a different piece of the puzzle, each piece of information on its own would be useless to most people, and so would appear innocuous in the case that anyone did catch them out.

They never once questioned what they were doing. Each believed that they had been chosen for a higher task and that as such, any laws, legal or moral, did not apply to them. They did not even slow down during the coronavirus outbreak or the subsequent lockdowns, because they knew that the crisis that they had been called upon to address was bigger and more urgent.

In any case, Cecilia did not leave anything to chance. On the second weekend of each month, they would all gather at her apartment, sit around in a semicircle, and watch her dance as she reinforced her vision. The ritual had become the highlight of all of their months. They would compare notes on what they had each achieved during the month. They laid out the materials they had gathered and identified what was still missing. Then they drew up plans for the following month.

They were functioning as a team, their collective intelligence coming together to co-create something bigger than themselves. There were no fights, no arguments, just absolute focus on the task at hand.

At the end of the evening, their favorite part of the night would come. Each month, Cecilia prepared a speech, each more inspiring than the last. Each month, they were drawn deeper into the web of her cause. To the outside eye, they might appear cult-like, but what would any outside eye know? How could they judge the team, their objectives, and their methods of achieving them?

***

Sandy and Bale were working together at the very core of the project. What kinds of decisions would they need to influence in the unsuspecting masses? Would they need to be micro decisions, or major lifestyle decisions? Would they, for example, try to force everyone to recycle, or to persuade them to become vegan?

Bale was setting the strategy, and Sandy was drawing on her academic background and Penn's vast resources to sketch out the ideas that needed to be implanted and the decisions that were to be influenced in order to achieve the goal of creating more socially responsible individuals.

They repeatedly argued about whether there were certain moral 'rules', or standards, for instance regarding environmental harm, that, once implanted, would not need to be changed, or whether these rules and standards would need tweaking from time to time. Sandy was of the opinion that they should focus on a few major tasks. Bale, more cautious, wanted full and constant access so that they could be adaptable. He was worried about steering the ship too far in one direction, only to hit the shore on the other side, trying to do something positive but starting a chain of events that took them somewhere unexpected. Who knew, for instance, what the overnight eradication of the demand for meat would do to the ecological stability of the planet, indeed what the immediate practical solution would be, if the surplus of cattle that had been artificially inflated beyond numbers that would naturally have occurred were suddenly no longer needed?

In the end, it didn't matter what Sandy or Bale thought. While Wayne had made significant progress in decoding the electrical signals of neurons in order to intervene with the human decision-making processes, the team still had not discovered a way to reprogram the Microbees once they were inserted. Even if they eventually did find a way, it would be Cecilia's decision to determine how it would be utilized. She met with Sandy and Bale once a week to monitor and guide their progress.

***

Sandy had at times been concerned about the ethics of their research. Unlike John, Wayne, Amir and Frank, who had all been consumed by the scientific aspects of their work, trying to create the means to affect decisions, Sandy spent her days thinking about the decisions themselves, and the mechanisms at work in individual minds when they were making them.

Sandy had been keen to work on the area of the brain behind the right ear, which had recently been shown to control moral judgment. She had a theory that if the Microbees were inserted in that area, they could enhance an individual's moral compass, and that the collective good generated for the planet this way could be enough to enable sustainability.

Cecilia, on the other hand, had insisted on creating a mechanism to influence specific decisions. This was scientifically far more difficult because they would need to discover more about how specific decisions were taken, what electrical signals were sent, and how to affect them. It was a new and rapidly evolving field of research that Sandy, being a student at Penn, had privileged access to.

Setting aside the scientific difficulties, Sandy was, on principle, against influencing specific decisions. But Cecilia was adamant, leading to an early dramatic showdown between the two women late one winter evening in Philadelphia.

***

They were meeting where they had first met, in Houston Hall, at the exact same table. It was exam time, and students were pulling all-nighters. Sandy and Cecilia had exchanged a few pleasantries about Sandy's life now, and how it had changed since they first met, but there was a palpable tension.

Sandy brought the subject up first. "I understand what we want to do, and I support the cause one thousand percent. But I don't agree with the path. I think we should find a way to enhance the individual moral compass, rather than to directly control, negate free will. I know your intentions are good, but once we build this technology, if it falls into the wrong hands, we're all screwed."

Cecilia was amused by Sandy's defiance, the Greek girl who had been by far the least qualified when she was recruited. She played along, appearing to listen intently; she wanted all her team members to stay engaged. Plus, Sandy was doing exceptionally well in her role, totally surpassing Cecilia's expectations.

"Sandy, I think you're overestimating the human brain's ability to distinguish between right and wrong. What is morally right now was wrong just 50 years ago. Hell, 50 years ago, it was illegal to be gay in most first world countries, the same countries that now allow same-sex marriages."

"So what's your point, Cecilia? Our understanding of morality might be evolving and changing, but it's always the same part of the brain controlling it, as has been repeatedly proven. Let's focus on that, and allow people to make their own decisions, the right decisions."

Cecilia was speaking softly, because there were too many people around and because she did not want a confrontation with Sandy. "The fact that people are able to make their own decisions is what has brought us here, Sandy. We don't want to enhance their moral judgment. We want to replace bad decisions with good ones. We need to want to become their moral compass, not enhance it."

"But who are we to decide which decisions are good and bad?"

"There are certain acceptable moral standards. Forest arson is a crime. It's wrong not to recycle batteries. We need to affect directly these types of decisions."

"Listen, Cecilia, I support you, I support the cause, but I'm not convinced that we will stop at those decisions. How do I know that you won't use the Microbees to, for example, control population growth? We both agree that population control is a key sustainability issue, but is it within or outside the remit of the decisions we want to control?"

"Do you mean using the Microbees will reduce the drive to reproduce? I don't think we could do that, even if we wanted to."

Sandy retorted, "What about abortion, birth control or euthanasia. There are other ways to control population. We should just enhance people's ability to make the right decisions themselves."

"Humans had plenty of opportunity to make the right decisions, Sandy. And they made the wrong decisions every time. I thought this was made clear during our trip. I don't think that enhancing the world's moral compass would help those people in Papua New Guinea, or stop the deforestation in Indonesia. It certainly wouldn't stop the US government from destroying the ecosystem around Bikini Atoll. I think you are overestimating our ability to distinguish right from wrong. We need to implant the exact decisions we want people to make."

"But who are *we* to make decisions for billions of people, Cecilia?"

"Sandy, if you asked a billion people if they agreed that the sustainability of our planet is a huge problem, 90% would agree. And then they would go about their daily lives, making trillions of small decisions that doom our planet. You have said this yourself. So, we are not going against free will. We are creating a collective conscience to achieve a goal that all of us agree is important."

Cecilia paused for a second, and then said, "There is no free will. Free will is a myth. We live within boundaries and yes, in western societies, we can decide what to eat or whether to go to the movies. But can we live our lives exactly how we want? Not really. If we cross the socially accepted boundaries, we are frowned upon, even arrested. Mind control is exercised by parents over their children, by bosses over their subordinates, by governments over their people, by the media, by advertising, by big business. Anyone in a position of power inevitably engages in mind control."

Sandy joked, "So you think you're exercising mind control over me, right now?"

"You're damn right I am. It's called leadership. And people, yourself included, want to be led. They want to feel part of something bigger than themselves. They need their lives to be given meaning because in modern, developed societies, all meaning has been removed. Only religion provides meaning to some lives, and religion is the ultimate manifestation of mind control. What we are doing here Sandy is no different than what has been imposed on societies for centuries. The only difference is that we are using technology to get it done, to control the specific decisions that will determine the long-term future of our species."

Sandy agreed with what she was hearing. She was also mesmerized by Cecilia's passion, her ability to communicate complicated truths in a comprehensible way. Cecilia Stein was a true leader if there ever was one. Still, Sandy was not ready to give in so easily.

"You have a point. But how will we know where to draw the line?"

"Where would you draw the line, Sandy?"

Sandy considered this for a moment. She hadn't expected the question to be thrown back at her. It was a once in a lifetime opportunity for Sandy Papas to determine the future of the entire world. She felt privileged to be part of Cecilia's elite team. She was in awe of the talent she was exposed to on a daily basis. She truly believed in the mission, and she was confident that she could help make a difference in the world. But it had to be on her own terms.

"We ought to define the boundaries of the decisions we will be affecting in writing. We all need to agree to them."

"OK, that sounds reasonab..."

"We must make a commitment to *never* deviate from these decisions," Sandy cut her off. "We will pledge secrecy. We will not make our technology known to anyone else," she said, and Cecilia was now more convinced that she had made the right choice in bringing Sandy in the group, unconventional as this decision had been at the time. We need a constitution," Sandy concluded, and hence, thanks to her, the idea of a constitution emerged.

***

It took them a couple of months, and when it was concluded, the Constitution contained six articles. The first outlined the scope and the vision, which, after long discussions, was agreed to be, "To create a horizontal collective environmental conscience in human beings of all nationalities, religions, races, and genders." The word "collective" was added by Bale, whose theories were based on collectivism - the opposite of individualism - and is defined in Wikipedia as the moral stance, political philosophy, ideology, or social outlook that emphasizes the group and its interests. The word "horizontal" was used to distinguish it from vertical collectivism, which forces people to act for the "common good," usually enacted within authoritarian regimes.

Article 2 committed everyone to total secrecy. For as long as they lived, regardless of the circumstances they found themselves in, they would never reveal the project, or any aspect of it, to anyone. A side issue relating to secrecy was security. The Constitution forced the team to take all actions necessary to secure their project from external infiltration.

Article 3 discussed governance. It was decided that within the group, everyone would be equal, each with one vote. Deadlocks could not be reached in this group of seven, unless one member died or was otherwise unable to cast a vote. The Constitution went as far as to discuss what would happen in such cases.

One challenge regarding governance that they could not easily get around was the issue of enforcement. In democratic constitutions, there were three branches of power: the executive, the legislative, and the judicial. In their case, they could not really split power into three without contradicting Article 2. In the end, it was decided that the whole group would exercise the legislative power to make choices about their project and the way forward. The executive power would be controlled by technology. This meant that any decision, rule or amendment ratified by the team would be programmed into a system in such a way that would allow no room for deviations. It was not a foolproof solution, of course, because systems could be hacked into, as they well knew, but it was the best they could think of, and it helped that they had a top-tier hacker working with them to ensure that theirs was impenetrable.

The issue of judicial power was discussed, but no concrete solution was found. They struggled to identify and decide upon appropriate penalties for violating the Constitution. A group member could be expelled if the rest unanimously voted for it, but that was as far as the Constitution went on this topic.

Article 4 concerned the scope of the project. Here, the decisions they would be able to influence were laid out. During the weeks they spent discussing and drafting Article 4, they decided to categorize decisions into clusters. In the end, they came up with the following:

1. Recycling & waste management
2. Energy
3. Consumer habits
4. Diet
5. Water conservation
6. Use of chemicals
7. Forestry and wild animals
8. Activism

The final cluster of decisions had been added after Cecilia and Bale convinced the others that it would not be enough for each person to change their own behavior. They needed people to become advocates of the environmental movement, in order to influence those around them and create a ripple effect. Missing from the list was the proposed cluster of overpopulation. The team failed to agree on this because of the moral nature of the decisions that would be involved, so it was left out.

Each cluster would later be broken down into the specific decisions that would need to be influenced. For example, the decision to buy recycling bins, to stop using plastic bags, to switch to more energy-efficient light bulbs and to participate in environmental rallies. Each cluster was further split into corporate and individual decisions. Therefore, apart from individual decisions, the team aimed to control the environmental decisions made by centers of power, whether it is those at a corporate or a governmental level.

Through Article 4, everyone made a commitment to never influence any decisions that could not be reasonably classified under any one of these clusters.

The selection of the people who would receive the Microbees and the method in which they would get them was the subject of Article 5. In its initial form, Article 5 was largely left empty as they had not yet discussed or decided on this. They would need to amend this Article sometime in the future.

The rules of such amendments were laid out in the final Article 6, which required nothing less than the unanimous agreement of all members. The team would find themselves making several amendments to the initial Constitution, which would become their guiding light, the document that united and bound all of them under one purpose: to save the planet from destructive human activity.

***

The weeks turned to months, and Cecilia had already poured over a third of her fortune into this dream, putting her money where her mouth was. Wayne felt extreme admiration for the woman who, in her thirties, had decided to work her ass off to do something worthwhile, rather than retire and enjoy her fortune. Wayne was also a pragmatist. He knew that the money would end at some point, and that then the dream might fall apart.

He used his own exceptional business skills to ensure that Uniocom became profitable. Uniocom did not discover the cure for AIDS, but it did discover several drugs that changed the game of Big Pharma. It now employed 650 people, all scientists of the highest caliber, many of them working with a specific mission in mind, to decode the Microbees' signals, but having no idea as to how their discoveries would ultimately be used.

Sandy, who was still enrolled at Penn but had only taken a couple of classes, had made great progress with Bale on determining exactly what they needed the technology to do. They had decided that whatever was built would need to influence both input and output. This meant that the Microbees would need to get input from the human brain, evaluate it in a split second, and create a new signal to influence decision-making. As had been agreed by Cecilia with Sandy, they focused on the small decisions, things like: Should I throw this can of Coke in this trash bin or should I walk ten feet further to put it in the recycling bin? Should I buy this energy-efficient light bulb? Little did they know, the light bulb itself would become a crucial part of their plan.

***

A separate, but simultaneous development was Welit, an Israeli company founded by Amir Levy and funded by an unknown US-based venture capital firm called Invest.io, which had been created to support high technology startups, though as yet Welit was its only investment.

Welit had acquired Hilight, another Israeli startup, engaged in developing Li-Fi technology. Li-Fi was the future of Wi-Fi, much safer, with no electromagnetic waves. It used LED lights to transmit and receive data at phenomenally fast speeds. Safer and faster, Li-Fi was due to overtake Wi-Fi by 2030 – sooner, if Cecilia had anything to do with it. About half of the money Cecilia had funneled into the project was to make Li-Fi more prevalent, and faster. With Cecilia's help, Amir had managed to turn Welit into a profitable company by producing a market-leading LED light bulb that cost under $1. Welit's light bulb was Li-Fi ready, hence, enabling the transmission of digital signals via power grids.

While all this was going on, Frank and John had been working on the actual mechanism that would be used to start changing people's decisions. Frank was working on the Microbee software. John had graduated from Penn but, following a huge contribution by Uniocom to the Department of Nanotechnology, he was offered a research position to continue his research. This gave him access to one of the world's most advanced nanotechnology research labs.

Frank had also graduated, from Caltech, and moved to Philadelphia to work closely with John. Neither John nor Frank had any idea of what the strategy would be once the device was built; all they needed to do was to create a microscopic device that would attach to cells in the front cortex of the brain, where all decisions are made, listen in to the electrical signals created by the neurons and change them.

How the Microbee would be inserted into a human body and reach those cells, let alone on the scale needed, was unknown to them. What they did know was that the Microbee had the computing power of a standard calculator, and an input-output mechanism that would allow it to do what it said on the box. So to speak. The Microbee was so small that it was invisible to the eye. It would never go into a box.

A huge part of the Uniocom research was focused on how to influence behavior using external mechanisms. Combined, Uniocom and John's research would solve a big piece of the technology puzzle. It would not solve the issue of how the team would communicate with the Microbee once it was inserted into a human brain, but Amir was working on that. And it did not address the issue of what decisions would be affected. That was up to Bale and Sandy. And it did not address how the Microbee would enter the brains of billions of people... But Cecilia Stein was onto that...

CHAPTER EIGHT

THE TESTING

In the fall, the team decided that Sandy should return full-time to college. In the past year, she had only taken a couple of classes, and it was time to complete her studies. When she returned, unlike the other seniors, she opted to live on campus and share a dorm apartment with three other students: Maya, Kathy and Elizabeth.

Maya was a senior at Penn, a petite brunette originally from Hawaii who wanted to leave the islands as much as others wanted to go there. She had a nose ring, a couple of less than discreet tattoos on her right arm, and a straight A record at Penn. She had been dating a freshman (now a sophomore) for almost a year.

Kathy was a junior from Ohio, an all-rounder American lacrosse team player, blonde, tall and slightly overweight. Elizabeth – or Liz as she liked to be called - was British, an international exchange student with whom Sandy had hit it off immediately. She was in her third year of studies, a psych major, a brunette with a cute face and relatively short hair.

Maya and Kathy were settling into the two single rooms of the apartment, while Liz had already taken one of the beds in the double room, so when Sandy arrived, helped by the Slav with the scar, she headed for the last remaining bed.

The apartment was on the twenty-third floor of Hamilton College House, one of three high rise dormitories built by Penn in the 1970s as a "temporary" solution to an increasing student housing problem. From their room, they had a direct view of downtown Philadelphia, some twenty-five blocks away.

"Hey, I'm Sandy."

Liz got up from her bed and hugged Sandy, very European, Sandy thought. "Liz," she said, smiling.

"This is Darko," Sandy said pointing to the Slav with the scar, and Liz gave him a smile also, which was not returned.

"Darko, indeed," Liz whispered in her British accent, loudly enough only for Sandy to hear, who suppressed a laugh.

Composing herself, she told Darko where to leave her stuff and as she walked him to the door, they bumped into Kathy. "Hi," she said, and Darko mumbled something in return. "Sexy!" Kathy said to Sandy, as soon as Darko was out of earshot. "Yeah, right!" Sandy rolled her eyes. "I'm Sandy". "Kathy. This is Maya." And with this, Sandy began to get acquainted with her test subjects.

***

Over the past months, Darko had become a member of the team. His goal was not to help with whatever the team was creating. He did not know much about it, and he did not care. His sole responsibility was to keep the team safe, and he had assembled a sizable security detail to do so.

A Muslim by birth, Darko had spent a quiet, happy childhood in former Yugoslavia, with his father and brother. During his teenage years, he'd played basketball, and in his early twenties, he'd played war in Bosnia. He lost his family in the Srebrenica massacre when Serbian Christians murdered 8,000 Bosnian Muslims in what the UN described as the worst genocide on European soil since World War II. Darko had been captured, and he endured some of the worst forms of torture ever devised by man. Darko was more than familiar with the ugly side of humanity.

During the Bosnian war, Darko had sided with the Americans. He'd joined a special task force of CIA operatives who'd trained him to fly airplanes and to use guns and explosives. When the war ended, the same men helped Darko to resettle in the USA.

He had been running a private security firm when Cecilia Stein approached him and requested his services. Darko had by now cut all ties with the CIA, and his profile fitted what she was looking for. Over the past years, Darko and his men had become the security detail for Cecilia and her team. There was no reason to think that Sandy needed a security guard at Penn, but Cecilia – and Darko – were taking no chances. The project was entering its most dangerous phase yet.

***

Darko crossed Spruce Street to find his electric Tesla Model X parked where he had left it. It was parked legally. It was always parked legally. Darko never broke the speed limit, never ran a stop sign. He could not afford to be pulled over. It wasn't his gun that he was worried about. He had a license for that. It wasn't even the Uzi automatic weapon in the trunk. He had a license for that too.

It was the seat cushions, the spare tire, and the floors and ceiling of the car that he didn't want police taking an interest in. They all had been refitted with military-grade C-4. Ever since he had been trained by the US on the use of explosives, Darko never went anywhere without some of his favorite substance in the world. He didn't know where and when he might need to use it, but what he did know was that a couple of pounds of C-4 could always come in handy. And in this Tesla, he had packed much more than a couple of pounds.

Darko did not particularly care for the exterior of the car, but he loved the interior. He felt safe here, sitting on almost half a ton of explosives, just one random traffic accident away from being blown to pieces. Darko was indeed a dark man. He hadn't been born this way; he'd been made this way. In any case, he was more useful this way.

***

Testing the Microbees on humans had been the subject of a heated debate within the team. They were not going to attempt to run official tests for the Microbees, as obtaining a license for this from the FDA would be impossible. So, they got approval for a cover story. The tests themselves were complicated. The Microbees aimed to change the behavior of the human being in which they were implanted. Cecilia and the team could not possibly hope to obtain the informed consent of test subjects. They also needed to have a basis for comparing the changes in behavior. They needed to find test subjects, get to know them well, somehow insert the Microbees, run the initial programming, and then observe the differences.

They also needed to be close enough to observe any side effects. It was imperative that they be able to reprogram the subjects or to abort the process if they needed to. After several weeks of debate, it was decided that Sandy would lead this part of the project. She would return full-time to Penn to finish her studies, and she would use people whom she would get to know extremely well as test subjects.

It was important that the roommates were carefully chosen. Hacking into Penn's Residential Services system was a child's play for Frank. Finding the common thread amongst these students was just as easy.

***

The first semester unfolded uneventfully for Sandy. Sandy's class had graduated the previous year, so Sandy knew almost no one on campus. Hence, she hung out with Liz who was eager to get the most out of American college life. Sandy joined her to a range of frat parties, sometimes with Kathy and Maya, whose boyfriend Jason was a brother of the exclusive Zeta Psi fraternity. Incidentally, the Zeta Psi house was only a block away from where John was spending most of his days, at the nanotechnology building, which made Sandy feel a little awkward following Liz and Kathy's lead, ferociously flirting with drunk college students.

As the years had passed, Sandy and John had gradually grown apart, from a romantic perspective. Their relationship had turned into more of a growing mutual admiration for each other's intellect, which occasionally manifested in physical attraction, and they succumbed to old feelings. Neither of them had started any other relationship. In fact, none of the group had entered a serious relationship since they'd all met three years ago.

Though never explicitly stated, Cecilia did not encourage serious relationships. She didn't need the baggage that came along with partners. Their goal was a higher one, and everyone needed to make the relevant sacrifices. Not that she discouraged sex. "We are programmed to have sex," she had said once in a more casual conversation, "and sometimes we need to give into our programming."

Poor Bale was so engaged in the project that he'd actually separated from his wife and moved to New York. He was able to live comfortably and take care of his children under Cecilia's sponsorship, but he'd found that he couldn't be a committed member of the group and a committed husband at the same time. Such was Cecilia's influence that she could convince someone to break off a casual relationship, even terminate a long-term commitment, without uttering a word of encouragement. Of course, Bale was an extreme example, as it was *his* dream that was being put into practice. It was arguably a small price to pay to save the world.

Classroom work at Penn was boring for Sandy, who could have earned a Ph.D. twice over had she been able to publish the work she had done for Cecilia. Over the past year, working methodically with Bale and Wayne, Sandy had been able to decode the electrical signals sent from one neuron to the next when specific decisions were made. They had been able to successfully intervene and change these signals, forcing the subjects – rabbits, initially – to make different decisions.

With Amir's help, they had been able to engineer a way to communicate with the Microbees. They used LiFi protocols and took advantage of the one organ that reacts to light: the eye. The command was transmitted from regular LED light bulbs, manufactured by Welit. This was then picked up by the retina photoreceptor cells, decoded by the attached Microbees, and then travelled via the optic nerve, reprogramming the rest of the Microbees. It was a non-intrusive and readily available mechanism for reprogramming the Microbees at will. This was the single most important achievement they'd made so far, and it enabled them to start running initial tests. It meant that once the Microbees were inserted into the subject, they could follow a process of endless trial and error until they got it right.

While the programming of the Microbees had been solved through LiFi, a big challenge remained: how would they know that the reprogramming – or indeed the initial installation of the Microbees – had worked? Humans cannot transmit LiFi signals. The team considered various options and eventually came up with a simple yet effective method. They created a command that would force the subjects to say a single, specific word without consciously intending to. This command was sent in the form of light via LiFi, which was then "seen" by the subject and translated to electrical signals through the brain's normal processes. These signals were intercepted and decoded by the Microbees, and then new signals were sent to the brain's language center, and the subject involuntarily spoke the word. Their hope was that, since the command should reach the subject's language center, skipping the central parts of the brain, the subjects would not think twice about speaking the word, or wonder afterwards why they had.

The final challenge, of powering the Microbees, was overcome by Amir. After trialing several different methods, from using blood flow like a river mill, to biochemical electricity generation, he'd realized that these Microbees would be inserted into a human body, and the human body was in constant motion. This was more than enough. Thinking about how an automatic watch is wound by the movement of the hand, Amir solved the last and remaining barrier to implementing Cecilia's plan.

The only thing left to do was to insert the Microbees, which would inevitably require some kind of intrusive procedure. This was why the initial selection of the subjects was so important. They needed people who would volunteer to take part in a medical experiment. Maya, Kathy, Liz and Sandy had all lost loved ones to cancer and were all members of the Penn chapter of the Colleges Against Cancer student group. The 'Relay for Life', as it was also known, was a "collaboration of students, faculty and staff dedicated to eliminating cancer by working to implement the programs and mission of the American Cancer Society."

So it came as no surprise when, after Sandy brought home a flier about a revolutionary new treatment for cancer, they were all excited and eager to contribute in any way they could. It was great. They would even get paid: two hundred and fifty dollars each!

***

The procedure, indeed the whole process, was quite simple. The four women checked into four single rooms at the University of Pennsylvania Hospital, but only three of them were wired up to various monitoring machines. Sandy checked in too, but only to avoid raising any eyebrows. As soon as the other three girls had settled into their rooms, she left hers and joined the Uniocom team, who had set up a portable lab in a room next door under the guise of the fake cancer research. Cecilia, Frank, Wayne, John, Amir and Bale were all there, observing the experiments that they hoped would change the world.

Each room had several cameras. On the screens, they saw a doctor appear, administer the shots, which included the Microbees and whose real purpose was unrelated to cancer research. A pathologist was on call to address any immediate issues while they waited, but nothing of consequence happened.

As soon as the Microbees entered the body, they traveled through the bloodstream and, within twenty minutes, reached the cells they were programmed to attach to. The Microbees had undergone initial programming before they were injected, and through LiFi the team could communicate with them for three distinct purposes: to verify that the Microbees had properly attached to the cells; to send them re-programming code if needed; and, to shut them down, at which point the Microbees would detach themselves from the cells and be expelled from the subject using the body's natural mechanisms.

It was the first of these purposes that was put to the test when, a couple of hours later, the doctor reappeared in each girl's room holding a small device. He held it up in front of each of the test subjects, and pressed a button. A light appeared, and almost instantaneously, each subject said "Yiamas," confirming that the attachment of the Microbees had been successful.

The 'Yiamas test' was Frank's idea, but the word itself had been chosen by Sandy. "Yiamas" in Greek literally means "to our health," and is used as "cheers." It was easy to pronounce and meant nothing in most other languages. Of course, it couldn't be tested in mice. Liz was the first human being, indeed the first being of any kind, to undergo the Yiamas test. Just as the team had hoped, she thought nothing of it.

The girls spent the night at the hospital. The first results of human testing were promising. There were no visible side effects. A couple of the girls complained about headaches and were given pain killers, but in truth, the pain went away when the Microbees were reprogrammed to release different levels of electricity for each subject. John and Frank were taking notes furiously on things they needed to improve on. For example, to avoid causing headaches in the future, the Microbees would need to automatically adjust the intensity of the electricity output to be exactly as strong, never stronger or weaker, than the input. The next version of the Microbees would get this right.

The fact that the Microbees caused no detectable side effects was huge news. The next step was for the Microbees to be tested in various different situations. How did they interact with medicine? With alcohol? Drugs? Sex? CT and MRI scans?

CT and MRI scans had already been tested in mice early on. The CT scan was carried out with no consequence, as the Microbees were too small to be captured on the scan.

The MRI scan had posed a much bigger challenge. The initial Microbees had not been developed by John to be used in humans undergoing MRI tests, and so he had used ferromagnetic materials. When subjected to MRI, the heads of the first mice had exploded as the Microbees were pulled from all directions by the magnetic waves. So, John's team had gone back to the drawing board and built a Microbee out of non-ferromagnetic material.

Indeed, no detail had been overlooked. The team had done rigorous testing over the span of several months to perfect John's initial invention before any decision was made to implant Microbees to anyone's head.

***

When the girls returned to their dorm, Sandy got to work. She had produced an online reporting tool, where she would log all the activity of her room mates, from sleep patterns to toilet visits. Were the subjects more reserved? Were they more promiscuous? More relaxed or more stressed? She also had extensive discussions with them to try to assess if the Microbees have any effect on mood. Sandy was curious to find out how the Microbees interacted with drugs, fights, laughs, orgasms.

There was no scientific reason why the Microbees would have any adverse effect. It was probably overkill to undertake such rigorous testing, but the team were leaving nothing to chance. In the end, save for the minor adjustments for the headaches and some reported nausea, the team concluded that the Microbees posed no real risk and had no notable side effects. The only remaining question was regarding their effectiveness in changing environmental decisions. In order to test this, they had to reprogram the girls.

**

One cold morning, Sandy met with Darko at the corner of 41st and Market Street. They exchanged no words, just a package. Why this exchange needed to take place in such a CIA-like fashion was beyond Sandy, but this was the way Darko operated.

Sandy returned to her dorm room. No one was there. She opened the package to reveal a brand-new iPhone XV, complete with a custom application for reprogramming or, if necessary, shutting down the Microbees. The reprogramming code was already inserted. All Sandy needed to do was get the girls to look at an LED light for three seconds. That wouldn't be a problem, as the flash on the iPhone had been replaced with an LED light. All she needed was to take a picture of them.

She did it that very evening, as she didn't want to waste any time. They had gone through almost a bottle of red before Sandy proposed taking a photo with her brand-new phone. She held it up at the end of a selfie stick and they all raised their glasses. The flash flickered and all four girls said "Yiamas," though only one knew why, only one had said it voluntarily.

At the girls' request, Sandy posted the photo on Facebook and tagged the others. And thus, the moment in history when the first humans were reprogrammed to take more environmentally friendly decisions was captured and shared with people who would never recognize it for what it was.

Sitting in front of his computer at his lab, John was the first to see the post which Sandy had captioned "Looking forward to a bright future."

"We're on," he said to himself, as he 'liked' the post.

***

The first positive signs were apparent immediately, evident in a multitude of changes. Their apartment upgraded their recycling bins, now separating six different types of trash. They took more care conserving energy. They joined environmental groups, and became active members. One night, returning from a Zeta Psi party, Liz was so drunk that she could hardly walk. Yet, she had taken a two-block detour to find a recycling bin for her empty bottle of Miller Light.

So, it was apparent that the programming had worked. But would it make any difference to the world? With the three girls, not really. But rolled out to millions, or billions, the combined effect would be huge.

The Penn test was a huge success, and Sandy was ordered to end it. Kathy, Liz and Maya had played an important role in changing the future of humankind. No one had been hurt. It was time to move on to the next stage.

One night, Sandy returned to the apartment, ready to take another selfie, this time to shut the Microbees down. But she was met with unexpected circumstances. Recycling bins had been turned over, there was broken glass everywhere, and Maya was sitting in the middle of the living area, crying, and being consoled by her bewildered roommates.

Kathy's lips moved silently, "Jason dumped her," Sandy read. Maya had been going out with Jason for almost two years, and they seemed a match made in heaven. There had been no apparent signs that this relationship would come to an end anytime soon.

"Why?" Sandy whispered, but Maya heard. "It's these stupid recycling bins," she shouted as if it were Sandy's fault. In fact, Sandy had tried to maintain a neutral – bordering on negative – stance towards the new eco-friendly enthusiasm that had overcome her roomies. She didn't want her own bias to contaminate the test results.

"Is she kidding?" Sandy asked Kathy.

"Apparently, we've been spending too much time on pro-environment rallies and with the environmental groups. It turns out Jason is somewhat of a climate-change denier."

Sandy was appalled by this, but tried to hide her feelings. She liked Jason, and she was really sorry for Maya. Though she'd never know, her relationship breakdown was indeed Sandy's fault. Maya's feelings were oscillating between anger and sadness. "I'm not even a big environmentalist. Never have been. I'm not sure what's got into me," she said, sobbing, no idea how literal the answer was.

"It'll be OK," said Sandy, "we'll get rid of the bins, you can stop going to the meetings, and you'll get back with Jason."

Liz and Kathy shot bewildered looks at Sandy, as if she'd said something crazy. But it was Maya's reaction that really surprised Sandy. "That's the thing, Sandy, there's a rally tomorrow and I really want to go. And I don't want to stop recycling. Jason will have to accept me for who I am now."

Sandy urgently wanted to take the picture as planned, but this wasn't a moment anyone would want to remember. So, she just stood there, helpless.

For the first time it dawned on her. Changing people's behavior would eventually lead to changing their beliefs. It was called cognitive dissonance, the need for the mind to align actions with beliefs. The Microbees had forced a genuine mindset change in Maya.

Eventually, on another day, Sandy did take the picture. "Yiamas," all three girls had said in unison, a cheers to the end of the Penn test. But would the effects end also? Sandy spent another month with the girls before eventually graduating and moving on. The recycling bins never left the apartment. The girls remained active supporters of the environmental groups. Maya never got back with Jason.

CHAPTER NINE

THE PILOT

It was Saturday September 11, 2021. In Lower Manhattan, there were memorial services to mark 20 years since the attack on the World Trade Center. The US President was in town, and the city seemed to stand still for a day. But not for a team of seven in Midtown. It was their monthly meeting, and something as sinister was brewing at the top of the Metropolitan Tower.

It had been 2 years since they had first met here. Two impressive and exciting years. Years of creation and advancement for all of them. Even in the absence of the grand plan, the group would still be considered a success. Uniocom was now being noticed by big pharma companies, and top talent across the USA wanted to work there. Welit had taken the LED market by storm and was now the undeniable market leader.

John was also doing great, raising some eyebrows in the academic world, both in terms of his research results and his seemingly endless capability to find sponsors. Sandy, Frank and Bale, though equally successful, were working in obscurity, their work recognized by no one other than Cecilia.

They were all sitting in the usual semicircle, glasses of Malbec in their hands, spirits high, the sun setting in spectacular Technicolor before their eyes. Cecilia was wearing a short flowing green dress, and she looked fantastic. Everyone in the group was in love with her. She had become their boss, mentor, leader, friend, and employer. She gave meaning to their lives, meaning that they never thought they would have. She gave them power, and they gave it to her in return. It was an incredibly strong bond that each had with her and, through her, with each other.

Sitting down with her legs crossed and leaning forward with her hands on her knee, Cecilia announced, "We are now ready to roll out a major pilot."

This came as no surprise, as the preliminary tests at Penn had gone better than expected. Still, the team had many questions about how this would work.

Cecilia stood up and said, "We have the Microbee, ready and able to control neurons. We have the I/O mechanism ready to control the Microbee. We also have the Constitution" - referring to the set of rules and regulations that Bale and Sandy had drawn up and everyone had agreed to – "And we have the delivery mechanism ready to go," she said looking toward Wayne who, frankly, had no idea what she was talking about.

Circling around, Cecilia looked at Bale, who was working on his own side project, which would be revealed shortly. She pressed a button to turn on the 100-inch TV screen at the far end of the room. Everyone turned to face the screen, which showed a Google Earth image of an island.

Cecilia said, "This is Nauru, the smallest island country in the world. Population ten thousand, unemployment 90%. It is also the country with the largest number of overweight people; 97% of the population is overweight, with 71% being classified as obese, and 40% are suffering from diabetes," she said, flipping through slides showing the statistical data on the screen interspersed with pictures of obese Nauruans.

Cecilia turned to face Bale again, who got up and went over to the screen. "I've been on this island. People are fat and jobless. We can help them."

"In Nauru, virtually every light bulb is manufactured by Welit," said Amir. Cecilia had insisted on donating 100,000 LED light bulbs to this unknown country.

Cecilia smiled. "We have enough Microbees, as we have been using the Penn lab to produce trillions of Microbees," she said, looking at John.

"Yeah, we raised some eyebrows, but further donation from Uniocom has helped subdue any objections," he said. "But how will we inject these into the subjects?"

"We'll inject them," Wayne replied, who finally understood why he was so central to the deployment of the Microbees. "We'll put them into the shots of our new diabetes research drug. So what decision do we want to affect?"

"Oh, we'll start with something simple and entirely measurable," said Cecilia, smiling more broadly now. "We're going to put the Nauru people on a diet."

***

Within two and a half years, this group of scientists had broken through every single barrier to inserting a mechanism for controlling human behavior. They had created a small device, economically viable, able to connect to the human brain and capable of receiving signals from the outside using the body's in-built visual sensory system.

The ability to control dietary impulses involved a cluster of decisions that had been outlined in the Constitution as diet was a key discussion point in Bale's original sustainability papers. This meant that the diet the Nauru people were about to be put on was within the parameters of the Constitution.

It took some of Cecilia's cunning negotiations to convince the Nauru government to test the new promising Uniocom diabetes drug to the 4,000 Nauruans suffering from the condition. Batch AHR 224485 of Uniocom Inc's shots, destination Nauru, each contained five different types of Microbees. Once the dark red liquid was injected, the Microbees would attach themselves to the neurons that affect dietary decisions. They would be pre-programmed to cause different dietary decisions, but they could also be controlled via LiFi signals in case they needed to be reprogrammed.

All this had already been tested on Kathy, the unwitting participant of the Penn human tests. Initially, they had programmed her to lose weight and, indeed, she had lost some ten pounds over four weeks. Then, one night, Sandy reprogrammed her to gain weight and immediately after, Kathy had claimed she was "soooo hungry" that she'd rushed to the nearest twenty-four Burger King, a joint which the students affectionately referred to as Murder King, where she gobbled down a double whopper with cheese, drowning it with milk shake. She went on to gain a further eight pounds before Sandy put a stop to it.

So, they knew in principle that the Microbees could control diet. But the real test would be on the Nauruans. Here, the team would learn the true impact of messing with decisions on a mass scale in a closed society.

***

The Gulfstream landed at Nauru International Airport, as it was called, though there was no evidence that any international airlines flew to Nauru.

The full team was there under the cover of being a research delegation sent there by Uniocom to examine the effects of diabetes in a controlled environment. The government had given Uniocom permission to create a medical lab on the island and to study up to 4,000 diabetics. The lab itself was a building that looked uniquely out of place. A concrete two-storey building, it had small, narrow windows on the ground floor and large floor to ceiling windows on the upper floor. It was painted white and occupied an acre of land. When Cecilia's team arrived, it was already in place and fully staffed by international and local employees.

One of the benefits of having built their own lab on the island was that they also built accommodation for the team. They could, therefore, pass up the Menen Hotel, named after the main town of Nauru but looking more like the "Menace" hotel. Ranked number 1 out of 1 hotel in Nauru by TripAdvisor, it had 30 reviews and a 2.5-star overall rating, with comments ranging from "Extremely Average," to "Needs Love".

Thankfully, the Gulfstream team would be staying in nice rooms, on the floor above the lab. Of course, their arrival on Nauru island was big news for the locals, and the government made sure that camera crews were at the airport and ready to interview these foreign investors and researchers who had decided to take an interest in their little island nation.

Wayne Ross took it upon himself to give interviews. He was the CEO of Uniocom Inc, the American up-and-coming pharmaceutical company that had taken a great interest in curing diabetes and had built an impressive lab on the island, giving jobs to dozens of locals and supporting the local economy.

As the others walked towards the terminal, Wayne approached the President of Nauru, who he had met on a previous trip, and together they confidently approached the microphones. The President spoke first, in accented English, which was one of two official languages in Nauru. "We are proud to welcome Nauru's largest foreign investor to our island. The research they conduct may solve our biggest health problem, and contribute to the global eradication of diabetes."

He turned to Wayne, who said, "We are here to conduct non-intrusive tests on our new shots, which we consider to have therapeutic, not just symptomatic effects. Our new shots are also being tested in the USA and elsewhere, and we are grateful to the Nauru government for giving us the opportunity to test them here, where the environment is more controlled." It was true that the FDA had approved clinical tests of a new shot, produced by Uniocom. The shot was approved. Not the Microbees in the shot.

The state TV journalist, a fat woman who looked like she was diabetic herself, asked, "People here are worried that we are being used as guinea pigs. Is that what's happening here?"

"No, no, absolutely not," Wayne assured her. "On the contrary, Nauruans may be the first people to benefit from our new shots, and in this way, you will help make history in our quest to cure this disease." Of course, all this was a lie. Weight loss could help diabetes symptomatically, but it could not cure the disease. But Wayne Ross and the Uniocom team would be long gone before this became apparent.

"Dr. Ross, how long will you be here?" came the next question.

"The tests will take about a month. Personally, I've decided to take some time off and stay on in your beautiful island for a while, perhaps even the entire month."

This impressed the journalist, who turned towards the camera. "The CEO of a large American company staying on the island is an honor for us," she said, not realizing that in the group that had landed that day, there was also the CEO of a major Israeli company, as well as the former CEO of a global social network.

***

The following morning, they all rose bright and early. It was early October, the month with the least rainfall in Nauru. There was not much to see on the island, though the surrounding sea was inviting.

Darko had joined them to ensure they were safe. He'd had concerns about the Nauru test. It was their most dangerous mission yet. He would have liked to have his team with him, but they couldn't unload what was effectively a small army in the sovereign state of Nauru. He would have settled for his Tesla but that too was not possible. So he brought a small briefcase, the contents of which provided him with some comfort.

That same morning, the first Nauruans would be injected with Microbees. They had split the 4,000 or so diabetics into three random groups. Group A would include 2,000 people who would receive Microbees programmed to help them lose weight. Group B included 1,000 diabetics who would receive Microbees designed to get them to gain weight. To ensure that it all worked well, another one thousand Nauruans would form Group C, who would be injected with Microbees, but with no programming associated with weight loss or gain. They would form the control group. This was because they needed to confirm that the weight loss or gain was due to the programming of the Microbees, and not due to some other random factor involving the injection of the Microbees.

The process itself had been designed by Amir, Wayne and Frank, and was very simple. The patient would come to the lab, happy to enter one of the few air-conditioned buildings on the island. They would give their name and ID number and wait to be called.

When the patient was called, blood would be drawn and analyzed, and the shot administered. They would then be told to wait for another two hours before being called to a different room where they would undergo a Microbee-detection test. John and Frank had estimated that the maximum time it should take the Microbees to find the host cells was twenty minutes, which was enough time for the blood to circulate around the body at least twenty times. But just to be doubly sure, they made the patients wait two hours. With 90% unemployment, it wasn't like they had anything better to do.

The recently injected subjects were then directed to a room with a black floor and ceiling, and black sound proofing material on the walls. The subjects were told to stand in the middle of the room, and then the LED lights would flicker, transmitting a message. "Yiamas," the subject would say, confirming that the Microbees were in place and operational.

The subject was then considered "droned". Everyone agreed that the word was horrible, but the term had somehow stuck, so this was how they referred to test subjects. Each "drone" had a unique identifying number.

"Hey guys, we just started processing humans, much like the Nazis did," said Frank lightheartedly, at some point during the day, in what was a really bad attempt at humor. The group had not missed the similarities to Auschwitz, but their cause was benign and noble so, in their view, that justified their actions.

All patients in all groups were rewarded for their patience with a large buffet of food. The only thing they had to do was to pass through the till, where they gave their unique ID number and had their tray weighed. They did not have to pay.

Four hundred Nauruans passed through the lab on the first day. Three hundred received the "get thin" or "get even fatter" programming, and one hundred were not programmed at all.

The results of the first day already confirmed that the pilot was working. On average, the buffet trays of the "get fatter" group weighed 50% more than the trays of the "get thin" group, and 20% more than the control group. Just as they had predicted.

More importantly, there had been no side effects. As darkness fell over Nauru that night, the group retired, quite exhausted but excited. It had been a good day.

***

Nearly four thousand Nauruans went through the same process, except for a few hundred that did not give their consent or were excluded for medical reasons. By mid-October, they had all been grouped into A, B or C. The effects were measured during the following ten days when the Nauruans returned for tests.

The average weight loss of a Group A patient was 4%, which was impressive. Group B, the "get fatter" group had gained 3% in weight, and the control group was 0.1% heavier, which was well within the margin of statistical error.

The blood tests already revealed that blood sugar levels were also quite promising for the "get thin" group. The Nauru test was looking to be huge success. As the team were making plans to get out of Nauru, the President asked if Wayne would kindly stay for their national holiday on October 26. This was only a few days away and so Wayne reluctantly agreed, after consulting with Cecilia, of course. It was a decision that they would both come to regret.

***

It started the day before the national holiday as a small skirmish between Group A patient Nora Kun and Group B patient Reanna Adeang. Nora had lost 10lbs in the three weeks, while Reanna had ballooned from 170lbs to 182lbs. Though they were friends, their friendship was tested when Reanna's husband, a Group B patient himself, paid Nora a compliment.

This sparked fury in Reanna, not so much directed toward her husband, who was edging on obesity himself, but at Uniocom, who had "ruined" her previously "sexy" figure and caused her to gain weight. So, Reanna gathered her Group B friends, clearly distinguishable by their weight gain, and formed a protest team. One of the team members was a statistician who informed them that Uniocom was probably working with control groups, and that he was not in the group that was benefiting from the new drug.

Nauru was a small country, and news spread fast. Soon enough, the fat reporter from the national TV station joined the group. After making several failed attempts to contact Wayne, and knowing that she was risking her own job, she decided to open the evening news with a report on the "large number of guinea pig Nauruans" who were gaining weight. It wasn't difficult for people to figure out which group they were in.

A Facebook group was formed, and 450 people joined, each posting the number of pounds they had gained over the past month. Looking at the angry emojis under the posts, it was evident that the group had gained traction. Then someone posted the idea of staging a protest.

***

Darkness had fallen and Sandy, Amir and John were having a quiet beer at a small sitting area above the lab. Darko was also there, in a corner of the room, alone, speaking to no one as was his usual tendency. Then Darko noticed a large crowd approaching the lab from a distance, and his familiar instincts kicked in. "We have to go," he said calmly, and left the room to summon Bale and Frank.

Sandy looked at John and Amir with a puzzled expression on her face. They had already packed, as they were due to leave the following day, but Frank and Bale were still downstairs in the lab working on uploading the test results and destroying some paper evidence. Cecilia and Wayne had been invited to dinner by the President, and were at the Presidential Palace.

She looked out the window and saw the group, moving closer now. What were their intentions?

***

Frank was keying in commands on his laptop when Darko rushed into the lab and told them to wrap it up.

"I need 15 more minutes to get everything uploaded," said Frank.

"I need a couple of hours to destroy all this evidence," Bale objected, his face helpless, indicating to Darko the stack of papers he was feeding to the shredder.

"We don't have a couple of hours. We barely have fifteen minutes. Can you finish uploading upstairs?"

"Sure," Frank said, and picked up his laptop. The whole building, indeed, the entire country, was Li-Fi ready.

"We can't leave these behind," said Bale, gesturing at the stacks of paper.

"Go upstairs, leave these with me," replied Darko.

***

Bale and Frank joined Sandy, Amir and John on the top floor of the lab. From there, they had floor-to-ceiling window views of the crowd, who had by now gathered around the lab. They were singing and chanting, and some of them were brandishing tall lit torches. Their intentions became clear when they tried to break into the lab.

"What the fuck," said John, suddenly very worried.

"What the hell happened?" asked Bale who, like the rest of the team, had missed the whole Facebook commotion.

"Where is Darko?" asked Sandy, suddenly quite eager to have him close to her.

***

Darko placed his briefcase on a table bench. It did not contain a laptop. Nor did it contain research papers. He opened it calmly, removed the handgun and the automatic Uzi. He checked that both were loaded.

Below the two weapons was his old favorite, C-4. Not much, but enough. Feeling a rush of excitement, like a kid that was finally allowed to play with a coveted toy, he removed two blocks and set them around the stack of papers Bale had been in the process of destroying. All the while he could hear the crowds outside banging on the door. How long would the door hold, he wondered. He needed just a couple more minutes.

***

"How much longer?" asked John

"Five minutes," replied Frank

"In five minutes, a bunch of these fat Nauruans will get in and eat us!" John was terrified, but still attempting a joke.

"Is there a way we can stop them?" asked Amir.

"What do you mean?" Frank replied, cautiously.

"I mean, could we change their programming?" Amir said, a hint of panic in his voice now.

They could hear the angry mob outside the door trying to break in.

The windows on the lower floor were too narrow for any human to crawl through, let alone the obese Nauruans. Still, the mob broke some of them for effect, and then someone threw in a torch. If they couldn't get in, they would force them out.

It was sheer bad luck that the torch fell onto flammable materials, and the lab quickly caught alight. Smoke started flowing toward the top floor, and the entire team panicked. They could see the Nauruans outside trying to raise a ladder to enter the building from the first floor. Sandy and the others closed the windows, and effectively cut off their fresh oxygen supply.

"Oh my God, we are going to choke to death in here," Sandy exclaimed. They could hear sirens outside now, and a fire brigade showed up but couldn't get close enough to the building due to the angry mob blocking the way.

The police were also there, but the crowd was just too large.

Then, things got even worse. A huge explosion was heard from the lab, and the entire building shook as if it was going to collapse. It was Darko's C-4, at the floor below, but the team had no way of knowing this, and they panicked.

Civil unrest was unfolding right in front of their eyes, and they were responsible. People could die tonight, and not just them.

Bale, the most senior among the group with Cecilia, turned to Frank and said, "We need to stop this madness. Now."

Sandy looked at him and then at Frank, who nodded at Bale and picked up his laptop. "How? How are you going to stop this?" she asked, with a rising panic in her voice.

Frank began to furiously hit the keyboard keys and ignored her. She turned to Bale. "Richard, how are we going to stop this?" she screamed.

Bale spoke softly, "The Microbees."

John, also distressed, asked, "But how? We haven't programmed such a command. It doesn't fall under any of our clusters. And we don't have the LiFi setup."

Amir, looking over Frank's shoulders, said, "We don't need to. We have the street lights."

"Are you talking about a mass reprogramming of drones?" Sandy asked, alarmed, but desperate.

"Yes," Bale said, ignoring the ethical objection that Sandy was clearly grappling with. He needed to control the situation before it got out of hand.

"Got it," said Frank. "C'mon guys, let's do this before someone gets hurt. We can worry about the ethics of it later."

"What are we doing?" John asked.

"We're sending these lines of code to the drones. The programming should cause them to disperse. We run this, and that stops," Frank said, nodding toward the windows.

At that point, a shot was fired; the bullet hit the window frame and everyone ducked.

Bale gave the order. "Run it."

Frank pressed enter and the code was sent wirelessly to a mainframe that controlled the street lighting around Nauru. It went straight to the public power corporation and was instantly transmitted from all public street lights. The team had a prime view of its effects from the first floor of the burning lab.

"Yiamas," the Nauruans said concurrently. The chanting stopped. The efforts to enter the building stopped. Bale and the team had a front row view of what their technology was capable of.

"Run it again," Bale said, to ensure all drones had seen the LiFi. "Yiamas," the Nauruans said again in unison, and they began to depart peacefully.

At that point, Darko entered the room and forced everyone out, with a gun still in his hand. There was a police escort waiting outside. Cecilia and Wayne were waiting in a van. The group quickly got in, and the van sped off toward the airport.

Frank took out his laptop and confirmed that the research data was now safely stored in the cloud. Bale looked at Cecilia and said in a soft voice, "We need to shut this thing down before we go."

Cecilia looked away, outside the window, knowing that this test, while successful in many ways, could prevent her from achieving her ambition to save the world. She watched peaceful Nauruans returning to their homes. No harm had been done; indeed much harm had been avoided here. But they had discovered that if you introduce a big change to a society, you run the risk of disturbing a delicate social balance built over generations.

They had learned something in Nauru, but they had also experienced the darker side that they'd known the technology had. The cohesion of the group itself would need some mending. As she was having these thoughts, Cecilia looked at Sandy, who was sitting across from her, and the look on Sandy's face staring back at her was pure disappointment. *We will deal with this later*, she thought, and looked then to Frank, who had his cell phone ready and waiting for the order.

"Shut it down," she said, and Frank pressed the button. "Yiamas," the Nauruans said again in unison, and with that, the Microbees shut down and the Nauruans were de-droned, bringing the Nauru test to an end.

***

As they entered the airport, Sandy saw dozens of Uniocom employees scrambling to board the single Boeing 737, having been given the order to evacuate the island. The group of eight boarded the Gulfstream, and immediately the plane began the short taxi to the end of the runway.

As they took off, they could see the lab, still blazing. Despite the local fire brigade's efforts, it had been completely consumed by fire, destroying the largest single direct foreign investment that the country had seen in years. Sandy couldn't help thinking that they had left the place in a much worse state than they had found it.

Sitting opposite Sandy, Frank obviously did not share her concerns. "That was awesome, man," he said, exhilarated. "Yiamas," he lifted his hands and gestured as if he was the conductor of a symphony orchestra.

Sitting behind Sandy, John, said coldly, "Shut up, Frank."

"Hey, hey, chill," Frank responded, annoyed.

Sandy got up from her seat, burning with fury. "Don't tell him to chill," she screamed. "Didn't you see how we were controlling those people? Didn't you see how we just stopped them from fighting?"

"Yeah," said Frank, in a slow, patronizing tone, "and that was a *good* thing. What, did you want to let them kill us?"

"That's not the point, you bleeding imbecile. If we can make them stop fighting, we can also make them start fighting." Sandy shouted.

John added, more calmly, "The point is, we've created a remote control for people, and we've just handed it to wizkid Frank here." The singular incantation of "Yiamas" had send chills down John's spine, who was feeling uncomfortable like Oppenheimer, the creator of the A-bomb, who famously wrote, "Now I am become Death, the destroyer of worlds," after witnessing the first ever nuclear blast.

"Who gave permission to Frank to create that command?" asked Sandy.

"I did," said Cecilia bluntly. She was now standing up, her face dead serious. "There was always a possibility that something would go wrong with an experiment of this size. It was the right thing to do, so that we had the power to stop things from getting out of hand. Today, we saved lives. For the purposes of the experiment, and for our mission, it was necessary."

But Sandy wasn't letting it go. "We all should have agreed on this."

"You can't be involved in every decision, Sandy. I had to make a decision, and I did." She said this in a "like it or not" tone of voice that angered Sandy further.

John picked up the conversation, speaking more softly and in support of Sandy. "We have to agree to these things, Cecilia. It's one thing to reprogram one drone at a time, it's a completely different thing to have the technology for mass reprogramming using street lights. That power shouldn't be in the hands of any one person, not even yours."

The plane fell into heavy turbulence, forcing them to pause the conversation for a few minutes. *A mid-Pacific crash would be the perfect ending to this disastrous day*, thought Sandy. Before long, the turbulence stopped, and when the conversation resumed, everyone was calmer. Wayne spoke first.

"Guys, I'm not sure what you thought we were developing all this time. Yes, John, this is indeed a remote control for people's thoughts and decisions. We knew this from the start. Today we used the technology in a way it should never be used again."

Bale added, "Our mission is clear: to affect only those decisions related to the sustainability of our planet. And yes, the idea of mass reprogramming never came up before. But for the experiment, we had no choice but to leave a door to that open, and we should be thankful we did."

John was still furious, as was Sandy. For John, it was a grave misuse of the technology he had developed. For Sandy, it was a breach of trust. Both John and Sandy were deeply insulted, at a professional and at a personal level.

"I think we need to introduce a new rule in the Constitution," Sandy said. "I think that none of us should have the power or right to implement mass reprogramming."

"That's... really difficult," said Frank. "The only way this can be done without restricting us to reprogramming individual drones is to use the drone's unique identifier as a password of sorts in order to access the Microbees. But I don't understand the big fuss, anyway," he continued, getting to the substance of the conversation. "No one here wants to create an army."

"No one here, and no one now. But we can't have a technology that could give a single person that power," Sandy replied, firmly.

"But that kind of change would set us back months."

Cecilia intervened. "Frank, I'm the last person who wants a delay of months. But I have to side with Sandy on this one. We need rules governing mass reprogramming."

So, on the plane ride back to New York, they came up with rules. If mass reprogramming were ever needed, all members of the team would need to agree to the change, make it a part of their Constitution, and add their electronic signature to signal their agreement. To ensure that they would all indeed be present during the signing process, they agreed to use special security equipment to scan the irises of their eyes. Once all members had 'signed' via the iris scan, the message could then be transmitted to all drones without the need for unique drone codes.

If, however, all members of the team did not agree, they could still make programming changes on an individual basis using each drone's unique number. But even then, at least four out of seven team members needed to sign to make this happen.

These safeguards were put into place to protect against a rogue member deciding to use the technology for their own benefit. Once the team agreed, most members of the team shut their eyes to put this stressful day behind them. Cecilia stayed awake, happy to have passed through this hurdle, but worried about the team's cohesion. The plan needed to keep moving ahead, a little behind schedule, but ahead all the same. There was still one major obstacle to overcome and she needed everyone's buy in.

She got up to go to the toilet, and noticed that Frank was not asleep. Over the next minute, whilst looking at herself in the toilet mirror, she made a snap decision. Returning to her seat, she whispered something in Frank's ear. He smiled, pulled out his laptop, and started typing code furiously. Next, Cecilia went to the cockpit and knocked on the door. Darko opened it, she whispered into his ear too. He did not smile. He acknowledged the order with a slight nod of the head, and closed the door behind him, stepping into the main cabin. He moved towards the back. Frank saw him and winked, but got no reaction. Darko was just following orders. He didn't know that the team had crossed a line today. Or that another line was about to be crossed.

CHAPTER TEN

VIRAL DEPLOYMENT

12 months later

The child ran frantically towards her home, clutching the medicine her father had requested like her life depended on it. She burst into a dilapidated building and tore up a flight of stairs, which hadn't been cleaned for weeks. She barged straight into the apartment, her home, which had once hosted seven members of her family. It was as small as a studio apartment in any western city.

There in front of her, lying on a mattress on the floor, was her mother. Her face told the story of the pain she was enduring as she burned up with fever. Sitting dejected on the mattress next to her was her father. He had been crying, a show of emotion she had never seen from him before.

The teenage girl was overcome by the unfairness of it all. When had their luck run out, she asked herself? Hadn't they suffered enough? Years earlier, they had left their home country, fleeing on foot to avoid the civil war, narrowly missing a chemical weapon attack near their home.

They had survived in a Turkish refugee camp for three years. It had been a dangerous time, but her father had managed to keep them safe and together.

When the war was over, as they returned home, they witnessed families cruelly and literally torn apart by leftover land mines. Her family was one of the lucky ones. Back home, they tried to rebuild their lives, amidst the continuing terrorist attacks that killed hundreds.

This girl was no stranger to fear. In fact, she had been afraid for as long as she could remember. But this new threat, an unseen virus which had already claimed the life of one brother and two cousins, fueled a terror inside her like nothing she'd ever experienced before. She shivered to her core as she watched her mother suffering.

She sat down next to her father and hugged him. Trying to distract him, she enquired about her other brothers and sisters. He had sent them off to protect them, once his wife had been diagnosed. But not her. She refused to leave her mother's side. He respected that.

Life was unfair. First, a civil war that was fueled by a feud between foreign powers. Then a forced displacement. Radical extremism. How much more could they be expected to endure?

This global epidemic had already claimed thousands of lives around the world. By the most moderate estimates of the World Health Organization, the virus was by now statistically certain to infect a billion people, killing some 150 million, making it the worst pandemic in history.

Both the girl and her father took some small comfort from that thought, that it was a natural disaster at least, not a man-made horror. It was God's will. Or so they thought.

***

It had snowed in Manhattan over the Christmas holidays, and the city was dressed in white. The view from the top of the Metropolitan Tower was even more magnificent, as the sun set on the last day of the year. Feeling insulated from the troubles below, Cecilia, Wayne, Bale, Frank, John and Amir sat, not in the usual semicircle this time but with chairs facing the view. Sandy had flown back to Greece for a rare visit to her former benefactor over Christmas.

There were faint smiles on all their faces as each contemplated the past three years, the accomplishments and the failures. Two major and successful corporations had been established, groundbreaking research had been conducted, mass production of a world-changing device had taken place. By any standards, they were all already successful beyond their wildest dreams. But it was not enough for them. They were on the brink of setting the final part of their plan in motion and, like a sports team before a critical game, they were hyped, excited, and ready to roll.

John was especially elated. It was his discovery more than anything else that would be the foundation for the future of mankind. Of course, it was also reliant on Cecilia's cunning management, Frank's programming, based on Sandy's creative thinking, all under the supervision of Bale's steady hand. Wayne and Amir had played a crucial role in the delivery and management of the program, but it was John's discovery that had made everything possible. The Nauru experiment had put some doubts in his mind, but Cecilia had managed to alleviate his concerns, for the most part. She really was the most awesome woman, leading the most extraordinary team of people he could ever hope to meet. The plan was bigger than himself. As with any grand plan, there would be some collateral damage, but it was all for the greater good.

Tonight, John was missing Sandy. She too had had doubts following the Nauru experiment, but she too had eventually caved in light of the benefits of furthering the project. Cecilia had made several concessions, making the Constitution stricter. All this had taken a lot more than just Cecilia's Metropolitan penthouse dances. But the dances, a ritual by now, were also key to helping reduce tensions.

The fact that this viral outbreak was likely to make the world fall apart below them did not seem to concern any of them. It just validated why they needed to act.

***

On New Year's Day, the first glimmer of hope in the battle against the virus came when the FDA unexpectedly announced that it had approved a new vaccine against the H7N9 virus for mass use. A variation of the H1N1 vaccine, the new version had been shown in clinical trials to be 95% effective in reducing transmission of the virus, and 99% effective in preventing fatality. The FDA had rushed through the approval of the drug.

News channels from around the world praised the decision and other countries rushed to follow the FDA's example. Experts questioned whether enough doses of the vaccine could be delivered on time, but the producer made firm commitments.

Over the next ten days, the first batches arrived and mass vaccinations began. In the USA, where things were more organized, a system was devised. Medical students were recruited to administer the shots, and special rooms in universities and hospitals were set aside and equipped to handle the incoming masses. The US Department of Health asked people to turn up at allocated destinations based on the final digit of their social security number. Despite all this, the queues for the so-called

"Shot Spots" were miles long. Sometimes, they even crossed each other and people didn't know which way they were heading. But they were patient, and within the first 10 days, more than 50% of the US population had been vaccinated, exceeding the DoH target of 33%, which had been statistically deemed enough to halt the rapid spread of the virus.

By the end of January, almost every American had been vaccinated, on US soil and abroad. The USA became the first country in the world to eradicate the virus altogether, with a total number of fatalities fewer than 750.

In the European Union, things were messier. The European Commission initially failed to approve funding for the shots, leaving individual countries to make the decision themselves. By mid-January, with the individual governments stalling and the number of the infected rising, something unprecedented happened. The producer of the vaccines sent half a billion shots to the EU, on credit, with no official guarantee that they would ever be paid fair. It was the first time in history that a large corporation had shown less regard for profit than for the welfare of real people, and the first time they'd shown more concern for citizens' welfare than citizens' own governments.

So, Europeans got their shots, and they soon arrived in Greece, where Sandy still was. Panic had spread throughout the country, which had only seen a dozen of confirmed H7N9 deaths, but where nonetheless masses of people rushed to hospitals and doctors to be vaccinated.

One of these doctors visited Sandy's benefactor's house to administer the shot to the people and staff of the villa located in the suburb of Ekali in northern Athens. The family doctor sat on the leather sofas in the large sitting area, by the burning fireplace, as, one by one, relatives and staff were vaccinated.

Sandy stayed in the corner, after proclaiming that she had already been vaccinated. She stood there, filled with a sense of satisfaction and pride, mixed with overwhelming excitement, as she watched the doctor unpack the blood red shots, full of the secret ingredient produced on the other side of the world. Once everyone had been vaccinated, she walked over and picked up one of the empty vaccine boxes. Imprinted on it was the logo of the savior company, producer of the H7N9 vaccine that would eventually inoculate 1.5 billion people: Uniocom Inc.

***

Two days later, Sandy was back in New York. As she climbed up to the seventy-sixth floor of the Metropolitan Tower, she knew that now the real party would begin. 3C, the Command and Control Center, had been created one floor below Cecilia's apartment.

Sandy stepped out of the elevator and was immediately met by one of Darko's 24-hour security detail. Next to the single door leading to 3C was an access code keypad, in which she entered her unique twelve-digit code. She was then prompted to speak into the voice recognition system, and finally she looked straight ahead as her face was scanned and recognized. Straight away, what sounded like several sets of locks unlocked, giving her access to the entire floor.

Passwords had been given to only eight people, Darko being the eighth. Even the cleaning crew did not have access, and Darko was always there when they visited. The other residents of the tower speculated that someone famous must have moved into the building but none had seen anyone recognizable. Perhaps it was some Russian oligarch, they gossiped.

The open plan space included a large bench with seven workspaces grouped in the middle of the room. There was one space for each member of the team, and no visible hierarchies. When Sandy walked in, Frank was tapping away furiously at his keyboard, hopefully not hacking some government agency, most likely playing some weird game. Amir and Wayne were having a quiet discussion at a large Chesterfield sitting area at the far end, the corner with the best view.

"Hey guys," Sandy said walking confidently into the room. It had been a month since she'd last seen them and whilst they'd had highly encrypted video calls – with the encryption designed by Frank – they were cautious enough not to discuss anything over an open line. Nor did they exchange emails of any significance.

Amir and Wayne got up to greet her, but Frank stayed put, and Sandy realized that he had his Beats noise-cancelling headphones on. *Definitely playing a game*, she thought.

"What's up," she asked, high-fiving each of them.

"Quite a lot, actually," smiled Wayne who pointed towards the hundred-inch screen located on the middle wall and facing inwards, in case a passing helicopter could somehow read it. On the screen was a graph and something like a running chronograph below. The number on the screen briefly read 1,132,890,183, before the digits ticked over; the number kept getting larger.

"Is this the number?" She asked.

"Yes," said Wayne, letting out a laugh. Sandy and Amir also laughed, and the three of them embraced in a three-way hug.

"So we are live with 1.1 billion people and counting?" Sandy said, barely able to believe what she was saying.

"And it doesn't look like it's slowing down," said Amir. "At this rate, we could reach 1.5 billion, or even 2 billion – who knows?" They let the enormity of this sink in. A quarter of the population connected like never before. This stage of Cecilia's plan was her greatest success so far.

"And the cost?" Sandy asked, a little quieter.

The smile vanished from Wayne's face. "The official tally is ten thousand, but that could be an overestimate".

"Hey, that's good news, right? I mean, the original estimate had been 30,000 deaths for a billion drones," said Sandy.

"I guess. It now seems likely that we could get up to twice the number of drones at a third of the cost. Anyway, we decided some time ago that to do this much good, some people would need to take the fall," he said, half-heartedly.

***

It had been six months earlier that Cecilia had revealed the most sinister of her secret plans.

They had gathered at her apartment, and sat in the usual semicircle, but there had been no dancing – this was a different kind of meeting. Cecilia had spoken first, laying down the groundwork.

"We are ready to go live."

John reacted. "No we're not; we're still working on Microbee 2.0."

"We cannot wait any longer," Bale said impatiently. The average temperature of the planet has risen more than 1.5 degrees; we've reached the point of no return. We need to use the original version of the Microbees. We will have to find a way to upgrade to Microbees 2.0 at a later stage."

"But that would mean that gazillions of Microbees installed in human's brains would need to be physically replaced with the new devices. What a waste! How would we even make this costly change?" asked John.

"We can include the decision to upgrade to Microbees 2.0 in our constitution and in the original programming of the Microbees," Wayne said, suggesting that each drone would be eventually forced to inject him or herself with the new Microbees when these became available. No one offered an alternative and they were all eager to launch, so it was settled.

Cecilia then moved on to her choice of delivery method. First, she asked Bale to give a presentation on the current state of the planet. Bale was very well prepared. He had PowerPoint slides with impressive statistics about the level of pollution in the seas, the air, and on land. He referenced studies that made projections of future population growth, increasing levels of pollution, and waste management failures. It was all one sided, of course, but there was no need for a counter argument in this group. Everyone believed that the environment was on a clear path to total destruction. Still, the data was staggering.

The Cambridge professor then got to the heart of the issue.

"Every month, more than 85,000 deaths can be directly or indirectly attributed to the deteriorating state of the environment. This includes violent unprecedented storms, respiratory conditions caused by pollution, food shortages due to droughts, and many other dire and avoidable circumstances." Bale had a slide of statistics and graphical representations of these deadly phenomena, where one could see not only the clear and devastating scope, but also the steady upward trend.

Bale then went on to make projections regarding the possible benefits of a worldwide change in human behavior, focused on creating a more sustainable future. While they were only estimations, the numbers were impressive. Within one year, the number of deaths directly associated with environmental damage would reduce by 10%, or more, if people lived in ways that were more considerate of others and of the planet. He concluded his two-hour presentation with a slide showing a single estimate: 50-75,000. This was Bale's own prediction of the number of lives that would be saved within one year of the project launch.

Sandy was having trouble following why the number of lives saved was so relevant. They all knew that their solution to environmental destruction would have the collateral benefit of saving lives. She did not understand why Bale was going to such lengths to quantify that particular benefit.

When Cecilia took over from Bale, she laid out her plan to engineer a viral outbreak, and everything became clear: 30,000 people would have to die to save 50-75,000 lives, all within the same year. The long-term benefits in terms of lives saved alone would be enormous.

Amir, not Sandy, was the one to raise the obvious objection, "And who are we to decide who dies so that someone else can live?"

Wayne, already privy to the plan, had the answer ready. "We're not deciding who dies. We are substituting one natural disaster for another," he said coldly. Sandy was conscious now of just how much he'd changed since they'd first met.

"We're talking about biological warfare here," Amir objected. "This is no video game. Real people will die, like they did in 2020."

"No shit! Real people die every day. Didn't you listen to what Bale said?" came Frank's less than friendly reply. He really wanted to use the word dumbass, but he refrained.

Bale spoke next. "The human race is failing to deal with the destruction of the environment. Two people die every minute because as a species we are totally incompetent when it comes to dealing with this."

"There must be some other way," Sandy reasoned. "Why couldn't we try to convince people to volunteer for the Microbees?" She realized immediately after speaking that the level of penetration needed for the project to succeed could never be achieved through voluntary participation, and her query went unanswered.

"So when and where do we release the virus?" Frank asked.

"Summer. In the Middle East," Cecilia said.

"Why the Middle East?" Amir and Sandy asked in unison. It was too close to home for them.

When Cecilia explained, they got it. The World Cup was indeed a unique opportunity. They were also inwardly relieved that neither Greece, nor Israel had qualified. It shouldn't have made a difference, but it did. They were human after all.

They took a quick break, and all of them mulled over the consequences of what they would be putting into action. Sandy headed to the washroom to throw some water over her face. She had shocked herself. She was actually considering signing an order to murder some 30,000 random people. The WC was occupied, and Amir soon appeared behind Sandy, so they chatted while they waited. For Amir, his parents' deaths from a random bomb made it almost impossible for him to agree to this plan. *Good*, thought Sandy, Amir would take most of the heat in the inevitable disagreement.

The door unlocked and John emerged from the toilet. He seemed much more relaxed than the both of them.

***

When they reconvened, before anyone could speak, Cecilia got up.

"I know you all have concerns about this plan. I share those concerns. I have struggled immensely with the morality of the decisions we need to make.

As Richard has shown us, this talk of environmental disasters is not speculative scaremongering. This is happening now. People are dying, now. We're not releasing a virus that will kill thousands now just to hopefully save thousands at some distant point in the future. The balance will be outweighed within a year.

Humans have already made the decision to kill each other. Every time we start our car, every time we fail to recycle, every time we use plastic, or over-consume, we add to a problem that is already killing thousands of our fellow humans, people we have never met, in another part of the world."

Her voice was getting louder and louder as she moved through what was probably a well-rehearsed speech, impeccably delivered. As always, her eyes were constantly locked on someone else's, and were moving from one person to the next as she was turning around, dancing.

"We're not pushing a trigger, it's true. But we are still killing. It's like we're feeding someone nanograms of poison, each dose not enough to kill them, but..." She paused. They all got the point.

"So now here we are. We have a solution to this problem. It's a one-time opportunity. We can't wait; the situation will be irreversible in a year or two. We cannot get state sponsorship, because we cannot trust anyone else with this technology," she said, her eyes locked on Sandy's.

"We are a blip in the history of humankind. An outlier. If we don't use this technology, no one else will come up with a solution. Failure to act now will mean billions will die in the future. From this perspective, the decision is not so difficult. The decision is between action and inaction. The course of history is always changed by people who take action. Not by people who are afraid to step up and take responsibility."

Speaking more softly now, and moving more slowly, she continued. "We have a responsibility toward the human race. If we had never developed this technology, we could step away in blissful ignorance. But we did. We do have it. We know what it can do, and what it can do is a world of good.

So, we have a yes or no decision to make, it needs to be taken here, tonight, and it needs to be yes," she said, and stopped circling, her eyes locked on Bale, who looked back and smiled. Sandy turned and looked at Amir, who was watching Cecilia, transfixed. It was an impassioned speech; the best Cecilia had ever delivered. Neither Amir nor Sandy seemed ready to protest.

No one spoke for a while, and when the discussion started again, it revolved around how they could reduce the number of deaths, rather than seeking alternative deployment methods. Did the virus have to be deadly? Why did it need to be released on a global scale? Could the vaccine be released sooner?

There were logical answers to all of their questions. They couldn't create a global frenzy if the outbreak was local and non-fatal. A global crisis would provoke a faster reaction, thus risking fewer lives. The recent Covid-19 pandemic had created reflexes that would minimize the consequences.

In the end, only two concessions were made. First, they would delay the outbreak until September, giving it just a couple of months to spread before the World Cup. Second, if governments were too slow to approve the vaccine's cost, then Uniocom would provide it on credit, in order to minimize the number of deaths.

As they all gathered around the iris scanner to digitally sign the amendment to article 5 of their constitution, the outbreak had not yet started and it was still in their power to stop it from ever happening. Yet, they were satisfied that, through their discussion, they had reduced the damage that the virus would do. It was the simple decisions taken at the seventy-seventh floor of a Manhattan skyscraper that ultimately reduced the death toll by at least 20,000. It was a testament to the group's ability and willingness to make bold life or death decisions on behalf of, and for the collective good of all of humankind.

CHAPTER ELEVEN

THE SUCCESS

Mary is 33-years-old, happily married with 6-year-old identical twins. Mary wakes up, makes breakfast, and then cleans the dishes with an environmentally-friendly liquid soap. On the way to drop off the kids at school, she stops by the recycling spot and disposes of four different batches of trash, neatly separated by type: aluminum, paper, glass, general.

George is 45yearsold and suffering from a mild mid-life crisis. He is divorced with three sons, who he sees every other weekend. George travelled a lot during the week for work, but he recently took an interest in finding ways to reduce his carbon footprint. At first, he was appalled to discover that he had such a high-carbon lifestyle. Now, he conducts teleconferences rather than travelling. This way, he can also see his sons every week.

Sahib is 18 and ready to go to college. Like other boys his age, he is constantly preoccupied with sex. Being a late bloomer, he hasn't had any - with another person, that is. Like many youngsters, he is also worried by the direction the world is heading in, and he wants to do something about it. So, he joins a student science lab for environmental studies, where he meets Anny. Anny is a year older, on a year off before going to college. Anny is working on a project for more efficient disposal of batteries. Sahib is mesmerized. And totally in love.

Carlos is 72, a childless pensioner who is bitter about approaching the end of his life. His wife of 35 years passed away last year, and he is mad at her for leaving him behind to face death alone. But Carlos is completely healthy. One day, he wakes up and realizes that it may be another 20 years before he finally dies. He needs to be active again and he decides to work on an environmental project. An engineer by profession, he has worked all his life in the carbon-inducing energy industry. But he has an idea about how energy could be stored, though he's never had the chance to try and apply it. Now, at 72, revived by his sudden urge to recycle and conserve energy, he starts working on a project that will eventually lead to a major breakthrough in conserving the power generated by solar and wind panels.

Chuck is the plant manager of an aluminum factory. He is considering bids for a project to contain water pollution in the area. He has three offers on the table. One of them is 100% foolproof, but is also about twice the price of the other two. Chuck surprises himself by deciding to make a case for the more expensive bid. He is further surprised when his boss, a money-hungry SOB, agrees and pats him on the back as he leaves his office.

Carol is a career politician. At 54, she has been around long enough to be cynical about how she wins elections. She knows it's all about campaign contributions. It's all about helping big business interests over anything more meaningful, whether that's gun control or saving the environment. Yet, she turns down a major contribution from a chemical manufacturer who no doubt hoped to buy her support in maintaining their high CO_2 emissions.

Sandy is 25 years old. A recent college graduate, a Greek national living the most improbable dream with unimaginable power in her hands, she has been able to change people's lives, and the course of all humanity. Sandy is happy. Not just satisfied. Not just fulfilled. Happy. She enjoys her time with her on-and-off boyfriend John, the engineer behind her work, who is as astonished as she is by the impact they have together been able to have on the world in their short lives.

Amir and Wayne, hotshot CEOs, are living a dream that many would envy. But they don't care about status or power. Wayne has been able to achieve his lifelong dream of saving the world; his late partner Amy would have been proud. He is grateful that Cecilia convinced him to stay on board. He is also producing small miracles each day through new drugs developed by his company, Uniocom. But all this pales in comparison to the satisfaction he feels knowing that he has helped save the world.

Amir can't believe his luck. The work done by his company, Welit, and this team gives meaning to his life, meaning that he'd lost when he lost his parents. Amir once thought about taking revenge for his parents' deaths by killing a few Palestinians. He is proud and impressed that he has been able to emerge from that state of mind and do something meaningful, borne out of love for humanity, not hate.

Frank is 23 years old, and has been a hacker for as long as he can remember. He was behind some of the most notorious hacks, but only a select few know about his greatest accomplishment of all. Frank relishes the power. He's always known that he was destined for greatness. But he'd never dreamed that he would be the first human to 'hack' a human brain. And even if this thought had crossed his mind, "wouldn't it be cool to …" he couldn't have predicted that it would be billions of brains that he would hack into. For Frank, saving the world isn't so important. It's the power that makes him tick. He knows this is too much power for one man to hold in his hands. If he's to be truthful, he doesn't even trust himself.

Dr. Richard Bale is a philosopher, a sustainability professor whose theories have been put into practice, against all the odds, with phenomenal success. Dr. Bale is in it to save the world, and how this is achieved isn't important. He sometimes feels overwhelmed by the technology he's helped to developed, but mostly he is happy that his ideas, crazy as they once seemed, have found a profound and practical application during his own lifetime. These days, Bale spends his time travelling the world. He wants to watch first-hand how his great project is unfolding, and to assess if it has a different impact in different cultures.

***

The measurement of the success of the project had always been a topic of heated discussion. Bale's worldwide observations were purely circumstantial. The team needed a more rigorous approach to verify their success. Sandy and Frank were tasked with monitoring global news to see if there were any major Nauru-like disasters developing. Nothing hit their radar. The effects of their project were evident in social media trends - mentions of the environment had increased a hundred-fold in less than six months.

They also tracked progress via the environmental indexes on the stock market. They witnessed the expected growth in demand for things like recycling bins and for all products made of recycled materials.

For example, one area they monitored closely was the consumer preference, for example, for organic food. Mass food production was a huge contributor to greenhouse gas emissions, and the chemicals used to protect crops were also harmful to the environment, and to people. The preference for organic and other environmentally-friendly, sustainable food sources had been included in the cluster of dietary decisions, and Sandy was happy to see that global demand for these products was growing.

***

It was late in the morning, and Sandy was at 3C, coffee in hand, looking at three screens in front of her. She was watching the FTSE Environmental Technology Index, which tracked companies investing in new technologies that are designed to benefit the environment. She noticed that the index itself had jumped 8% since the market had opened in London. While this kind of trajectory was expected over time, a sudden jump seemed out of the ordinary.

To make their life easier, Frank had developed a unique global news article aggregator. Reportbrain, as he called it, downloaded two million articles a day from thousands of news outlets worldwide. It then analyzed the content and grouped the articles based on theme. Insightful analytics were created to compare the present day with the recent and more distant past. If the articles were in a language other than English, they were automatically translated. Using Reportbrain, Sandy was able to see that the number of press articles mentioning subjects related to the protection of the environment was on a steady growth trajectory. She was also able to figure out what was happening in the Environmental Technology Index within seconds. It was the sweetest piece of technology Frank had created since hacking the human brain.

That morning, a company called Envolution had launched its Initial Public Offering in London. Its stock price had doubled in the first few hours of trading, sending all related stock soaring upward. Sandy was reading through the articles, vaguely interested, when something out of the ordinary caught her eye. In an obscure article in San Antonio Times, one that she would never have seen without Reportbrain, she read that local investment company, Invest.io, "must be quite satisfied with the returns on their investment."

The name Invest.io rang a bell, but she didn't know why. She searched "Invest.io" on Reportbrain and, other than the same article from San Antonio, it returned nothing. Nada. "*Tipota*," she whispered in Greek. Strange.

Next she googled "Invest.io", and still nothing came up, not even the San Antonio article. The company didn't exist. She typed www.invest.io into her browser and was directed to a holding page that revealed nothing. She tried Whois to see who owned the domain name, but got no further information.

She got up, coffee in hand, and went over to the window. No one else was in at 3C to discuss this with. She returned to her desk, again typed "Invest.io" into Reportbrain, but this time there was nothing. Not even the San Antonio Times article. Now her curiosity was really piqued.

She tried searching for "Envolution", again the San Antonio Times article came back up, but this time there was no mention of Invest.io. It wasn't in the version published on the newspaper's own site, either.

With no further leads, she decided to focus on Envolution Plc. The company was growing in triple digits month on month, selling eco-friendly equipment from recycling bins to the large-scale machines used in recycling plants. It was involved in wind and solar, batteries, filters – anything and everything related to the environment. *Talk about perfect timing*, thought Sandy.

The phone rang. It was Vlad from the Metropolitan Tower reception. Her food delivery had arrived. She cleared the cache and history from her PC, as she always did. As no one was allowed on the seventy-sixth floor, she left 3C and took the elevator to the ground floor.

"Angelo," she called out, as soon as the door opened.

"Yiasou Sandy, ola kala?" came a man's reply, in perfect Greek.

"Yes, perfect, how come you're delivering this in person? Did your delivery guy call in sick?"

"I never miss an opportunity to see your beautiful face, Sandy. I'm just sad you never invite me upstairs," Angelo replied smiling cheekily.

Sandy returned his smile and said, "You do know I have a big strong boyfriend?"

"Keeps me up at night."

Sandy and Angelo shared a laugh, and Sandy paid for her delivery: dolmadakia, a taste from home. Sandy was a regular at LOI, Angelo's restaurant, which was the closest Greek place, also located between 6th and 7th Avenues, but one street north on 58th.

She went upstairs and continued her research, eating over her keyboard. By the time Frank walked in, she had moved on to reading about social unrest in Kinshasa, which turned out to be unrelated to the project.

***

Interestingly, even though there is a common belief that different cultures think and act in different ways, this mass experiment had proven beyond any doubt that the biological process of thought was the same from one culture to the next, and, for that matter, from one human to the next. Bale had known this from the start, and indeed it was the foundation of their global plan. Still, Bale was worried that the actions resulting from the Microbees would have different effects in different cultures. This was what had motivated him to travel around the world and witness first-hand the effects of his project. What he discovered was a universal sense of a common purpose. Everybody was doing just a little more to help the environment than they had done before. The common effort was visible to everyone, and was picked up and reinforced by mass and social media. This collective network, with all humans focused in one direction – a massive social network transcending culture, race, sex, color - had been Bale's initial vision, the basis for what he was now witnessing.

From Istanbul to Panama City, from Santiago to Manila, Bale was witnessing the effects of the project at ground level. In the first couple of months, evidence that the plan was working had been scarce. Following the Nauru disaster, Bale and Sandy had worked with Frank on a progressive algorithm. The behavior of humans - would not change dramatically from one day to the next. Rather, small changes would take place initially, and these changes would accelerate over the course of one year. But Bale could still see the initial effects around the world, and they were no different than in London or New York.

***

One day, at the beginning of spring, just a couple of months after their project had successfully kicked off, Cecilia invited Bale to her apartment for dinner. It had just changed to summer Daylight Saving Time, and the day had grown longer by an hour. It was Cecilia's favorite day of the year. Cecilia had decided to cook for Bale, a rare treat indeed.

They spent dinner discussing the progress of the project, Cecilia very interested to hear about his travels and first-hand experiences. They were devouring the New York cheesecake that Bale had brought when

Cecilia asked him suddenly, "Richard, what more do you want from life?"

Bale laughed. "I've got everything I ever wanted out of life. Thanks to you."

"Thanks to you, too, Richard. Seriously though, is this it? Have we achieved everything can do?"

"We can't get complacent. The proof that things are changing for the better is scarce. Let's make sure that this works before we consider any next steps," said Bale.

"I believe that this is going to be a huge success. And it's even bigger than what we set out to do. But I understand what you're saying. Just hypothetically, though, what would be our next move?"

This sounded to Bale like a rhetorical question, so he threw it back to her.

"I don't know," she replied, cryptically. "We have the ability to influence people's minds. Perhaps saving the environment was just the first step," she said carefully, eyeing him closely.

"To save the planet and all of humanity is no small feat, Cecilia. Although only we know it, you are the most influential person in history."

"I'm not looking for fame, you know that. I'm worried, Richard, that humanity is still moving in the wrong direction. Look at radical extremism, renewed nuclear proliferation, and our sub-standard leadership. We cannot trust these leaders to steer us away from disaster."

"A lot of these problems are related to poverty and inequality, which are largely driven by scarcity of resources," Bale said, not sure where Cecilia was going with this. "They are also driven by the geographic dispersion of environmental disasters, which more often than not hit the poorest regions of the world. We should expect our project to have a profound medium-term side-effect of alleviating inequality."

Cecilia leaned back, visibly not convinced, glass of wine in hand, and then continued. "The world has been moving in the wrong direction for decades. Wealth has been accumulating in the hands of the few, and then the fewer. The middle class is shrinking away to almost nothing. Hunger has not been eradicated. Social cohesion is fragile. I don't think we can wait for any medium-term effects of our project."

She took a sip of wine. "The rich need to start sharing, and not just in terms of doing what's right for the environment. I know that this is a very anti-capitalist point of view. I also know that it's ironic coming from me, a child and beneficiary of capitalist society. But I just don't get it. How can people be so content with their lives whilst so many others suffer? How can people enjoy riches that have been acquired through the suffering of others?"

She paused. Bale was intrigued, and a little worried. "We cannot solve all of the world's problems, Cecilia."

"But we can, that's just it. What's the point of saving the environment when it's still likely that some nut could nuke Central Park?" she asked, and Bale instinctively glanced in that direction.

Not giving Bale the chance to answer, she carried out, ranting slightly now. "People need to understand that in order to continue to exist, they need to co-exist. They can only achieve this if they share, in the sense of compromising their own lifestyle for the benefit of others. What we've seen over the past many decades is the exact opposite. People are selfish. They hold onto what they have, be it their inheritance or recently acquired riches. The technological revolution will only concentrate wealth further. Robots are taking away jobs, and there's no social safety net. Is this the world we want to live in?"

She pressed on, not allowing Bale to interject. He didn't have to. She knew he agreed.

"What we have achieved so far is to get people to share a bit of their time, energy, and money to benefit the environment. But we can do so much more. We can reduce social inequality, feed the poor, end all wars. Is it socially responsible, morally responsible even, for us to stop here, now that we have the power to do so much good?"

"Where is this coming from, Cecilia? If I didn't know you as well as I do, I would be worried that power has corrupted you," Bale said, politely, though in truth he was very concerned. "Power is the ultimate aphrodisiac, you know. It's what people yearn for when they don't know how to be happy. Is that what's going on here?"

"Oh, cut the crap, Richard," she replied scolding as she stood up from her chair. "The world as we know it will have to change. We both know this. Redistribution of wealth will happen, one way or the other. What I'm suggesting is helping it to happen in a peaceful way. In a way that doesn't involve humans killing other humans."

"I see no imminent threat of war," Bale objected. "We don't have the sense of urgency that there was with our environmental project."

"That can change from one minute to the next. You know this," visibly annoyed that he was not eager to accept her arguments. She sat down again and shifted the conversation.

"I want you to spend more time disseminating your theories and ideas worldwide. While people will never know what prompted their sudden change of behavior, I think that they need someone to look up to, a prominent figure. A face of the environmental movement would help amplify the effects of our project," she said. "I think that face should be yours."

"I would rather not do that," he replied.

"I know, but you have to. You are the one who has been advocating change all these years."

Reluctantly, he asked what she had in mind.

"You will keep travelling around the world, but at every stop, you will give an interview with the local media. You need to keep spreading the word. After all, we've only implanted Microbees in one-fifth of the earth's population," she said, as if this was a small feat. "We need the other four fifths to follow suit, to join the current trend."

"Don't you think that there's a risk of exposing our project?" Bale asked, still searching for a way out, though he knew that Cecilia had a point.

"It's a risk we have to take," replied Cecilia, in a way that did not allow a "no" answer, not even from Bale.

***

In the months following the dinner at Cecilia's apartment, Dr. Richard Bale, the professor and philosopher who had first argued that people needed to work together if they were to save the world, became the face of the project that, unbeknownst to the world, their team of seven had been working on for years. It was clear to the media and politicians that the environmental movement was picking up pace. Bale was just there to fuel its growth. As he flew from country to country, city to city, he gave interviews to the press, highlighting the importance of the change in people's attitudes.

In one such interview in autumn 2023, with CNN Turk in Istanbul, he was challenged about his role. The reporter was one Okan Celik, a well-known figure in Turkish media. It was a 60-minutes style one-to-one interview, conducted in English, in Bale's hotel, Soho House. Soho House is a London private members' club, where Bale was a member. Its Istanbul site is housed in a building that had been built in 1873 by Ignazio Corpi, a powerful Genovese shipbuilder, who used imported marble from Carrara and rosewood from Piemonte. Famous artists provided the decorations, with wall paintings depicting Greek mythological scenes. In the 20th century, it had served as the residence of the American Ambassador, and then became the U.S. Consulate. CNN Turk had to obtain a special permit from Soho House to be allowed to bring a camera inside.

It was fitting that Bale, a citizen of the world, but born in the UK, was sitting here, at a private British club, the former consulate of the country in which his theories had been turned into practice in a city that represented the crossroads of civilizations, discussing the future of the world.

Okan's crew had set up in the second-floor lounge, a room with high ceilings and windows offering a majestic view of the Golden Horn. Okan and Bale sat opposite each other in comfortable leather armchairs.

Okan looked at the camera and spoke first in Turkish, "We are here in Istanbul's Soho House, the former US consulate, with the man whose theories about the world have found profound, if unexpected, application in 2023. Dr. Bale, thank you for speaking to us today."

"Thank you, Mr. Celik, for having me."

"So, Dr. Bale, 2023 has been an astounding year for the environment, and I would like to first hear your assessment."

"Well, Mr. Celik, I'm happy to report that I think we're finally moving in the right direction. And this is not driven by our governments, but by the will of ordinary men and women to do their bit to protect our environment."

"And through all of our small and seemingly insignificant actions, we produce a profound aggregate effect. Is that right, Dr. Bale?"

"Yes, indeed it is. Environmental problems were never going to be solved by governments. Not within our current political structures, where the people in power rule with a time horizon of four years at most. Even here, where the ruling party has been in power for more than twenty years, the steps they've taken towards a more sustainable future in the first nineteen years pale in comparison to what has been achieved in the last year, by normal people."

"So I take it you have some numbers to support this?" Okan asked.

Bale smiled. "As a matter of fact, I do. According to the Global Environment Watch, carbon emissions in Turkey have increased every year since the change of the millennium. This is normal, as Turkey experienced a high growth rate throughout these years. Plus, the three million Syrian refugees who added to the population fleeing violence and war also played a role. Turkey was about average, in comparison to the rest of the world, all things considered.

"2023 was the first year that carbon emissions actually reduced. And this wasn't just the result of cleaner energy or new technologies. It was the adoption of these technologies at a faster rate, even when they are more expensive, that has made the difference."

"But one could argue that it's anti-capitalist to buy more expensive energy," said Celik.

"On the contrary. This is capitalism at its best. This is the ultimate proof that capitalism works," Bale lied, knowing that had it not been for the Microbees in a billion plus people, capitalism would have made this impossible to achieve. But he needed his host and his viewers to believe that there were no secret forces behind the changes. They had to believe it, or they would turn to conspiracy theories that could risk the entire project.

"But why now? What was the spark? Why was 2023 the year? Our path to environmental destruction has been a century long. We've known for at least 30 years that climate change is a huge issue. People did nothing for 29 years, and then suddenly, this year, they completely change gear. Why?"

Bale had been expecting this question, though interestingly, in at least twenty interviews, this intelligent Turk had been the first to ask it.

"It couldn't have happened in any other way, at any other time," was Bale's measured response. "Think about it. We may all share the same concerns, but was each of us doing small things to make sure we didn't further contribute to our global problem? Or that we contributed less? No. We didn't do it, because we knew that whatever each of us did, it wouldn't be enough."

Bale's tone was firm, professor-like.

"It didn't matter if I recycled. It mattered if millions, billions of people recycled. It only takes a little more effort from each of us, but we were cynical because we believed that whatever we did, it didn't make a difference."

"It's only when all of us, together, collectively started taking the same small actions that things changed. And then the positive reinforcement began. The small gestures each of us made created a big wave of change. And then we became part of something much bigger. We created a social network that transcends religion, nationality, race, sex, all of these things that work to divide us."

"And what would you call this new, environmentally conscious social network?" Celik asked.

"Excellent question, Mr. Celik, and one that hasn't been asked before. I would call it humanity. It's the realization that there are more things than bind than tear us apart."

"Still, you haven't answered my question: why now?"

"In my view, it will have been totally random. I don't know exactly what it was," Bale lied again, "but I do know that all that was needed was a spark. It's growing now because it's given people a sense of purpose. And because they're witnessing the positive results."

"So, you don't think we're going back to where we were before?"

"I'm optimistic that the course of history has changed. But we need to keep at it. We need to fight complacency."

"Do you think you were the spark, Dr. Bale?"

"Absolutely not," Bale lied for a third time. "I certainly don't want to take the credit."

"Some say that the H7N9 virus outbreak at the World Cup last year was the spark. Everything seemed to start after that."

Bale had hoped this question would not come up even though he knew that Turkey had been one of the more seriously affected countries, with more than three hundred deaths from the virus.

"I don't think so. The issue there was a disease, one that we were lucky enough to eradicate quite quickly. Environmental issues are much more pervasive, and a different type of challenge."

But Celik didn't let it go, "But perhaps the pandemics of recent years caused people to realize that, as you say, they have more things in common than not, that we now live in a globalized world where diseases affect us all equally, just as we will share in the effects of environmental damage."

"Perhaps. I'm not sure the spark is even relevant, to be honest. People were ready to do the right thing, and now they're doing it. That's all that matters. A single assassination sparked World War I. Was that spark really so significant, or were the conditions for war already there?"

"Dr. Bale, while you don't want to take credit, you are undeniably now the face of a historic change."

Bale smiled awkwardly, breaking eye contact as he looked down, embarrassed. This kind of limelight was not something he'd ever aspired to, but Cecilia had convinced him, as she always did, that it was important for people to have a face to unite the movement, a face to rally behind. And it certainly could not be her face. It had to be Bale, who had decades of publications to his name where he espoused the importance and benefits of collective action to save the planet. He was the authority on this matter, and it was his role to take on.

Of course, Cecilia had left nothing to chance. She funded his fame to make sure he did in fact become the global authority on the environmental changes currently unfolding.

Bale looked back up to his host and said humbly, "I'm sure that many theories devised by many philosophers have seen real-life applications before me. I'm just lucky that mine found its application during my own lifetime."

"I think we're all lucky for that, Dr. Bale," said Celik, closing the interview. "Thank you for all that you've done for humanity."

***

They still gathered once a month in Cecilia's apartment. These days, such was the elation of the group that they all danced well into the morning. The monthly meetings still began with an update from each member of the team. Today Bale, just back from Shenzhen and Bangalore, went first.

"Things are progressing well. I visited a couple of recycling plants and their business is going through the roof. You can see recycling bins everywhere, and this is in countries that have not yet mastered general waste management. So, overall I'm satisfied."

"Satisfied? That's the fucking understatement of the century. No, the millennium," Frank laughed.

Everyone smiled. They shared Frank's feelings, wanted to stand up and scream their lungs out in satisfaction. *The power to change the world really is the ultimate drug*, thought Sandy. But to do it alongside this unique set of people, and for a cause so noble, was beyond anything she could have dreamed of.

"I'm worried that our little secret may be exposed," Wayne said, bringing them all back down to earth.

"How's that?" Cecilia asked.

"I don't know exactly. It's just, what's happening is too good to be true. I'm worried that someone's going to wake us up from this dream, is all."

"I wouldn't worry," Frank reassured him. "What we've done is unbelievable, literally. Even if you told someone yourself, they'd never believe you."

"I agree with Frank," said Cecilia. "The strength of our secret lies in the improbability of what we've achieved."

"I'm not worried about any of us revealing the secret. I trust everyone here fully. It's just that when you have live technology in 1.5 billion people, a random event or chance occurrence could expose everything."

"Such as?" asked John.

"I don't know, maybe an MRI scan, a curious doctor, an autopsy. We can't think of all the possibilities."

"But we've tested the Microbees in an MRI scan, we know they can't be seen," said John. "A pathologist would need a super microscope, as powerful as the one at Penn, to detect the Microbee in an autopsy."

"Relax, man, you worry too much," said Frank lightheartedly. But Wayne wasn't giving up.

"Guys, we can't predict or stop a random event. We have to accept that something could jeopardize the entire project. What I'm saying is, we can't just sit back and relax, believing this will last forever. It won't."

CHAPTER TWELVE

THE RANDOM EFFECT

Christmas of 2023 was approaching and almost a year had passed from the go live date. Nothing had gone wrong. In fact, many things were moving in the right direction.

The most important piece of news was that Dr. Richard Bale has been named Time Magazine's Person of the Year. The front cover showed Bale with a backdrop of Mother Earth. The words "Dr. Richard Bale, Person of the Year 2023." And below, in smaller print, "The man who lit the spark," copying the line from Bale's Istanbul interview.

Bale could no longer go anywhere without people approaching him to thank him. There were collateral benefits to his new-found fame. His kids were now looking up to him, following five years of questioning his choices. During the year and his travels, he'd also had more chance to spend time with them. His son, Michael, was finishing school this year and wanted to study environmental engineering in the USA, a choice his father deeply approved of. He was a good student, and his father's fame would certainly help him get into the college of his choice. His daughter, Cornelia, still had a couple of years of school to go, but it was already clear that she would follow in her father's footsteps and study something related to sustainability.

So, fame and recognition were providing some benefits, although Bale still resented it, believing that the credit was collective, and not for him to claim. They needed his face, he realized this, but the progress that had been made was the result of the efforts of literally billions of people. He thought Time magazine had missed the point entirely.

Sandy felt blessed to be the closest associate of Time Magazine's Person of the Year. She didn't get any recognition herself, but she took immense satisfaction from Bale's recognition. She finally decided to reward herself by taking some time off and visiting her home country again. Her last visit, when she had seen her benefactor's family being vaccinated and receiving their Microbees, seemed so distant now. But this time, she wouldn't be visiting them.

This time, she was travelling with John, and they planned to visit some of her country's rural winter destinations. But not before visiting Amir in Israel. He had invited them to stay at his beachfront villa, and would not take no for an answer.

They landed in Tel Aviv on Christmas Eve, a holiday not celebrated in this city. Everyone in Cecilia's group was now a top one percenter in terms of wealth, but Amir was doing even better, due to the success of Welit. He'd bought a beach-front hotel, closed it, and remodeled it to create a 10-bedroom villa. "Money talks, but wealth whispers," he was often heard saying at 3C – apparently this wasn't a philosophy he adopted himself.

Despite his wealth, Amir himself was there at the airport when Sandy and John exited the security controls. He guided them to his brand-new self-driving E-class Mercedes, and they made their way to his new home. The double iron gate was already open for them, and they drove up the pebble stone driveway to a small square outside the main entrance. The house itself looked as if it had been airlifted from Tuscany. Square, stone-built, with bay windows covered in ivy winding its way up towards the tiled roof.

"Wow," said Sandy, who was not usually impressed by material riches. "Are you sure it's prudent to live such a lavish life? I mean, do we really want the spotlights on ourselves?"

"I have to," Amir said, sighing, as if he was incarcerated in a high security prison. "Welit is one of the top Israeli companies. People expect me to live a certain lifestyle. I'd raise more eyebrows if I didn't."

"It's a tough life but somebody's got to live it," laughed John as he entered the house. The ceilings were at least twelve-foot high, and right in front of them was a large staircase leading to a small internal balcony and from there, no doubt, to the bedrooms. But what John was most attracted to were the windows overlooking the other side of the building. He made his way over, and there it was, the Mediterranean Sea. A beach before it. A private Olympic sized pool before that, immediately in front of the house. Despite the time of year, temperatures were in the mid-70s and it was sunny.

"Wanna go for a swim, hon?" John asked.

"Yeah. Skinny dip? Sorry, I didn't think to pack my bikini in December."

"Hey, we can take care of that," said Amir, and a member of the house staff appeared from nowhere. Amir spoke to her in Hebrew, she nodded, took a quick look at Sandy and John and gestured that she would show them to their rooms.

"Get settled in. Your swimsuits will be waiting for you at the pool. And when you come down, please do me a favor and leave your cell phones in your room."

***

"So, what's up," asked John, when they were all settled in the poolside sitting area with thick white cushions and a marble coffee table.

"Nothing much," said Amir, unconvincingly. He clearly had something on his mind, something he was struggling with.

"C'mon man, tell us," John insisted, taking a sip of iced coffee.

"Well," Amir hesitated, "everything is just going so well. Don't you think that things are going a little too well?"

"I'm not sure I follow," said John, amused. "Sure, things are going exceptionally well, but aren't we happy about that?"

"We are. But do you ever think about how we got here? What we did to deserve this? Why us?"

"I've thought about that a lot," Sandy reassured him. "I understand why you, or John, are here. I'm not so sure about myself."

"But that's exactly my point, Sandy. You did an incredible job with the decision analysis. But when we started, were you the obvious choice?" The question was left hanging for a few seconds. They all knew the answer.

"I guess that there is something special about the Mindalikes algorithm, right?" said John, in support of Sandy.

"Is there? Or is it Cecilia's use of it that was special? Did we ever find out what keywords she put into it? She talked vaguely about environmental consciousness and other crap, but what else did she want?"

"What difference does it make?" asked John, visibly annoyed that they were sitting here, indulging in what he considered to be their hard-earned riches, having saved the world from itself, questioning the motives and methods of what Cecilia had done half a decade ago. "Who cares? I'm just happy I was chosen."

"So am I," seconded Sandy.

Amir went quiet for a while, and looked out at the horizon. The sea was light blue in color today, and seemed to merge with the sky at the horizon.

"What if I told you that you had never had free will?"

"What do you mean?" Sandy asked.

"I mean just that. It's a hypothetical question. What if whatever you had done for, and as part of, the group, wasn't your own decision, but someone else's?"

"That's a little too hypothetical for me, man," said John, shrugging off the question.

"Humor me."

"Well, I'd be pissed off, for one. I'd like to think that the impact I made, my contribution to the plan, was my own. That decisions that I made were crucial to its success."

Sandy, suddenly realizing what was being discussed, said, "Oh honey, of course you made an impact. Your discovery was crucial. We all had an impact"

"Yes, but how would you feel if I told you that throughout the entire process, you were just a pawn. A smart pawn, an important pawn, but just a pawn, following orders. Being played."

Sandy, upset now, objected. "That's not the case, and you know it. Cecilia was the leader, of course she was, and I followed her most of the time, but I also had a fair number of fights with her."

Amir smiled, in an effort to defuse the tension that was building. He was still being infuriatingly cryptic.

John was getting impatient. "Why don't you just go ahead and tell us what you're thinking?"

"I don't know, really. It's just that if I found out that I had been manipulated into this, I'd be seriously pissed off. And I'm starting to wonder if I was."

John was skeptical. "Leadership is a form of manipulation, Amir. Cecilia had a vision. She needed us to implement it. She chose carefully. She implemented impeccably. And here we are. Why question all that now?"

Amir stood up, took two steps toward the pool and then turned around to face them. "Because, my friends, we are responsible for the deaths of tens of thousands of people," he said, before turning around and jumping into the pool.

John turned to Sandy. He was perplexed. Last time he'd checked, the number of people who'd died from the virus they'd spread as part of their initial implementation, had barely surpassed 10,000. There had been no side effects from the project since then that they were aware of. The Microbees were working well. What was Amir talking about?

They waited patiently as Amir did four laps of the pool. When he finally got out, John asked, "Who? How?"

"Oh, they're not dead yet, but they will be."

"What do you mean? How will they?" John persisted.

"More people will die to fulfill Cecilia's dream."

"Cecilia's dream has already been fulfilled," John countered.

"How can you be so naïve? How could all of us have been so naïve?"

John was getting angry now, offended. "What are you talking about, Amir? You're not making any sense."

"If you were Cecilia Stein, and you wanted a group of people to believe in your cause, and to do what you asked them to, what would you do?" Amir directed this question at Sandy.

"I guess I would enter those keywords into the Mindalikes algorithm. But how is that different from finding people with common interests?"

"There's a bloody big difference between searching for people with common interests... and searching for people with common weaknesses," Amir argued, conspiratorially.

"What do you mean?" asked John again, though this time he sounded curious, rather than annoyed.

"Every member of our group has suffered a major loss or a major crisis in life. We have all questioned our own existence. We all needed to believe that our lives mattered. To make our dead families and partners proud, to make a difference in the world."

John, looking thoughtful, said, "But that's a weakness and a strength at the same time. It's people like us who bring about change."

"True, but think about how we did it. We didn't really influence anyone. We didn't argue our cause, we didn't persuade. We discounted completely the possibility that humans could find their own way, and instead we fucking droned them. How would you feel if you found out that you'd been droned?"

"I'd be livid, of course I would, but I haven't been, so what does that have to do with anything?"

"It has everything to do with everything..."

Sandy interjected here. "Amir, what are you getting at?"

"Come on, I want to show you something," he said, walking toward the house. Sandy and John reluctantly followed Amir inside. John pressed on.

"I just don't get why you are having second thoughts now, Amir. Where have you been these last five years?!"

"I'll show you," Amir replied, as he took a small staircase to the basement. Once below ground, they walked down a long dark corridor with black wall-to-wall carpets, black walls, and black ceiling. They were still in their bathing suits as they entered a dark room, with no windows, and no lights on. Before the door closed behind them, John saw that the walls were made of padded soundproofing material, the kind used in recording studios.

Then they were in darkness. Amir hit a switch, and a light flickered. "Yiamas," all three of them said, in unison. Then the light switched off, leaving them silent in the darkness, shocked.

***

3C was quiet at this time of night. Darko was the security guard on rotation. He liked the night shift. Not that he had a choice. She demanded that he work nights. Most nights were uneventful. But occasionally his services were required.

This was one of those nights. She appeared from the door to the staircase. It was only one flight down from her apartment. She walked towards him, wearing a silk negligée. She enjoyed these games, once in a while.

Darko unlocked the door, and let her inside. He paused for a moment at a panel next to the door. He flipped a switch, and 3C went into complete lockdown. No one else could enter. The lockdown was one of many security features Darko had implemented. You could lock 3C from the inside, preventing people from entering, or from the outside, preventing them from leaving. It could only be unlocked from the same side.

Cecilia walked towards the far window, overlooking midtown Manhattan. She leaned forward and placed her hands on the window.

Darko quietly approached her from behind; now half undressed, and wrapped his hands around her, caressing her breasts. He kissed her neck, her body. Her right hand found its way behind her and unbuttoned his pants. He pressed himself onto her and she let out a short, soft cry of pleasure, as she spread her legs.

Still standing with her hands on the window overlooking one of the most famous views in the world, her back to her lover, Cecilia exercised the particular power she had over this one man. Billions of unsuspecting others were under her direct influence. Unbeknownst to her, half way around the world, there were at least three people who had discovered her secret.

***

"Oh my God," said Sandy, as Amir turned on the light. As soon as they could see again John sank to the floor and leaned back against the padded wall.

Sandy sat next to him, holding onto him and staring at the opposite wall. For effect, Amir flicked the switch again, and again all three said "Yiamas."

"Stop it," John shouted.

"Do you see where I am coming from, now?" asked Amir pointedly.

"But how? When did this happen? We removed the Yiamas command after the Nauru experiment."

"True, so our Microbees are from the Nauru experiment."

"Oh my God," Sandy said again, realization coming in waves. "So all the decisions we made afterwards, all those could have been influenced?"

"They could, and they were," said Amir coldly, who'd clearly come to terms with this devastating betrayal much earlier. He was still standing, watching them.

"No. Surely not all of them. Just the decisions in the eight agreed clusters," said John.

"But they could reprogram the Microbees using the Li-Fi. And they did."

"So Frank was involved," said Sandy, in disbelief.

"Wayne too," Amir said. "They would have needed Wayne to crack the neural code for these new decisions."

"But none of this is in the Constitution," Sandy said, struggling to grasp the new reality she was being confronted with.

"Forget your fucking constitution, Sandy," shouted Amir. "It's a goddamn meaningless piece of paper, it always has been. We've been pawns from the very beginning."

Sandy started sobbing. John wrapped his arms around her and hugged her tightly.

"So, does this mean that we're de-droned now?" asked John, remembering how they de-droned the Nauruans.

"No, this is just a drone detector."

"So how do we de-drone ourselves?" asked John.

"But why would we want to de-drone ourselves?" asked Amir sarcastically, returning to the argument they'd had by the pool. "We live under the illusion that we control our fate, that we have free will and that we can exercise it. And no doubt about it, it is an illusion. But we need this illusion to survive. Once we know that someone is playing mind games with us we go crazy, just like you Sandy over here."

Amir paused for a second and then said, "We have to be careful. The evidence that we have been droned is still in our bodies. Do we really want to destroy it? We may need it, when the time comes"

"For when the time comes for what?" asked Sandy, barely able to speak.

"For when we face justice for the crimes we have committed. The crimes against humanity," Amir said, and Sandy burst into violent tears.

***

Darkness was falling in Tel Aviv. Sandy had spent the day by the pool staring at the sky, a million thoughts going through her mind. Since their initial and brief discussion following Amir's revelation, she hadn't uttered a single word. Eventually, she dozed off. For her, sleep was the only antidote to extreme stress.

Amir had left for a few hours, to go to work. John had done more than 20 laps of the pool to try and release some tension and think through the events of the day. Finally, he dozed off too on a deck chair by the pool, overcome by jet lag.

When it grew dark, Amir returned and brought out some blankets, as it was colder now. They were numb, but ready to address the situation.

John spoke first. "I've been thinking, what if we're jumping to conclusions here? The only thing we know for sure is that we were droned. We don't know why, and we certainly don't know if we have been re-programmed."

Amir was not going to be reassuring. "Don't be naïve, John. Why would Cecilia drone us, and not use that power to get her plan approved with no contest from any of us? And why would she not de-drone us, if she'd regretted her decision to drone us in the first place?"

Sandy replied to this, her voice cold, coarse, angry. "She couldn't have. We would have said "Yiamas," and then we would have known we'd been droned."

John added, "In which case, she couldn't reprogram us, either. Yiamas is spoken even at reprogramming," he reminded her. "Remember Nauru?"

Amir interjected, "Actually, that's not true. When I worked with Frank, we left a back door open for reprogramming where the drone wasn't forced to speak the word. So, she could reprogram us, and I think she did"

"There's no basis for that assumption. Let's just ask her," John said, still desperately clinging on to the hope that he hadn't been so deeply deceived.

"Are you crazy? Are you blind? You're in denial John," Sandy shouted, who'd progressed from shock and disbelief to anger. "And you're missing the point. Droning us was completely out of line. It's a complete breach of trust. We can never side with that woman again. It's over!"

John, not convinced, said, "I don't agree with you. I certainly don't want to throw away the past five years of my life without at least giving Cecilia a chance to explain."

"You'll be putting yourself at risk. And us," said Amir. "Plus, if you tell her, that limits our options considerably."

"As if we have many," said Sandy sarcastically.

"Well, I don't blame you for thinking that. It's your first day. I was like you for several days. And then I realized that there was a way out of this. It's why I needed to involve you guys."

"How did you find out we were droned?" asked John.

"I didn't. But I knew that if Cecilia was going to drone anyone else, it would be you two. You were the most vocal in opposing parts of her plan. There was something else, too…" here Amir hesitated.

"What?" Sandy asked, dreading another chilling revelation.

"I don't want to burden you…"

"No, tell us," said John, and Sandy nodded in agreement.

"Well… Remember that night at Cecilia's apartment, when we were discussing the outbreak of the virus in the Middle East, and the anticipated deaths?

They both nodded, fearful.

"Well, I was 100% opposed to it. I couldn't agree to a plan that would kill 30,000 random people, even if it would save millions of others. It contradicts all of my deepest held beliefs. It makes a mockery of my own parents' deaths," he said coldly, "who were the random victims of terrorism."

"Hey, I remember that night," said Sandy. "I thought you told me that you were going to veto that decision. What happened there?"

"Well, my dear Sandy and John, you may also remember that all three of us had objections but then visited the bathroom during that break. I think something happened in that bathroom that weakened our resolve to oppose one of the most sinister plans ever conceived in the history of humankind."

At that point something snapped in Sandy's and John's head, as if the normal moral values they had held prior to being droned suddenly took over from the Microbee implants.

"Oh my God. We were responsible for the deaths of all those people," Sandy whispered, shocked.

***

After denial comes anger, then bargaining, depression and finally, acceptance.

It was bargaining that Amir had to deal with the next morning. Both John and Sandy looked dreadful. Sandy had had violent nightmares, but they'd both had a rough night.

The conversation started at breakfast. John once again took the lead.

"OK, so we know that we are responsible for those deaths. We knew that already. It's just that our understanding of the morality of that decision had been interfered with, clearly by some clever code created by Frank. So let's discuss morality. Is it really so bad, what we did? I mean, the fact is, we are still well on our way to saving the world. Perhaps the end does justify the means."

"I wondered the same thing," Amir said. "And we need to consider the consequences of our actions from now on in this respect."

"Cognitive dissonance," said Sandy abruptly.

"What?" Amir and John turned to her.

"Cognitive dissonance. It's a common human reaction; we need to match actions with beliefs. Usually, we do something because we believe in it. For example, we go to church because we believe in God. But this cause and effect mechanism also works the other way around. We believe in something *because* we do it. We believe smoking is not going to kill us because we smoke. We believe that recycling is not effective because we don't recycle. In the human mind, beliefs and actions need to be aligned. It's a common cognitive error."

"How is this relevant? I'm sorry, I'm missing your point, babe," John said, confused.

"You have already taken the action. That action resulted to the murder of ten thousand people. Now your poor little head is trying to convince you that it was the right decision."

"But it could be," John persisted. "We could be at a turning point in human history. The point when humanity decides to save itself from annihilation."

"Plus, the deaths have already happened. There's nothing we can do about them now," Amir added.

"But if we have been droned without our knowledge, we cannot trust Cecilia," Sandy said. We don't know her at all. How can we be sure she won't use her powers to do more than just save the environment? What if the end never stops justifying the means?"

"More importantly, what is the "end" for Cecilia?" Amir asked. "Do we really know?"

They were silent for a while. They were making progress, at least.

Then John said, "One thing is for certain. We need to de-drone ourselves."

"But we can't," said Amir, sending chills down his guests' spines.

"As set out in the Constitution, we need to find the special drone code for each of us in order to de-drone ourselves," said Amir.

"That's right," said Sandy. "We introduced that rule after Nauru. To stop us from carrying out mass reprogramming."

"And we need four signatures to gain access to the codes. We need one more member of the team," John realized.

"I don't think anyone else is droned," said Amir.

"Frank and Wayne must be in on this," John agreed. "Cecilia couldn't drone them; she needs Frank for the reprogramming code and

Wayne for the translation of this code to electrical signals recognized and transmitted via the Microbees."

"I just can't get it into my head that after all these years, these guys can turn out to be such two-faced bastards," said Sandy. "I still have my iPhone from the Penn test. Do you think that would work without the code? We didn't have codes back then."

"Doubtful," said Amir. "We updated everything with the new rules, including the app that's on your phone. But the phone will still work as a drone detector so hold onto it, we may need it."

"But hey, are we sure that the rules of the Constitution have been programmed by Frank? I mean, seeing as we know now it's just a worthless piece of paper, perhaps we don't need four people," asked Sandy.

"Unfortunately, we do," replied Amir. "It was the first thing I checked, three weeks ago, when I discovered I was droned."

"What about Bale? Do you think he was droned?" asked John.

Amir had been expecting this question, and smiled. John and Sandy were following the exact same thought process he himself had gone through. He let them play it out, to see if they came to the same conclusion he had.

Having worked closely with him throughout the project, Sandy knew Bale better than anyone.

"I don't think so," she said. "Bale is so committed to the project he doesn't need droning. Plus, on the night that we discussed the outbreak, he gave the main presentation, remember? It's one thing to dampen negative reactions and doubts, and an entirely different thing to plant strong beliefs into someone's brain."

John agreed, "Yes, you'd need Microbee 2.0 to be able to do that and…fuck, the plans for Microbee 2.0. They are still at my office at Penn!"

"Let's focus on one problem at a time," Amir prompted him. "I agree with you guys; Bale is too committed to need droning. But do you think he knows about us? Does he condone it?"

"I think he'd do anything to see his theory put into practice," said John.

"I don't agree, he would never agree to this," Sandy objected. For now, at least, she still had faith in Bale.

"You're being naïve, babe."

"Maybe. But think of this from Cecilia's perspective, why would she risk telling him? She doesn't need him to reprogram us. He might see it as a breach of trust. Then he'd worry about himself. She couldn't risk him becoming a loose cannon."

"I agree with Sandy," said Amir. "I'd be happy to bet that Bale is not droned, and he doesn't know that we are.

"Me too," said Sandy. "But would you bet your life on it? Because that's what I think you're suggesting we should do."

"Do we have a choice?" asked Amir. None of them had an answer.

***

Sandy and John spent the entire day struggling with anger and frustration. John felt like screaming his lungs out in desperation, which he did a couple of times, standing at the edge of the ocean. Their conversations lacked coherence, and led nowhere.

Amir didn't press them. He knew they needed some time. In fact, he was impressed at how well they were coping, under the circumstances.

He thought that the lavish environment they were in and the seclusion probably helped.

In the evening, though, he decided they needed to start discussing their options.

"Let's go to the FBI," said Sandy.

"And tell them, what? That we intentionally killed ten thousand people, and droned a billion?"

"OK, so let's tip off the press. We can tell them what happened. We can show them facts."

"What facts? Our story is too wild for anyone to believe."

"What about the recent explosion in environmental concern. I saw recently a new company IPO'd in London, Envolution I think it was called. Huge, stock soaring," Sandy said.

"It's just circumstantial evidence. It doesn't prove anything," Amir objected.

"Well, at least someone is making big dough off the back of our plan," said John, in an attempt to make a joke. Sandy giggled, but Amir looked dead serious.

"What?" John asked him.

"Who do you think might be making serious dough off the back of our plan?" Amir whispered, in a moment of realization.

Then Sandy remembered the San Antonio Times article.

"It was about an investment company called... Wait, what was it called? Invest ... something"

"Invest.io?" asked Amir.

"Yes, that's them. You know them?"

"Of course I do, they're the backers of Welit. Cecilia is behind them."

"So, are we thinking that the "end" here is to make Cecilia a trillionaire?" asked Sandy, disgusted.

"Could that be why she wants Microbees 2.0?" asked Amir.

"Why, what's so special about Microbees 2.0?" asked Sandy.

"Quite a lot. Microbees 1.0 attach themselves to the synapse of the neural transmitting cells and interfere with information as it travels from cell to cell, effectively changing decisions. Microbees 2.0 work differently. They create messages that are sent to the memory cells. With Microbees2.0, you can create memories. And by creating memories, you can create ideas."

"Ideas like 'buy products from Envolution?" asked Amir.

"Hypothetically, yes," replied John. "Though I didn't make that connection until now. I was working on the assumption that the ideas we would be planting would further our environmental cause, not Cecilia's wallet."

"We can take Cecilia's association to Envolution to the press," said Sandy. "This is more than just circumstantial."

"No, we can't," Amir insisted. "Cecilia has hidden herself well behind complicated corporate structures, including bearer shares. But I know who we can take this to."

***

When John and Sandy went to bed that evening, there was a glimmer of hope on the horizon. Yet, they were still overwhelmed by the devastating discoveries of the past few days. Hope was the only remedy they had for the guilt they were feeling.

They knew that they had screwed up. They knew that the chance of fixing things was slim. But they couldn't do anything right now, so they did what humans often do to release tension. They mated.

***

The London Stock Exchange had just opened, and Cecilia was sitting in her Metropolitan Tower apartment, watching the screen. Envolution stock soared, as it had been doing for several weeks. It was riding a wave – or rather a tsunami – that no one had seen coming.

Through the cash generated by Envolution – and Welit, and Uniocom – Cecilia could have topped the Forbes billionaire list, but she did not want Forbes, or anyone else, to know about it. She had spent nearly her entire fortune on the project, and now, finally, she was seeing a return on her investment.

The financial return had never been the goal, and that was still true. She was planning to reinvest and reinvest until all of the environmental problems of the planet had been solved. This would be done through new technologies such as solar, wind, energy storage systems, and artificial photosynthesis. Through more recycling. And through the emergence of a species that governed and coordinated itself in a more efficient manner.

***

The next morning, they'd stopped feeling sorry for themselves. It was time for action. They boarded a plane, destination London. Sandy's thoughts were racing during the five-hour flight. In the past few days they'd had to come to terms with betrayal, murder, and the likely reprogramming of their own minds. They had felt anger, fear, and desperation. There were few options, none of them promising. They could very well be walking into a trap. A fatal trap.

Yet, she felt alive. Excited. Driven. Hope had overcome guilt. They could still fix things. They would find a way. They would prevail.

The thought of taking the simpler road, of talking to Cecilia, trying to understand what had happened and why, didn't cross her mind. She already knew the answers to these questions.

CHAPTER THIRTEEN

THE UNIVERSAL CODES

It was cold, cloudy, and windy in London, but at least it wasn't raining. Sandy had insisted on meeting Bale alone. While this was a confrontation she was not looking forward to, she believed - and the others agreed - that she had a better chance of reasoning with Bale, given their long history of working together in the development of the project.

They met in Hyde Park where Bale walked his dog, a 12-year-old whippet. He always picked up the dog from his family when he was visiting the UK. He had bought a flat in Knightsbridge, and was just a stone's throw from the park.

As they walked toward the lake, they discussed nothing of consequence, though it was clear that something serious was looming. Bale could see it in Sandy's eyes.

The weather really was rather unpleasant, Sandy thought, and as they arrived at the lake, they could see ripples in the water caused by the strong wind. They arrived at the coffee place, got themselves a couple of cappuccinos, and sat at a table outside. The dog was on a long leash sniffing the nearby tree trunks, oblivious to the tension in the air. She was a mid-size ultra-thin dog with short hair, the kind they use in races. Many years ago, Bale had been dragged by some friends to one of these races, and had been appalled at the cruelty of the sport. He had never understood why people used animals for their own entertainment. He couldn't save a bull, could not afford a horse, so he adopted a whippet.

Once they'd sat down, Sandy got straight to the point. "Richard, John, Amir and I believe that Cecilia has manipulated us all along, to get us to agree to her plans."

"But of course she did, my dear, that's just what Cecilia does."

"Yes, but she used an unfair advantage."

"I agree, she used every trick in the book to persuade us to buy into the project," Bale said, smiling.

"And a trick that's not in any book," Sandy continued, eyeing Bale carefully.

Bale was silent, so she continued. "She droned me, Richard." His jaw dropped. His reaction made her 100% certain that he didn't know. Even the dog barked.

"What? How? When? Why…?" was all Bale could muster. He didn't challenge her. If Sandy had told him, it must be true. His mind raced back to the conversation he'd had months ago with Cecilia. Had Cecilia moved ahead with the next part of her plan, he wondered?

"John, Amir and I are all droned. We don't know yet if you are. Or Wayne, or Frank. But we suspect that none of you were. Just us. Amir figured it out, and showed us using a drone detector. We know we are droned," she repeated for emphasis.

Bale was shocked. He knew he shouldn't be more shocked by the droning of three people than of a fifth of the earth's population. But for Bale, as for Sandy, secretly droning members of the team was a huge breach of trust.

"Do you mind if we do a drone detection test on you?" Sandy asked, pulling her modified iPhone from her handbag.

He nodded numbly, and she held the iPhone in front of his face and took a photo. Nothing happened. As Sandy had suspected, Bale wasn't droned.

"Richard, what do you think Cecilia was thinking?"

"I don't know," he replied unconvincingly, not wanting to reveal the conversation he'd had with Cecilia months before. "It was a bloody stupid thing to do. I guess she wanted to control you. To make sure you voted as she wanted you to."

"But she didn't need me. She could have just thrown me out of the group. Why go to all this trouble?"

"She needed John and Amir, so while she was at it, she droned you too."

"Do you agree with what she did?"

"Droning you? No! I think she could have convinced you to agree with her without droning you."

"That would have never happened, Richard. I know I would never have agreed to the outbreak plan. As soon as I found out I'd been droned, something clicked in my head. I never would have made that decision."

"My dear, I hate to disappoint you, but very few decisions you make are truly your own. How you dress, what you do for pleasure, where you work. All of these decisions are influenced by others."

"Yes, but they're minor decisions. We made a decision to kill thousands of people. How can you live with yourself, knowing that you made that choice?" Sandy asked Bale, looking him in the eyes.

"We made the decision to upgrade the human race, Sandy. The drones are an amazing evolution of the human species, connected and aligned to a common cause. It was worth it."

Sandy looked away, not convinced. For her, there was a pretty big line between being influenced by TV advertising, the media, and society, and an implanted device in your head directly controlling your decisions. Curiously, after working for several years on the project, specifically on which decisions should be affected, she only now truly realized what she had done, only now she herself had been droned.

Still, Sandy was reassured by Bale's reaction, although she was concerned by how committed he still was to this project, concerned that his view of Cecilia was still too favorable to realize that he'd been used. She pressed on.

"Have you heard of a company called Envolution?"

"Of course, they were listed on the stock market a couple of months back, here in London. They've been in the news quite a lot lately."

"It's funny how well they're doing, because of ... us. They must not believe their luck," said Sandy carefully.

"We knew that we would have this effect from the beginning. Some companies win, some lose, but in the end all of humanity wins."

"True that. But have you ever thought about the people who might be behind the winners?" she asked, eyeing him carefully.

Bale was an intelligent man. Sandy didn't need to say any more. In an instant, she saw despair in his eyes. The idealist philosopher confronted with reality. Bale was also British, showing his emotion wasn't in his culture. He broke eye contact.

"So, you suspect Cecilia is behind Envolution," he said, coldly. Sandy didn't bother replying, knowing he would draw his own conclusion.

"That would mean that Cecilia is in it for the money," he said, in a voice that betrayed his deep disappointment. What Sandy didn't know was that some of this disappointment was with himself, for his failure to keep Cecilia on the right track. "We have to stop her," he said, "Get her back on the right track. She's lost her way."

He smiled at Sandy. "You are our moral compass, my dear. You may not realize it, and I may never have told you, but I am quite proud of how you have grown during this project, and how, with your interventions, you kept us all in check. Or, at least some of us."

She smiled at his kind words. "If only I could be sure which of those decisions were mine, and which were Cecilia's."

"That's less important now, Sandy. What's important is to get these things out of your heads."

"For that, we need your help, Richard," Sandy said, and she told him their plan.

***

Bale dropped the dog off at home and they met John and Amir in the restaurant on the top floor of Harvey Nichols, the historic department store.

As they stepped out of the lift onto the restaurant floor, Sandy took in the tall glass ceilings, impressed. No light was coming through, as it had suddenly got dark outside. A combination of an early sunset and ominous dark clouds. *Fitting*, she thought.

The place was packed with people, but they found John and Amir sitting at the sushi bar. Sandy was thankful; she was starving. They ordered some wine and, for a moment, it was like the good old days. Only that it wasn't.

Bale explained to the others that he was disgusted by Cecilia's premeditated attempt to control a group of seven people who were already united under her leadership. With you three always aligned with her, Cecilia could use the technology in any way she liked. He was also appalled by her attempt to make money through Envolution.

"So, how do we get de-droned?" asked Sandy.

"We talk to Cecilia," came Bale's surprising answer.

"No!" said the other three in unison. "We can never tell Cecilia that we know," Sandy added.

"Why? It could have been a momentary lapse in judgment. She made a mistake, that's all. We need to give her the chance to fix it."

"I can't face that woman again, not after what she did," said Sandy.

"You must confront her to keep our project going," said Bale.

"Our project is over," Sandy said.

"No, it's not. Those ten thousand people are already dead, but the world is moving in the right direction, a direction we all agreed – pre-Microbees – was essential. Would you really do anything to jeopardize that? It would be like pulling the trigger to kill millions. We can't undo what's already been done."

Sandy and the others hadn't thought that far ahead. All they'd been able to think about for the past few days was how to regain control of their own decisions.

"So, you're saying we shouldn't abandon the plan?" she asked.

"No, we shouldn't, my dears. But we do need to make sure that your decisions are not controlled, and we need to confront Cecilia about this. We still need to be part of the plan; we need to keep Cecilia on the right path, and we need to keep the project moving forward."

Sandy wondered if Bale was still in denial.

***

It was their third flight in four days, and it took them back to New York. At the restaurant in London, they'd reached a compromise. Bale would provide the final vote they needed to de-drone themselves without telling Cecilia, but afterwards they would confront her, and try to keep the project moving.

They checked into the Salisbury Hotel, conveniently located right across the street from the Metropolitan Tower. They took a two-bedroom suite located on the sixteenth floor.

John walked to the window. Across 57th street was the tower where it had all started. He wondered if it would be the place where it all ended.

They sat around a wooden coffee table by the window, and Amir laid out their plan. "The problem we have is that Cecilia thinks we are all abroad, in three different countries. We can't just show up or she'll know something's up." They all agreed that was true.

"Also, for me, it's not just about being de-droned. I need to download our logs to see what she did to us."

"That will be difficult," said John. "The logs are kept by Frank, and I don't think we can access them without his help, or at least without his knowledge."

"We have to try. Getting de-droned without seeing the logs is not enough. We need to know exactly what Cecilia did. We need to know what we're dealing with here, how far she's prepared to go."

"My first priority is to get this thing, this thing that I developed, out of my head," said John, acknowledging the twist of irony.

"I agree that the priority is to get you de-droned. We need to look to the future, not the past," said Bale.

"Guys, I *need* to know," Amir said, his voice revealing the strength of emotion he had been trying not to show.

"Know what?" asked John.

"He needs to know if the decision to release the virus was his own, or programmed by Cecilia," said Sandy quietly. "I need to know, too."

Bale, visibly irritated, said, "You have to get over this. It was the right decision, whether you made it or she did."

"But if she did, I need to know. And I need to have proof," said Amir, regretting it immediately.

Bale reacted immediately. "Proof? To do what with? Give to the FBI? The CIA? The NSA? The press? No one will ever believe you, Amir. Agreeing to release the virus is just one of dozens of crimes you committed to set this plan in motion. Even if you get absolved of responsibility for releasing the virus, you'll be convicted for the Nauru experiment, for the Uniocom vaccine you helped tamper with, for the LiFi programming, for conspiracy to commit crimes against humanity. No immunity agreement in the world would give you a get out of jail free card for what we've done, what you've done."

"No!" Amir exclaimed, defensively. "I need the logs to use as evidence when we confront Cecilia."

"You need to put the past behind you, all of you!" Bale was shouting now. "You're judging this situation based on today's values. But posterity will judge this moment as a turning point in human history. The ten thousand people who unknowingly died to save the world will be heroes." Bale was trying hard, but he was less persuasive than Cecilia. "There will be no happy ending to this if we don't enter the discussion with a view to forgiving... and forgetting." The others were not convinced.

They turned their attention back to the plan. All they needed to do was gain access to 3C, find their individual codes, sign off a programming change, and use the modified iPhone to relieve themselves of the tiny devices inside their heads. Amir and John would also try to gain access to the logs.

All four needed to be there in order to access the system, and to authorize the reprogramming. The de-droning process should not take more than fifteen minutes. Or so they thought.

*****

Over the next two days, they took turns watching the entrance to the Metropolitan Tower. They took notes when the guard shifts changed. They watched Frank and Wayne come and go. Luckily, the back entrance at 56th street was closed due to road works on that side of the tower.

Over those two days, Sandy watched Bale closely. Watched him go through the phases she and John had - denial, anger, bargaining – but he was still struggling to accept that Cecilia had an ulterior motive other than saving the world from environmental disaster. Bale now seemed stuck in the depression stage, and Sandy was worried.

On New Year's Eve, Bale made a call to Cecilia to wish her a happy New Year, and to confirm that she would be attending the New Year's Eve celebration she was always invited to, which was organized by an exclusive circle she still maintained contact with at Mindalikes. It was important that she was out of her apartment, which was hooked up to cameras installed in 3C. He also established that Wayne and Frank had change of year plans elsewhere in the city.

At 9:13pm, they saw the Tesla Model X arrive in front of the building. There was light rain that night and Vlad, one of the 3 or 4 building doormen always on duty, escorted Cecilia to the car, holding an umbrella. They almost missed her, but then, for a split second she emerged from under the umbrella and got straight into the car.

They had to wait another hour before it was safe to make a move. They knew from their surveillance that the 3C guards switched at 10:30 every night. They had decided not to show up all together as this might raise suspicion in the guard, so Bale and Amir went first, at 10:15pm.

John and Sandy left the Salisbury Hotel at 10:47, exactly 73 minutes before the turn of the year. They walked into the Metropolitan Tower, dressed for a party, to look as inconspicuous as possible. They said 'hi' to Vlad.

They waited thirty seconds for the elevator door to open, and by 10:51 they were on the seventy-sixth floor. They said 'hi' to the guard, who appeared somewhat surprised to see them.

Sandy looked straight into the face scanner, entered her code on the keypad, spoke into the voice recognition panel, and entered 3C.

Bale and Amir had been waiting anxiously. One by one they went to the iris scan next to the main terminal and had their eyes scanned. Within a few seconds, they were logged on.

***

Darko had dropped Cecilia off and was planning to celebrate the New Year within the confines of his Tesla as he waited for Cecilia's party to end. At 10:53, he received a text on his mobile. "Authorized access to the 3C main terminal database." *That's strange*, he thought. In the course of a normal day, he would receive several such messages, which Frank had made sure would be sent to Darko as an extra security measure. Darko employed a large security detail to take care of the project, but given the fact that there had been no security threats or breaches in five years, he had decided to allow most of the security detail to see the New Year with their families.

**

Inside the 3C, John and Amir were trying to figure out a way to find the unique code of their Microbees. It wasn't like you could search by name, as it was not stored in the database.

"There is a serial number and an activation date for each code. We were likely droned right after Nauru. Let's look at codes activated after the Nauru test, and before the outbreak," John suggested.

Interestingly, there were more than a hundred of such codes, leading them to wonder who else Cecilia had droned without the team's knowledge. Amir then tried to find a blanket method of passing all those codes through the de-droner automatically, so that they wouldn't have to enter them all manually, using up precious time.

Bale and Sandy, well prepared, went directly to the darker, south side of 3C and set up three chairs with their backs to the window. The ambient city light was brighter than usual, as New York prepared to welcome the New Year, but the room was dark enough.

Back at the terminals, Amir was frantically keying commands into his laptop, which was connected to Sandy's iPhone.

Meanwhile, John sat at the main workstation, searching for ways to hack the system to find the logs. He started from the screen with the codes, trying to access the logs for any random drone. Hopefully, when they found their unique codes, he would then be able to download their logs. As he was looking through the codes, he noticed a peculiar pattern. "Strange," he said. "What?" asked Sandy.

"Done" said Amir interrupting John's train of thought. They all quickly moved to the south side of the building, Amir, Sandy and John sitting in the three chairs while Bale held up Sandy's phone. At 11:23, Amir instructed Bale to press the button on the de-droning app.

***

Darko looked at the message again. He remembered that the security protocols demanded that for an authorized entry, four members of the team needed to be physically present at 3C. That was strange, on New Year's Eve. He called the security guard on call, who reported that he'd only seen two members go in, a lady and a man.

***

Nothing. No "Yiamas," nothing. "We put all the codes from the specified period through the de-droner. Nothing," Amir said, shocked.

"Could it be that the de-droning app isn't working?" asked Sandy.

"No, there's no reason why the app would be faulty. We might not have the right codes," replied Amir.

"Could we pass all the individual codes through the de-droner?" John asked.

"We can't, there are too many. We can probably upload no more than fifteen thousand codes to the iPhone's memory at a time. To run a billion and a half codes through the iPhone could take weeks," Amir said.

"What if we just run all the codes from the Nauru experiment? Perhaps we were droned while we were in Nauru."

"OK, I'll try that," Amir said, and literally dashed back to the terminal.

John, pleased with himself, returned to the log search. He had a lingering concern that he needed to return to.

Each unique Microbee code was a sequence of four numbers, followed by six letters. So, a typical code would be something like 1234ABCDEF. As he had been scrolling through the codes, he'd noticed the code 7982YIAMAS, then, further down, he'd seen 7983YIAMAS. And then 7984YIAMAS.

Now that he looked further, the same appeared to be true for each number in the sequence. He showed it to Sandy. "What do you think of this?" he asked.

"Could it be randomly generated by the code system?" she asked.

"Yes, of course it could. It just seems strange that I'm finding this "YIAMAS" in every number in the sequence. Hold on, let me try something."

He typed in a query to the system. Sandy wasn't overly familiar with databases, but after spending five years with this group, she could understand the basics. John was trying to isolate all the codes that included the word YIAMAS.

As he pressed enter to run the query, Amir once again declared, "Ready," and all of them returned to their chairs. Bale didn't wait for the order this time; he just pushed the button. It was 11:32, and they needed to stay there for a few seconds, looking at the light, while the iPhone de-droner ran the de-droning sequences through the thousands of codes that were created in the year of the Nauru experiment.

***

Darko was unsure of what to do. He could not leave Cecilia to head back to 3C on her own. So, he decided it was time to report this to his boss. He dialed her phone number, but there she didn't pick up. *Damn.* He then texted her.

***

"Nothing. How is this possible?" cursed Amir. They needed to make this work.

"Can we hack the LiFi system in the 3C and run the de-droning sequence through all of the codes?" asked Sandy, trying to figure out a way to overcome the iPhone's capacity limitation.

"It will still be too slow," Amir replied.

John went back to the terminal he'd been using, and there on the screen were the results of his query: "9999 records found."

"Hey, guys, check this out," and he quickly explained what he'd found.

"Could this mean what I think it means?" asked Sandy.

"A universal code for each of the number sequences," Amir said.

"No!" said Sandy, "Surely not."

Bale looked bewildered, so Sandy explained. "They are suggesting that any number with the YIAMAS at the end refers to all the individual codes with that number. So 1234AAAAAA could refer to you, 1234BBBBBB to me, but 1234YIAMAS could be a back door for reprogramming us together."

"What else could it be?" Amir confirmed. He turned to Bale, and asked directly, "Could it be that Frank created a code for reprogramming a large number of drones at one time?"

"We said that we would never do that again after the Nauru experiment," Bale said, repeating what they all knew.

"We certainly did," said Sandy. "But maybe Frank only went halfway. Perhaps he left a back door."

"How do you know for sure?" asked Bale.

"We don't, unless we try it," said Sandy.

"What do you mean?"

"Let's run all 9999 sequences through the portable de-droner. Is there enough memory?" she asked Amir.

"Let's do it," he answered, as the clock showed 11:56. They quickly downloaded the codes from John's query, and ran back to the chairs.

***

As midnight approached, and the party guests started the countdown, Cecilia instinctively looked at her Apple watch. She saw the missed call from Darko, and then froze as she read the text. An authorized system entry could only be gained if four people were physically present at 3C. That meant at least some members of the team had returned early from their overseas Christmas holidays, and were meeting at 3C on New Year's Eve without her knowledge.

***

"Three, two, one" was the countdown at 3C, but not for the change of year. Finally, the light on the de-droner lit up and within seconds, Amir, John and Sandy said, "Yiamas," in unison, therefore, confirming that the universal YIAMAS codes could indeed be used for mass reprogramming, or, as was the case here, mass dedroning. As if they had given the signal, New Year's fireworks lit up across the city. The New Year had arrived and, with it, the trio resolved never to allow their decisions to be controlled ever again.

***

"Hi, boss" said Darko, who was frantically anxious now.

"We have a problem," said Cecilia coldly. But everyone was cheering behind her, and she couldn't be heard.

"What?"

"Darko, we have a problem. Lock 3C down!" she shouted.

"Did you say lock 3C down?" he asked.

"Yes, NOW!"

"OK boss," he hung up, and called George, the guard on duty, to relay the message. George got up, went to a panel on the wall, opened it and flipped a manual switch. No one could get out of 3C now.

CHAPTER FOURTEEN

THE LOCKDOWN

The fireworks were still there in the background as Amir, John, Sandy and Bale hugged each other, thrilled that they'd successfully been de-droned. But their mini celebration did not last long. They could not access their logs without their own individual codes, and since they'd used the universal Yiamas codes to de-drone themselves, they still had no idea what each of their specific codes were.

"Realizing this, Amir prompted them to get out. They quickly rearranged the chairs as they found them and rushed to the door. But the door would not unlock. "What the fuck?" Amir exclaimed.

"We're locked in. How?" asked John, perplexed.

He knocked on the door. The faint voice of George, the guard, could be heard on the other side. "Sorry, I've been instructed to put 3C in lockdown," he said. "Clearly there is some threat to your security."

"No! We need to get out of here!" John shouted.

"Sorry, I can't ignore my orders. Believe me, it will be for your own safety."

"Shit," said Amir, sliding down the wall to the floor by the door. "So close, and yet so, far. Now we'll have to confront Cecilia."

"And Darko, probably," said Sandy, suddenly terrified. "What do you think she'll do to us?"

"Nothing, probably," said Bale, but he didn't sound convincing. Locking down the 3C was an extreme measure, a clear indication that her intentions were not good.

"Perhaps there's another way out?" offered John.

"No, there isn't. I went through the security protocols with Cecilia when we were setting up 3C. We are truly locked in," Amir explained. "The only way out of here is if someone flips that switch on the other side of the door."

They were silent for a moment, then Sandy, still terrified, but still determined, said, "Then maybe there is a way out."

***

The Tesla was stuck in New Year's traffic as Darko tried to get them to midtown. Cecilia was sitting on the edge of the back seat, as Darko furiously tried to avoid the traffic while making calls to all of his security people. Calling the police wasn't an option. Cecilia knew by now that both John and Sandy were in 3C, as the guard on duty had seen them go in, but she didn't know who the others were, as the guard on the previous shift could not be reached.

But at least they were all locked in. She would get to them, sooner or later. *Probably later*, she thought, as she surveyed the traffic ahead.

***

Sandy was back at the terminal, keying in search commands. The others were standing behind her, not sure what she was trying to find. And then, there it was. The list of all the decisions they'd affected along with their Enigma code and corresponding LiFi programming. This was a working folder that Sandy had been given access to earlier on in the project, as it had been related to her specific tasks.

She looked through the list. They were organized in eight main folders, corresponding to the constitution clusters:

1. Recycling& waste management
2. Energy
3. Consumer habits
4. Diet
5. Water conservation
6. Use of chemicals
7. Forestry and wild animals
8. Activism

She clicked on each and found the subfolders that contained smaller clusters. Within each of these were thousands of micro-decisions, but she had a hunch, so she kept looking.

Finally, she opened the last folder 'Activism'. She found two subfolders, named 'Individual' and 'Corporate'. This was the structure they'd used in all of the folders to separate individual choices from decisions made by individuals on behalf of the corporations and governments they worked for. Sandy clicked on 'Individual' first, and saw a list of subfolders containing decisions such as 'Attending rallies', 'Sharing supportive stories on social media' etc. All of these were familiar to her, so she returned to the root folder and clicked on 'Corporate'.

Here too were decision clusters that were familiar to her, such as 'Corporate Social Responsibility', 'Legislation', 'Internal regulations' and so on, all the decisions aimed to influence corporations and government officials so as to make environmentally friendly decisions.

But then there it was. As she was scrolling through the list of folders, she saw one that she didn't recognize, called 'Leadership'.

"Interesting," she said, and clicked on it. In it were five commands that she'd never seen.

1. CEC VR
2. CEC CAE
3. CEC CAC
4. CEC CAA
5. CEC PAS

"What the hell are these acronyms?" asked Amir.

"CEC could mean Cecilia," Bale suggested.

"VR, could that be virtual reality?" asked John.

"What would virtual reality have to do with our project?" asked Sandy, confused.

"I don't know, sometimes I feel my entire life is virtual reality," John said, attempting a joke.

"How about voice recognition?" Amir suggested next.

"Can we program voice recognition? Isn't that a memory stimulus?" asked Sandy.

"True, we can't implant a memory with the Microbee 1.0. But we can program the Microbees to recognize the specific frequencies of a voice, and send a signal of recognition. It's a decision of sorts: do I recognize this voice or not?"

"OK, and the assumption here is that it is Cecilia's voice that this command recognizes?" asked Sandy, not expecting an answer, and already fuming that Cecilia would have created such a command. "What about the rest: CAE, CAC, CAA, PAS. What are those?"

"Let me see the code behind it," asked John.

Sandy clicked and the screen filled with what to her was incomprehensible gibberish, but John seemed to be able to make sense of it. After a minute of dead silence, he said, "I'm not sure how this translates to electrical signals for the Microbees, but I have a hunch that one of the Cs is the word 'Command'.

"That would make sense," said Amir. "First the drone recognizes her voice, and then they obey her commands. I'd hazard a bet that the other C is for 'Control'."

"Command and control," whispered Bale. "Command and Execute. Command and…"

"Whatever," said Sandy. "Cecilia has created algorithms to verbally command and control others, us. We can use these."

"How?" asked Bale.

"We can edit them so that the drones recognize one of our voices, and then follow our commands," said John, suddenly understanding Sandy's plan.

"And we can reprogram the security guard outside that door, to obey our command. To unlock 3C," said Amir, as it clicked for him too.

"Hold on," said Bale. "Are we sure the guard outside is droned? And are we really ready to cross this line?"

"He's droned. Nearly all Americans are. We don't have time to worry about crossing the line now. We can always reverse it," said Sandy, anxious to get out of there, and quietly determined to beat Cecilia at her own game.

***

Cecilia was seriously pissed off now. The traffic in Manhattan was unbearable, and showing no signs of letting up. The rain had stopped and it seemed that everyone was on the streets. It was 12:30, and according to Google Maps they could expect to arrive at the Metropolitan Tower at around 12:58.

***

Amir was sitting at a terminal trying to gain access to the Metropolitan Tower LiFi lights. John, in the meantime, was trying to edit the commands.

He worked first on the voice recognition algorithm. He'd figured out that the Microbees attached to the auditory vestibular nerve were programmed to recognize certain frequencies, no doubt those of Cecilia's voice. He confirmed this assumption by playing a recorded video of her speaking that he'd found - they were the same frequencies.

"I'm ready," he said eventually. "Who wants to play God?" he said. No one laughed.

"How about you?" asked Amir, looking at John.

"No. This thing freaks me out, man. I don't want the responsibility. Sandy?"

"These are the commands that Cecilia's used to control the three of us. I would prefer if someone else did this," she said.

"I'll do it," said Bale, in a cold, angry voice. It was like he was a different man. While the others had been trying to find a way to escape 3C, Bale had had time to consider the implications of what he'd seen, which in the context of the conversation he'd had at dinner with Cecilia, made all too much sense. This wasn't just a breach of trust. It was Cecilia's attempt to gain more power than any human being who had ever walked the earth. That was what these commands told him. And he was furious. He needed to confront Cecilia, but on his own terms, in his own time. Now, he just needed to get the hell out of here.

"OK, speak here," said John, and before Bale could change his mind, he handed him a microphone. John put in the recorded frequencies of Bale's voice into the algorithm he had called 'Bale VR'. All the other commands followed the master VR algorithm, overriding the previous settings and giving Bale the power to command and control any individual programmed with this code. The team still needed to authorize the new command before they could use it.

***

Darko received a new text message and passed his mobile phone to Cecilia. "Authorized new command at 3C." She looked at the message in disbelief. What were they up to? It couldn't be good.

***

"Amir, how are we doing?" John asked.

"Got it, guys. I can't isolate the seventy-sixth floor lights though. Any drone in the building will be reprogrammed, but it won't matter, as they'll never hear Bale's voice."

"Ok, here's the code, let's do it," John said, hurriedly. "We'll use the universal Yiamas codes, and run them all through the LiFi. The whole process should take about a minute."

Bale ran by the door and ordered George to laugh, and then cough, so as to verify that the LiFi programming had been successful.

Eventually, at 12:47, George coughed. Then the guard's mobile phone rang, and he moved away from the door. A chime could be heard in the distance. The elevator door opened, and then closed. George was gone.

215

***

Darko hung up and informed Cecilia that he'd safely removed the guard from duty, and that 3C was still in lockdown. Two of his other guards were also on their way to the Metropolitan Tower.

***

"Shit, shit, shit," said Bale. "He's gone."

"Now we're fucked," said Sandy.

"No, we're not," said John, holding the receiver of the landline. "I have Vlad, the building doorman, on the line."

Bale dashed to the phone and commanded Vlad to come up to the seventy-sixth floor. A minute later, Vlad could be heard outside the door. With careful and quick commands, Bale guided him to the manual switch. Within a minute, 3C was unlocked.

***

In the rush to find out what was going on in 3C, Darko broke his own rule and parked illegally across the street from the Metropolitan Tower. He opened the trunk of his car and for a brief moment admired its contents. He considered what he needed, and opted for a Kevlar vest and the Smith & Wesson handgun. He checked if it was loaded, and then stocked up with ammunition. Before closing the trunk, he looked under the floor and caressed the C-4 hidden down there.

He crossed the street with Cecilia, where he was met with two more members of his security detail who had just arrived. They were joined by George, the seventy-sixth floor guard who had been guarding 3C moments earlier. It was 12:58.

***

Everyone moved towards the open door when John shouted, "Stop. Come back. We need to do something."

"What?" asked Amir. "We need to get outta here, man!"

"Come back, now!" John shouted, and they all returned to the terminal where John had plugged in a USB.

"I need you to authorize this," he said.

Sandy and Bale instinctively leaned forward over the screen. "You're copying the commands and the universal Yiamas codes? Why?" Sandy asked.

"We may need them to stop this madness. And one thing I can guarantee you is that we'll never step foot in here again," he said, ominously.

Bale was the first to move towards the iris scanner. He knew that they were crossing yet another line. Getting access to the codes gave any one of them the power to change drone programming without the need for authorization from the rest of them. But he was confident of the good intentions of this new group, and was by now deeply distrustful of Cecilia, so the way he saw it, he had no choice. This was the lesser evil, so to speak.

Amir followed, anxious to get out of there, and then Sandy and John stepped forward in turn. John removed the USB memory stick from the terminal and put it in his pocket. Finally, they all rushed towards the door.

***

Cecilia, Darko and the security guards entered the elevator just as Darko received another text. "Good," Cecilia said when he showed it her. "They're still up there."

***

Once out of 3C, the four ran to the elevator. Then Sandy stopped suddenly. "Guys, what if the elevator opens and Cecilia is inside?"

***

The elevator door opened, and Cecilia, Darko, and the guards rushed out. Cecilia went through the security procedure to enter 3C while Darko and George both pulled their handguns, waiting for the door to open.

As soon as the click sounded, Darko kicked the door open and stood back, though he didn't really expect armed opposition on the other side. But there was no one to be found, armed or otherwise. Cecilia rushed to the landline and called down to the lobby. Within seconds, the whole building was locked.

***

On the seventy-fifth floor, the elevator chime sounded and four people entered quietly and pushed the button for the ground floor. When the door opened at the bottom, they were in for a surprise.

"Sorry people, we have orders not to let anyone in or out of the building," said Vlad, blocking their way, as soon as the other doormen informed him of the situation.

Sandy cried, "No, you don't understand, we have to get out of here right now. It's a matter of life or death."

"I'm sure you'll be able to get out of here in just a moment. It's probably all just a misunderstanding," Vlad said in a reassuring tone.

"Let us leave," said Bale. The command reached doormen's ears, and from there, as it had done before, it travelled to the auditory vestibular nerve, where it was intercepted by the Microbees, which altered the signal with the algorithms with which every drone in the building had been reprogrammed.

Vlad stepped aside.

"Unlock the front door," Bale said, and as the doorman dashed to do so, the group quickly sped after him.

As the building's front door finally opened, they heard the elevator chime behind them. Cecilia, Darko, and the security team rushed out as Darko held up his handgun.

"Don't let them out of the building," Cecilia shouted, as Darko rushed towards the exit.

"Stop them," Bale told Vlad, instinctively, giving a direct and unambiguous order, as the four of them ran out of the building.

Vlad moved to stop Darko as George, who'd also heard Bale's command, grabbed Cecilia's hand, pulling her back. The security guards who had just arrived pulled their handguns out and one of them fired a warning shot.

A second shot was heard, and one of them fell to the floor, flat on his face. Darko turned around and saw George, a gun in his hand, bewildered by what he had just done. A second later, another loud bang was heard and George fell to the ground, shot by his other colleague.

As he rushed to cross 57th street, Bale turned around. Vlad was fighting a security guard. Vlad was a former wrestling champion, and it didn't take long for him to take the security guard down. Darko didn't have time for this. He raised his handgun. A shot echoed from the entrance of the building. Vlad the doorman drone, who had accidentally been reprogrammed just a few moments ago, fell to the ground, grabbing Darko's leg, still desperately trying to obey Bale's order, the last thing he would ever do.

Darko struggled to pull loose, and by the time he'd made it out of the building, Bale and the rogue members of the team were nowhere to be seen.

As police sirens approached, Cecilia backtracked and got back into the elevator. She was safely in her penthouse apartment before the first police officer entered the building.

***

Sandy, John, Amir and Bale reached their suite at the Salisbury Hotel at around the same time. John and Amir fell onto the couch, while Sandy rushed to the toilet where she threw up violently.

Bale moved quietly toward the window and peered outside. Police lights had now pretty much blocked 57th street. Out of sight of where Bale was standing were the bodies of Vlad, George and another security guard. Three people he liked, and would never have wished dead. But now they were dead, the result of following his own command. CaE. Command and Execute. He had commanded, and they had been executed.

***

Cecilia was also struggling to see the street from her apartment. She saw the commotion, of course, and she saw ambulances approach. But she wasn't sure of what was going on, or what had happened to Darko. Then she noticed something that made her smile: there was no Tesla on the other side of the street.

***

The street was quieter now. The police cars and ambulances had just left. It was four in the morning, and Bale still had not moved from the window. Amir was checking the local news. Sandy and John were in the bedroom next door.

Bale was staring outside blankly. In this past week, he had watched his world collapse. From learning about the droning of the team, to realizing Cecilia's true aspirations, and then discovering the special commands she had created just for herself. It was too much for him to bear.

A thousand thoughts circled in his mind. This technology was indeed dangerous if it fell into the wrong hands. But for the life of him, he had never imagined that the wrong hands would be his. He'd started a gunfight, and people had died trying to protect him. Those decisions might be easy for politicians, but not for the philosopher professor whose primary goal in life was to save people, not send them to their deaths. Yet he'd had a hand in many deaths, now. Too many.

But what he was struggling with most, what was now crystal clear to him, was that his vision had not ever been put into practice. Bale's theory called for a non-hierarchical social network that no one could control. By contrast, what Cecilia had apparently developed was a social network of which she could - would - take control. In his blind ambition to see his life's work realized within his own lifetime, he had downplayed the importance of this very distinction and tried to bury it under the constitution, a document that was too easily circumvented, meaningless, really. It had served only to facilitate their own self-deception.

***

Amir suddenly felt a rush of cold, holiday season air. He turned around. Bale was standing by the open window. Amir didn't move, and then he said softly, "It wasn't your fault, Richard."

"It was. It was all my fault," Bale whispered, looking down at the street.

"We're all to blame," replied Amir.

"My theories, idealistic fantasies, set this whole disaster in motion."

"It wasn't about your theories; it was about Cecilia, and her thirst for power. Properly applied, your theories really would have saved the world."

"But that's the thing, Amir," Bale said, turning now to look at Amir. "I never thought about the down side, about the danger. I never even considered the possibility that a network of connected human beings could be susceptible to control by other humans. My theories, complex though they were, failed to predict the Cecilia Stein phenomenon."

For a moment, Amir couldn't find words. "It is the inherent nature of every man, woman and child to seek ever more power," was all he could muster.

"I should have predicted it, should have known. I should have stopped Cecilia when I had the chance," Bale whimpered, now shivering from the cold wind coming through the window, and from the realization that his life's work had amounted to nothing, worse than nothing. That he was a failure. He turned again to look outside.

"It's not too late," said Amir, desperately trying to pull Bale back from the brink. "It's never too late."

"I agree," said Bale. "It's not too late to change things. But it's you guys, the younger generation who are now responsible for making the change. This isn't my world anymore," he said, echoing the sentiments of most of the older generation who, at the end of their life, absolve themselves of the responsibility to make the world a better place.

And with that, Dr. Richard Bale, brilliant philosopher, face of the greatest environmental movement the world had ever seen, who'd provided untold hope for the future, leaned over the window ledge, and took his final step on an unknown journey.

CHAPTER FIFTEEN

THE CHASE

Amir rushed to the window, shocked and speechless. He saw Bale's body, sixteen floors down, splayed across the pavement. Then he looked across the street and saw Darko. On instinct, he pulled out his smartphone and took a video of the scenes that followed.

Amir then ran into the bedroom and shouted, "Guys, we've got to move," and showed them the video.

***

It was four in the morning and Cecilia was still standing at her window, directly overlooking the Salisbury Hotel. She didn't notice the man jumping to his death. But soon people gathered around the body and another commotion on 57th street began.

Then her phone rang, "Thank God you're OK. I thought he got you," she said, breathless.

"He didn't, but why did he do it? He was one of my most loyal guards."

"They messed with his brain, Darko... They messed with his brain," Cecilia told him, looking down at the floor.

"Well, we have a new problem. But I know where they are now, at least," he said, and filled her in.

***

Cecilia put on some athletics gear and rushed down to the ground. She approached the small but growing crowd. She could hear the returning police and ambulance sirens in the distance. She took a brief look at Bale's lifeless body. Under normal circumstances, she would want to take a moment to grieve. But things were not normal.

Darko had found out the room number. They had to rush.

***

"Oh my God," cried Sandy as soon as she saw the video. "I can't believe it."

"Well you'd better believe it, and soon – it won't take long for Cecilia to find out which room we're in."

They grabbed a couple of essentials and rushed out of the room.

"Where to?" asked John.

"Let's head to the roof," replied Amir, a plan forming in his mind.

***

"They've been here for two nights. They're staying in suite 1605," said Darko.

"Two days?" exclaimed Cecilia. "This is pre-meditated, then."

Darko agreed. "But why? What happened?"

"I have no idea. Let's go find out," Cecilia said, leading the way toward the elevator.

"Hold on. Are we just going to knock on their door and ask them?" said Darko, dubious about the wisdom of such a direct approach.

"We sure as hell are," said Cecilia, and she stepped into the elevator.

The exit to the roof was a fire exit. As soon as it was opened, an alarm would sound.

"Shit, shit," said John, panicking. "They'll hear this, and know we're up here."

"I don't care," said Sandy and she pushed the door open.

***

They argued about the best approach on the way up to the sixteenth floor. It took the relatively old and slow elevator a minute to get up there. Had they been on the ground floor, or if they'd gotten to the sixteenth floor quicker, they would have heard a distant alarm. But the faint noise went unheard inside the elevator.

***

They stumbled out of the doorway straight onto the roof of the Salisbury Hotel. On the west side, they could see the humongous One57 tower, the third tallest residential skyscraper in New York. The south end of the building was overlooking 57th Street. There was no building on the north side either, so that left the Landmark Gallery building to the east.

With no other options, they rushed to the tall brick wall that separated the rooftop of the Salisbury Hotel from the neighboring building.

"It must be ten feet tall," John exclaimed in desperation.

"Over here," shouted Amir, who was dangerously close to the north edge of the building. They moved carefully toward the edge and Sandy looked down. She could not see the ground from up here but guessed that it must have been a two-hundred-foot drop.

Amir was pointing to a fire escape intended for the occupants of the building next door. It was a steel, vertical wall mounted ladder that descended into the darkness below them. It was mounted about four feet away from the edge, just out of reach.

"I can jump and grab it," said John.

"No honey, if you miss, then…" Sandy stopped mid-sentence, as John had already made his move. Without a second thought, he leaned over the edge of the building and for a moment he looked as if he was about to jump, head first towards the darkness below them. But then, his right arm grabbed the vertical rod of the steel ladder and, for a split second, he was dangling horizontally between the roof of the Salisbury Hotel and the steel ladder on the edge of the Landmark Gallery building. His feet slipped and the full weight of his body began to fall, until it was stopped by his right hand on the ladder. He quickly turned around and grabbed at it with his left hand, and within a second, his feet were securely on the ladder.

"Wow," was all Amir could say, and then he let Sandy go next. Between Amir helping on one side and John's extended arm, she too was quickly onto the steel ladder and on her way down. Amir had to make the jump, but even with John's extended arm, he was hesitating.

"C'mon, man," said John, eager to get out of there.

Amir got close to the edge, avoided looking down, focused on John's extended hand and leaned forward. As he did so, he lost his concentration for a split second, and his hand didn't lock with John's. Realizing this, and before his feet left contact with the Salisbury roof, he instinctively pushed forward.

As he began to fall, he grabbed the ladder as John had done, but much lower. He had already picked up some speed and was unable to keep hold with his right hand. He frantically searched for something to grab onto with his left hand and just as it seemed he'd missed his last opportunity, he grabbed one of the horizontal rods. His entire weight fell onto his left arm as he swung and hit his face on the lower steps.

He let out a cry of pain, but swiftly got up and moved downwards, following Sandy and John in his wake.

***

Darko kicked the door open and they both rushed into the room. It was clear they'd been there just minutes earlier. There were suitcases in the middle of the room, half full. They had clearly left in a hurry.

Darko rushed to the open window. "Damn, we missed them."

"They must be close. Perhaps they're leaving the building right now."

"I can't see them on the street," said Darko still looking outside the window, up and down 57th Street.

"You go to the roof; I'll go back to the ground floor."

***

They reached the ground behind the Salisbury Hotel and took a moment to catch their breath. Amir, having just had a near-death experience, was shivering. The cold did not help.

They hugged each other for a moment, to warm up. Cecilia's group might be broken, but this piece was holding strong together. Then a faraway but familiar alarm startled them.

***

Darko reached the roof and quickly determined that the only way out was on the Landmark Gallery side. So, he rushed to the east side of the roof. The wall was too tall. He walked up and down, trying to figure out how they would have got away.

He walked to the 57th Street edge and looked down. He could see Cecilia, crossing the street, looking up and down.

He ran to the north side and again looked down. It was dark, and he couldn't see anything. Then he spotted the ladder. *They couldn't have...*

A sound echoed from the surrounding buildings. There was only one way to find out. He pulled out his gun, pointed it directly downward and fired a single blind shot.

***

The sound of the gunshot echoed loudly in the silent darkness. The bullet itself must have landed just a few feet from where they were hiding.

Sandy let out a small cry of fear. It was inadvertent and not loud, but it echoed around the buildings.

It was all Darko needed to hear. He pulled out his cell phone and called Cecilia. Then, he made the same jump John had made earlier and started his descent.

***

They knew immediately that they'd been found. The problem was that they were in a courtyard stuck between the buildings on 57th Street and 58th Street. It seemed like there was no way out. It was dark and cold, and they could hear the screeching sound of the steel ladder as Darko approached.

Sandy was the first to bolt. She started running westward towards the One57 building. Thankfully, she'd had time to adjust to the darkness and the lights of the surrounding buildings were enough to help her avoid tripping on the way.

John ran behind her, and Amir quickly followed. None of them had any idea where they were going, but putting some distance between them and Darko seemed like a good idea and no one could think of a better plan.

They were in the space between the buildings, a place where none of them had ever been. Sandy hadn't even realized that such a gap existed behind the buildings.

As she ran, she looked for open doors. On her left, she passed by the Salisbury Hotel, and on her right it looked like there was a restaurant, or a bar, judging from the empty bottles of liquor which were producing a nasty smell from a nearby dumpster.

She moved on, and tried a couple of doors. John did the same on the opposite side, and Amir farther on. Then, a flashlight appeared from the direction in which they had been hiding. Darko had reached the ground. They had run out of time.

Just as all hope had vanished, and desperation was settling over the small, unarmed group of three, a door opened from the bar Sandy had tried just a moment ago. Someone exited carrying two black garbage bags. Even in the darkness she recognized the face.

Angelo! We're behind LOI, the Greek restaurant, she realized.

"Angelo," she shouted and she ran towards him. Angelo was a big guy, clearly he spent time at the gym, but the voice of a woman, coming from the darkness between the buildings at five in the morning on New Year's Day startled him.

He stepped backward and almost fell down.

"Angelo, it's me, Sandy," she said in Greek.

"Jesus, Sandy, you scared the hell out of me. What are you doing here?" Angelo replied in Greek, and then spotted the others.

"Quick, we're being chased, we need to get in," said Sandy and then a shot sounded from somewhere behind them.

They did not wait another second as they climbed up a small ramp and entered the building, the door closing behind them. He immediately placed a horizontal security rod across the door, making it impossible for anyone to break through.

Turning around, they walked into the main restaurant area. "Fuck," said Sandy when she saw who was waiting for them.

***

Darko fired another shot, but it missed again. He tried pulling and pushing the locked door but it would not move. Suddenly he realized that he was trapped between 57th and 58th street possibly with no way to get out.

***

"What the fuck," John blurted when he saw her. "What the fuck, Cecilia!"

There she was standing, by LOI's open front door some 30 feet away, her cold demeanor, colder than ever. Angelo saw her and feeling like a cop in a movie, he walked up to her. "Just one thing," he said and motioned for her to raise her arms so he could frisk her. She didn't react as his hands moved up and down her body. It was five in the morning and Angelo had had a long night, after hosting a New Year's party for New York Greek diaspora. He'd had a bit to drink, and his hands roamed a bit more freely than was acceptable. But she didn't complain. Didn't flinch. She just stood there completely motionless. Expressionless.

He took her cell phone and invited her in, mildly aroused by their brief encounter. She stepped forward confidently, as if it had never happened, sucking the air out of the room as she approached the three traitors. Feeling trapped, John, Amir and Sandy sat at the back of the room around a round table where Cecilia joined them. Angelo too sat down, beside Cecilia for good measure. His evening had taken an exciting turn and he wasn't going to miss it. A stained tablecloth was still set on the table, not having been cleared up.

"What the fuck, Cecilia?" John repeated.

"Hi, John. Nice to see you, too."

"You used my technology to control people? To control us?" John cutting right to the chase.

"I didn't," she replied.

"So, what the fuck was all that about, in the lobby of the Metropolitan Tower?" asked Sandy, already furious at Cecilia's denial.

"If I'm not mistaken, that was *you* using *your* technology to *your* own benefit. Whatever that was," she replied, still looking at John.

"Then why did you drone us?" Sandy asked.

"If you mean the Microbees installed in your brain, yes, I was responsible for that, but I didn't drone you," she insisted.

Angelo's jaw dropped, not believing what he was hearing. He got up and picked up a carafe from the next table. It contained raki, the Greek version of grappa, but stronger. He served everyone in shot glasses.

"You're saying that you didn't program the Microbees to affect our decisions?" asked Amir. "That's what they're for. Why else would you inject Microbees if not to drone us?"

Failing to understand the references to bees, injections, and drones, Angelo smiled, took a look at his short glass, and downed the contents. This was getting better and better.

"It was a spur of the moment decision on the plane back from Nauru. I was worried the group was going to fall apart, so I instructed Darko to use the shots from Nauru. Frank recoded them so that they were dormant."

"Bullshit. You wouldn't have done this and then not used it. Plus, I would have never given my consent to do... you know what ... to ten thousand people of my own free will," Sandy said, hesitating, as she glanced toward Angelo.

Cecilia turned to Angelo now. "Angelo, right? You will keep this conversation to yourself." It's more of an order than a question.

"Yes ma'am," Angelo confirmed.

Cecilia turned back to Sandy, "You would, and you did," she said, her eyes piercing through Sandy's, who eventually looked away.

"But what about all these other decisions and commands you have programmed into the Microbees?" asked Amir.

"What about them?" asked Cecilia.

"They weren't part of our plan," said Amir.

"Or our constitution." Sandy found the opportunity to strike back.

"They are beyond the scope of what we set out to do," said John. Cecilia was now facing rapid fire from across the table.

"So what? I left a back door open to use only in extreme circumstances, if they ever arose. I had to protect the project." Cecilia was on the defensive.

"That's more than a backdoor, Cecilia. You gave yourself the power to instruct drones to do anything. Without our knowledge," said Sandy.

"Yes, I have that power. But so does a president. Or a CEO. Or the manager of any small business. Angelo, do you give orders to your staff here?"

"Of course I do," Angelo replied, excited to be a part of the conversation.

"And why do they follow them?"

"Because I'll kick their ass if they don't. I'd fire their asses."

"So, you threaten people, who depend on you to make a living. You tell them that if they don't do what you say, you'll throw them out onto the street?"

"I don't see how that's relevant," interrupted John.

"Bear with me," Cecilia said, as if she was asking for the patience of a court. Turning back to Angelo, she asked, "And do you ever do it?"

"I have once or twice. But mostly no."

"You're not a bad person, are you, Angelo?"

"No ma'am, I'm not."

Cecilia turned to John now, a smirk on her face for the first time.

"So, your point, Cecilia, is that you have the power to instruct people on what to do, but you're not a bad person because you don't use that power? I don't see the relevance of Angelo, here," said John.

"It's entirely relevant. Any leader, anywhere in the world can instruct people to do things for them."

"It's entirely different, actually," Sandy objected. "These leaders have earned the right to lead. And people obey of their own free will."

"Really, Sandy?" Cecilia's voice took a nasty tone, heavy with sarcasm. "Just how naïve are you, my dear? The leaders you're talking about have normally bought their power or got lucky in the political game, and hide behind tons of money and fake promises. More often than not, they instruct us to do things that no one in their right mind would ever do. Including to kill someone else. Or to fire them. Or to ignore scientific evidence and take decisions that destroy the environment. It is these leaders who are abusing power. Not me."

"But having the power to abuse means that one day, you will eventually abuse it, even if you haven't done so already. It's human nature," said Sandy.

"But it's human nature we're trying to change here. That's the ultimate aim of the project," replied Cecilia.

"Only in respect to the environment. We can't affect free will. We had long discussions and agreed on this early on".

"We don't have free will," said Cecilia, in a loud, scolding voice. "We believe we have the ability to make our own decisions, but the world makes these decisions for us. You cave to social pressures or maybe you get into an accident, get drafted, have an unwanted pregnancy, or you break a stupid law, whatever. It's the decisions and attitude of our parents, our education system, our friends. In the end, we are confined to a very narrow track, where the only decisions we can actually make for ourselves are which channel to watch on TV. All our lives are similar. We share the same timetables, the same habits, watch the same movies, dress in the same clothes, buy the same stuff. We despise and fear diversity, and we oppose it whenever possible. Anything and anyone different from us is a threat. We are already drones. Whoever droned us, whether it's God or pure chance, did a much more effective job than I did."

The team was listening intently. Cecilia's stare was moving rapidly from Sandy to John and to Amir, never looking anywhere else than directly into their eyes. No one dared interrupt her.

"And occasionally, we revolt. Then all hell breaks loose. We vote for the wrong people just because they promise to bring about change. We are suckers for their empty promises. Or, we take our guns and go to war, and the misery bestowed upon the world is unthinkable. Children are killed or injured, and our leaders call it collateral damage. Yet still we follow them, because the end, which is always, *always* just around the corner, justifies the means. Half of a happy family, dead, because someone ordered a bomb to be dropped. That someone sitting on the other side of the world, with an army of secret service agents guarding *his* life. So, yes, I do have the power to affect decisions. But I don't use it. My goal is to weaken the current mechanisms of power, for the benefit of everyone. I'm giving people back their free will, not taking it away."

"But we had an agreement, Cecilia," said John. "And you're using *my* technology."

"True, John. I saw an opportunity and took it. This isn't just about the environment anymore. It's about ending war. It's about population growth control. Income distribution. Feeding the poor. The world has so many problems. And we have the power to solve all of them." Her voice was unwavering, her stare intense.

***

For a brief moment, Sandy had been swayed by the power of her arguments. The ambition behind her vision. Yes, she had made mistakes, but there was a reason behind them. If only they had talked to her earlier, they would have avoided all the drama… and Bale would still be alive, she thought. But then something clicked in her head. Cecilia was a leader if ever she had met one, and as such, she was a deft manipulator. She had said everything that they had secretly wanted to hear.

She'd almost fallen into the trap. She didn't require Microbees to influence the decisions of this group, because they had been carefully selected by the Mindalikes algorithm, and molded through years of efficacious brainwashing at her monthly dancing performance atop the Metropolitan Tower.

With a renewed sense of rage, Sandy looked up, locked her eyes onto Cecilia's and said.

"No."

"Goddamnit Sandy! You are such an ungrateful *bitch*!"

Sandy, unfazed, continued. "You don't have the right to solve all the world's problems. You're not that person. You don't have the authority."

"If not me – us – then who?"

"Governments. Elected officials. The people. Revolutions."

"You're an imbecile, Sandy. We have self-selected our leaders for centuries. Look where it got us. Dictatorships are even worse. People abuse, oppress, and trample over others to remain in power. The human race is not equipped to share. We can't live in an interconnected world. This is what drew me to poor Bale's research in the first place."

"But what you suggest is that *you* become the leader. This time of the whole world. What makes you so much better?"

"You still don't get it, Sandy, do you? Whoever created us made a mistake. I know some consider it wrong to question the Supreme Being, call it God, Allah, Zeus, whatever. But He made a mistake. He put a flawed system – the human being - into action. It was His mistake that put us in this position. What we're doing here is fixing it. Only, our power will remain a secret and it will remain so - lest our friend Angelo here decides to speak out.

We don't need palace courtiers. We can just take pride in the results. And we can have these conversations - and disagreements - peacefully. But look at us. A group of seven, and even *we* can't coordinate ourselves to bring about a social good."

"It's your fault, Cecilia, you broke our trust," said Sandy, coldly. And now it's too late. I don't want to control anyone, or have anyone control me."

"This is utter bullshit, Sandy," said Cecilia. "You think that you're not taking advantage of others because you pay them peanuts to gather your garbage or clean your apartment. Do you think that if they had the opportunity to take advantage of you, they wouldn't? It's human nature to take advantage of each other. And as technology proliferates, we'll have more and more tools to do so."

"Take Angelo, here." She turned her ice-cold stare directly to him. "How did you like feeling me up when I came in?" she asked, and Sandy raised an eyebrow, having missed that encounter.

"Busted," said Angelo, with a guilty smile.

"What gave you the right to put your hands all over me?"

His smile disappeared.

"You were in a position of power over me. You're bigger than me, and I had to get past you. Right?"

Angelo nodded, looking ashamed.

"Did that make you happy? Are you satisfied with yourself?"

"Listen, lady," Angelo began, but Cecilia cut him off.

"Tomorrow, Angelo will be able to tell his friends about how he felt some chick up at five in the morning. He might embellish the story a bit, too. It will make his friends laugh, maybe high-five each other. Does it make them happy? Are you happy, Angelo?"

"Sure am, a bit tired is all."

"Bullshit. People aren't happy. They don't know how to be happy. Humans pursue happiness, but all they ever achieve is momentary satisfaction. They confuse satisfaction with happiness."

"We live in the most peaceful period in the western world and yet we're still not happy. We have everything we could possibly need and more, but still it's not enough. And when we get more, we find out that we didn't really want it anyway. Then we start exploiting others. We humans are horrible beings. And it's His fault, whoever He is," she said, pointing up at the ceiling.

"And now, we have the chance to change it. We have the chance to bring happiness to the world. To save us from ourselves. To stop abusing each other. It's all in this beautiful technology you developed, John. There aren't 1.5 billion drones in the world. There are 1.5 billion beautiful beings, with so much potential. We need to give them our unconditional love, and nurture them to do good. Not so that they can reach paradise in life after death, but to find paradise in this life. This is the vision; it always has been."

"So, what do you call this new method of government, Cecilia? Enlightened despotism?" Sandy asked.

"I just want this to work, and to bring happiness to the world," came the reply in a warmer tone.

"According to your own set of values," Amir remarked, still not convinced, to Sandy's relief.

"According to a set of values that we all co-create."

"So, who are we in this arrangement? God?" Sandy asked, incredulous at Cecilia's arrogance.

Cecilia replied in a measured way, showing that she had already considered the answer to this question: "If by God, you mean a supernatural creature that lives forever and watches all over us, then no, we are not God. But if by God we mean a being that created humanity, able to co-exist and work together for a better future, then yes, that's what we are. What we can be."

"Are you guys for real?" Angelo asked.

They ignored him, then John said "You're insane, you know that?" and Sandy relaxed a bit.

"Change is always driven by people who see opportunity where others fail to. Others may judge these people as crazy. History brands them as visionary."

"We can't let you do this, Cecilia," says John.

"You don't have a choice," said Cecilia and at that moment, LOI's door opened and Darko walked in, gun at hand.

***

They walked out of LOI and entered Cecilia's Tesla, John at the driver seat and Darko beside him. "Where to?" John asked. "Philadelphia," Cecilia replied.

"Philadelphia? Why?" asked Amir.

"I need some fresh Microbees produced at the Penn lab," replied Cecilia.

"What for?" asked Sandy.

"I need to get you redroned. You are useless and dangerous to me as you are," came the reply, her tone final, the alternative unthinkable.

***

Angelo locked the door behind them and sat down to consider the conversation he'd just witnessed. He was strangely drawn to this Cecilia woman, and by what she'd said. She really was pursuing something good in this world. He didn't understand all that about drones and Microbees, but it didn't sound like they were talking about anything terrible.

One thing was for sure. He had a story to share in the morning, although, for some reason, he was compelled to keep it to himself. He couldn't wait to get back home. He took out his phone and ordered an Uber. A friendly Pakistani face appeared on the screen, and a car was on its way.

When it arrived, it parked directly in front of the restaurant, so Angelo didn't have the chance to verify its license plates. Nor did he look twice at the driver, who definitely did not look Pakistani.

"Happy New Year," he said, as he got into the car but he never got a reply. There would be no New Year for Angelo, let alone a happy one.

CHAPTER SIXTEEN

THE SEIGE

John was driving on the New Jersey Turnpike heading for Philadelphia, as he considered his options. He could not let Cecilia re-drone him, only hours after he managed to get rid of the damned Microbees. He would not let Cecilia have complete control over his decisions and ultimately his memories and beliefs. He would rather die before that happened. He briefly considered crashing the Tesla with the intent to kill everyone on board. He would gladly get rid of Cecilia, that was the level of his rage, but he could not make this decision for Amir and Sandy, and this was not the place to discuss it with them.

Over the past few days, he had also realized the devastating effects that Microbees 2.0 would have if they were ever used by the wrong people. He wondered how far Cecilia would go in her quest for power. Would she use Microbees 2.0 to amass a greater fortune? For some reason, John was not convinced that Cecilia was after more money. Whatever her ultimate goal was, she could probably achieve it more easily if she could directly implant ideas into a drone's head. He could not let her get her hands on Microbees 2.0. He needed to find a way to get the three of them safely out of reach of Darko and his guns, and to have enough time to destroy the research and designs of Microbees 2.0.

As they crossed the Walt Whitman bridge into Philadelphia, with time running up, a rough plan started to formulate in his mind.

***

They reached the nanotechnology building, just as the sun was rising. They parked across the street and were met by one of Darko's sidekicks, Ayman. The army was growing and John thought that his plan became all the more difficult.

It was strange for these six people to be here at this time in the morning of New Year's Day. John looked around but there was no one around to see them, let alone stop them, or help them.

As they made their way towards the building, tired as they were, he wondered if this was the last time he would ever see this building, the temple of his life's work. He took a long last look appreciating the beauty of the mostly glass structure, and the bewildering lack of vertical columns joining the floors together. He looked up and once again admired the really unique feature: the protruding rectangular cuboid that formed part of the second floor, which appeared to be suspended in mid-air in front of the main building, seemingly unsupported.

John had twenty-four-hour access to the building. At Cecilia's direction and with Darko's gun-at-hand prompt, he walked up to the locked front door, stepped next to the fingerprint reader and placed his index finger on it. The sliding door opened momentarily and Sandy walked into the building. The door closed immediately behind her. At off hours, access to the building was restricted to one person at a time, John explained. Amir went next, then Cecilia walked towards the door.

"Wait," said Darko and pointed to Ayman to step inside first. As Ayman made his way to the door, for a split second, he blocked Darko's line of sight. At that precise moment, in one bold, swift and coordinated move, John placed his finger on the reader and shoved Ayman towards Darko. The door opened, John jumped into the building and the door closed behind him before Darko could fire a shot.

Cecilia threw a furious look toward Darko and, knowing that he had let his master down, he fired three shots towards the window. He was surprised to see that it didn't break. John felt confident as he approached the window.

He came face-to-face with Cecilia, only three feet and a bullet-proof nanotechnology-engineered window separating them. "You can't get in," he shouted, with a satisfied smile.

The windows were soundproof, but Cecilia read John's lips. She returned John's smile and mouthed, "You can't get out."

And so the siege started.

***

Frank was at the 3C. He had been working non-stop since Cecilia had called him earlier in the night, trying to figure out what the others had done.

He had taken just one short break to hack into a cell phone and get the details of an Uber transaction. He then cancelled the transaction, and removed all trace of it from the Uber system. The things you could get done as the world's foremost hacker.

The phone rang. "So what did they get?" Cecilia asked Frank.

"They certainly got access to the codes. They seem to have accessed the commands, and they found the Leadership folder. It's not clear though why they gave a new authorization before they left. I need to keep searching."

"Hurry up. I need to decide what to do next."

***

Sandy and Amir followed John as he rushed down the stairs, straight to the basement. There, in one corner of the building, they found the office of Senior Researcher John Walker, PhD. He had the largest office, all paid for by his grand sponsor, Uniocom Inc.

Sandy sat on the black leather couch that dominated one side of the room. John powered up his PC and three separate screens came to life. Two monitors on his desk, and one 55" flat screen on the wall.

It took John five minutes to locate the Microbees 2.0 files and select all of them. Then, he paused.

"Delete them, man," said Amir, who had been watching all of this on the flat screen.

John looked up and hesitated, "Once this technology is gone, it will be years, decades perhaps, before anyone comes close to achieving this."

"Good," said Sandy. "We don't want people to get their hands on this. That's the point."

"It's my life's work," John said in despair, looking at Amir for some support.

Amir himself was torn. The project was his life's work too, his chance to leave a mark in the world. He looked at John and recognized the despair. In a moment of weakness, he said, "Just upload it to Welit's secure servers and then delete it from the local drive."

John didn't wait for Amir to change his mind. Amir logged onto his private space on the Welit server and downloaded an encrypting algorithm. It was a function built by an Israeli startup, which Welit had acquired. Once the files were encrypted and uploaded, he used another function to execute a hard delete on the local drive, making sure no one, not even Frank, could recover the files.

***

Cecilia answered the phone and got the lowdown from Frank. The infidels had looted his system. Sandy was right that the technology could fall into the wrong hands. It already had.

Cecilia thought about her options and saw only one. She could not let these 3 loose cannons free to decide to jeopardize the future of her project. If she could not get them re-droned, then there was only one alternative.

"Do whatever it takes to make sure that they don't get out of there alive," she told Darko.

For Darko, that left only one option, one for which he was well prepared.

"You need to get as far away from here as possible," he told her. "You may need this," he added as he handed her a switchblade.

"I don't think I will need it," she said confidently, but then took it anyway.

***

John was reflecting on the events of the past few hours; the invasion of 3C, the gunfight on the ground floor, the death of Vlad, Bale's suicide, their close call atop the Salisbury Hotel, the heated conversation with Cecilia, their trip to Philadelphia, and finally Darko's ongoing siege of their current location. It was a lot to have gone through in less than 10 hours. But he knew that they needed to keep moving.

So he went off to try to find a way out of the building. Fire exit signs all led to a long corridor that connected this building with the next. They all had double doors which, if opened, would set off an alarm.

This would not only alert Darko to what they were up to, but also the fire brigade and the campus police.

Penn had the largest campus police of any university in the USA and, for that matter, the world. It would take Penn police less than three minutes to reach them. It was a risk that they might have to take, but he needed to discuss it with the others first. For now, he was just working out their options.

***

Back in John's office, Sandy picked up a conversation with Amir.

"Tell me, Amir, theoretically, if we wanted to de-drone everyone on earth, how would we do it?"

"Do you think we should go that far, Sandy?"

"That woman is crazy, Amir. And with tons of power in her hands. Anyway, I'm just wondering if it's an option."

"Well, we could use the generic YIAMAS codes and run the de-droning algorithm through public LiFi. Some counties use Welit LED lights in their subway trains, others in the streets, like Nauru. Another option could be LED TVs. It's an idea we toyed with at Welit."

"Talk to me about that. How does it work?"

"We can mask the LiFi algorithm behind a video that everyone watches. If the video is watched via a LED screen, the effect would be the same as the portable de-droner."

"And most TVs in the world are LED, right?"

"Yes, but how could you make sure that everyone watched the video? Make some kind of Hollywood blockbuster?" joked Amir.

"I don't know," said Sandy, but an idea was developing in her mind.

"There's no way out," declared John as he re-entered the office. "We can't leave without getting caught."

"Should we call campus police?" asked Amir.

"I think we would have a lot of explaining to do. Why are we here on New Year's Day? Who are you guys, and what are you doing here? I think campus police would have a few questions for us," replied John.

"Yeah, but we could get rid of Darko and his friend out there."

"Sure, but only for a moment."

***

Stu Spencer was driving up 33rd street having just left the University hospital after being on call. It had been a busy night, as New Year's Eve always is. Alcohol-related traffic accidents had been the cause of major and minor trauma cases and he also had to tend to several cases of alcohol poisoning. Not a great way to start the year, he thought.

He drove up to the corner of Walnut Street and stopped at the traffic light. A knock on the driver side window made him jump but then his eyes settled on this benign, good looking woman. What could she possibly want, he thought, eager to get home. But as a nurse, it was his natural tendency to help people, so he lowered the window of his Hyundai Elantra.

"You need to take me to New York City," the lady said. Her request was his command. He unlocked the door and let Cecilia Stein in.

***

Sandy absently-mindedly picked the remote control for the TV on the wall and switched channels. She stopped cold at CNN, when she saw the photograph of a familiar face. The caption underneath read "Dr. Richard Bale, found dead in NYC."

"Hey, look at this." Sandy jumped out of her seat and turned the volume up.

"...on 57th Street, New York. Dr. Bale, a British national and naturalized American became the face of the environmental movement last year when his theories on global coordination via social media suddenly became mainstream. Many have dubbed him the 'savior of humanity', though he has always maintained a low profile. He was 63 when he seemingly fell from the 16th floor of a hotel on New Year's Day, right here in New York, just a couple of blocks from here. The circumstances of his death are being investigated by the NYPD."

The anchor turned to face his guest. "So, what do you think this shocking and unexpected development will mean for the environmental movement?"

If only you knew, thought Sandy, who was deeply saddened by Bale's death.

"Well, Jonathan, I think that it's a great shame. This is a man who changed the course of our planet and possibly saved our species."

Sandy wiped a tear from her eye, and she retained her focus to the task at hand. She looked at her watch; it was 8am.

As the situation currently stood, they were locked in a maximum-security building with a crazy murderer lurking just outside. They were being chased by a woman who had more than a billion drones under her command. Their comrade and guiding light was dead, and here she was with her two scientist friends and no weapons. No matter how she looked at it, things were pretty desperate.

She sat across from John's desk, picked up his keyboard and mouse and, looking at the large screen, she typed in "Richard Bale" and clicked on "news".

New Year's Day was a slow news day, and Bale's death was making headlines across all traditional media. Next, she checked social media.

Bale's death was trending here too, with hashtags like #Baleforever, #ThankyouDrBale etc.

One in particular caught her eye: #VigilforBaleHydePark. She clicked to see what was being said. It seemed that some people were organizing a vigil at Hyde Park in the afternoon.

Sandy suddenly felt reinvigorated. An idea formed in her mind and she was back to being a girl on a mission. She had a plan. And with that plan, came hope. And hope was all she needed.

She got up and looked around John's office. Despite being his girlfriend and his project partner, it was the first time she had been in here. She found his backpack and opened it.

"What are you looking for?" asked Amir.

"This," replied Sandy, showing him a USB stick.

"You're not thinking of using those to get us out of here, are you?" Amir asked. "You do remember what happened last time we used those codes, right? Somebody got killed."

"We're not going to kill anyone, Amir. We can't, anyway, we are limited in what we can do with these codes," said Sandy, though she didn't reveal the plan just yet.

"Amir, can you give me your smartphone?" she asked him.

Amir handed his phone over to Sandy, who connected it to John's PC.

***

Darko and Ayman were busy at work. Using Ayman's 5-inch switch blade, they cut the seat cushions, the spare tire, and the floors and ceiling of the car.

"Do we really need so much of this stuff?" asked Ayman, looking at all the C-4 they were pulling out.

Darko did not reply. He was in no rush. They were right across the street from the nanotechnology building and he knew the three people in there could go nowhere. Furthermore, he wanted to give Cecilia enough time to be safely back in New York City before he used any – or all – of his favorite material.

For Darko, this was a game and he was damn good at it. Why rush and spoil the fun?

***

The old dog was crying. She wasn't in pain; she was just sad. Sad because her owners were sad. Little did she know that her master had just killed himself on the other side of the Atlantic. But her owners knew.

Suddenly she heard a familiar happy noise. Someone had just opened the drawer where her leash was kept. She was going for a walk. The happiest time of the day!

They left the flat and she kept pulling to go towards the park. Her favorite place in the world. That's where Michael and Cornelia were heading. Their mother, Beth, was leading the way.

It had been a rare sunny and dry mid-winter day. They walked through the narrow streets of Mayfair, and could see more people walking in the same direction. A car was coming toward them from a distance, and then it stopped and parked. Four doors opened and five people got out, a family of five with their dog.

There was some commotion as she stopped to sniff the new arrival. This gave their owners a chance to exchange a couple of words.

"Are you heading to Hyde Park, too?" asked the man.

"You too?" Michael Bale replied, in a surprised tone.

"Terrible thing, what happened in New York," the man said.

"Terrible, indeed," was all Cornelia could muster.

The man saw her choking up and took her in his arms. "It's OK, I'm sure the world will continue to walk down the path that Dr. Bale has paved," he said, oblivious to the fact that he was talking to the man's daughter.

They approached Hyde Park and, from a distance, they could see the traffic jam on Park Lane. Then, as they reached Park Lane, they saw scores of people coming from the direction of Hyde Park Corner tube station. Looking across the street, they could see lots of people already in the park. What was going on?

***

The TV media picked it up quickly. ITV News were the first to send a crew out to the park. After being stuck in traffic for 30 minutes, the van finally reached the park from the Marble Arch Side. It looked like thousands of people were crossing Bayswater road to enter the park.

Sensing that they were already too late, CNN sent in a chopper with Joanna Miller, CNN's reporter on call. As soon as she saw what was going on, she phoned her boss. Within minutes, Josh Cotton, the network's primary anchorman, was summoned to the main studio in Atlanta and the live feed began. It was almost 2pm in London.

***

At the basement of the nanotechnology building, three people waited patiently for the clock to hit 9am. When it did, the CNN feed from London flickered on to the screen.

"Approximately five hundred thousand people have taken to the streets to participate in a vigil for Dr. Richard Bale," said Cotton, seriously underestimating the figure. The image on the screen showed the true scale of the event. There were parts of Hyde Park that were as densely packed as you'd expect at a sold-out concert. But all around the park, you could see people converging towards the lake, where Sandy had met Bale less than a week ago.

"Can you believe this?" Cotton asked his guest, an astrologist who happened to be there in the studio for a scheduled New Year's segment. "Could the stars have predicted such a turnout?"

The astrologist fumbled a reply to this ridiculous question, trying to draw some loose connection to Bale's star sign, Aquarius, and his death on New Year's Day.

"Did we do this?" asked Sandy looking at the crowds gathering on TV.

"We certainly did," came the reply from Amir. "And now is the time to light this spark all around the world."

***

Stu Spencer was not sure why he had taken this woman in his car, or why after a long sleepless night he had decided to drive her to New York. He hated this city; it was too crowded for his taste. Even this morning, on New Year day, he could see thousands of people in the streets, curiously all walking in the direction of Central park.

They drove all the way up 6th avenue towards the park. The woman finally spoke, "This is where I get off," she said and he pulled over on the side. Before she got off, she made a move as if to kiss him on the cheek. Stu was tired, but single and attracted to this mysterious woman so he also moved towards her. He never saw the switchblade that slit his throat. As a nurse, he immediately knew he would be dead within the next minute or so. "Why" he tried to ask, but Cecilia Stein was long gone, lost in the crowds heading for the park.

***

"So, what's next?" asked Sandy.

"Well, we have to look at the time zones. And we need cities with large parks."

"In any city east of Delhi it will be too late, I think," said Sandy.

"Do you want to do this in Athens, too?" asked John.

"Why not?" she said. "The new park at the old airport site just opened, and it should be large enough to hold half the city."

***

As the news of the vigil in London spread, other hashtags began to spring up on Twitter. #NewYorkVigil, #SanFranciscoVigil, #ParisVigil. Every five minutes or so, a new city seemed to pop up in people's feeds.

New Yorkers started to flock towards Central Park as early as 10am. CNN switched their feed to New York for the 10am news, with a reporter on the ground asking people why they were attending the vigil.

"We have to make sure that our governments and the citizens continue in the direction set by Dr. Bale," said one respondent.

"I understand that people are emotional, and I know that 2023 has been a turning point in environmental history," said Cotton on CNN, "But can you remember any other occasion where so many people from around the world took to the streets united by a common cause?"

"No," came the firm reply from the distinguished historian who they had managed to patch in at a moment's notice. "I guess the closest to this we have seen were the anti-terrorist marches after the attacks in Paris."

"You might also remember the One Million Voices against Farc, the Colombian terrorist group. It was one of the first times that social media was used to spark mass protests across the world."

"But this today seems much bigger. What role do you think social media has played in this turnout?" asked Cotton.

"Well, I think that there are a number of factors in play here. Dr. Bale's popularity, the sad occasion of his death, the importance of his cause, and the fact that today is a public holiday everywhere. These are all contributing factors," the expert said, not knowing the main contributing factor.

John turned the volume down and said, "OK, on top of London we've got Athens, Paris, Madrid, Berlin, Rome, Dublin, Brussels, and Amsterdam. We have enough European capitals. Let's focus on the US now."

"That may be easier than we thought," said Sandy, looking at the first live pictures from Central Park.

"Well then, let's fuel these fires," came John's reply.

***

The pace was picking up. Cecilia was now back at the 3C and from atop the Metropolitan Tower, they could see Central Park already packed with people, while scores of others were on their way.

It was real, tangible proof that their project had indeed made an observable difference in the world. They had changed the course of history. People from around the world were now coming together to make sure that the legacy that they had begun would never subside.

People were celebrating the sudden change of course humanity had taken towards living in a more environmentally friendly way. These were Cecilia's people. Her drones. She had immense affection for them. Her life's goals were being realized, and there was no bigger testament to the gravity of what she had achieved than the huge gathering of people in Central Park on the first day of the year 2024. Little did she know that the stage was being set to end her project, not to celebrate it.

***

"Cognitive dissonance," whispered John, looking at the crowds, remembering what Sandy had said about the inherent human need to align behavior with beliefs.

"By changing their behavior, we influenced their beliefs," said Sandy, only now realizing herself just how far-reaching their initial impact had been.

***

The global news channels were now broadcasting live from several cities around the world. The vigils were taking place in more than 100 cities across the world, in Europe, Africa, North and South America. East Asia and Australia were asleep but would tune into the news in the early morning and impromptu vigils would no doubt be organized and gather pace in many key cities there, too.

Of course, it was impossible to explain why the death of one man had sparked this global gathering of millions of people. It was impossible to estimate the exact number who'd felt moved to leave their houses and show their respect for the man, and their continued commitment to his cause.

Politicians across the globe were paying close attention, and some scrambled to join the crowds so as to ensure they were seen and captured on camera. Whatever was their motivation or their own personal beliefs, it was clear that sustainability was creating a huge wave of public approval, and they were there to ride it.

**

Amir and John were sitting behind John's desk. The film editing software they had managed to download was not the most user-friendly, but it would do the job. After all, they did not need top quality to hide their message. The images on the screen were causing them distress; they wanted to get this done as quickly as possible.

**

At3:00 pm in London, conservative estimates put the attendance figure at approximately 2 million people in Hyde Park. It had been an astonishing day in Dr. Bale's hometown.

Of course, the attendance numbers were not entirely organic. Sandy had seen the vigil hashtag and she knew the idea was trending on social media. Left alone, a few thousand people would have shown up in Hyde Park. But she hadn't left it alone.

She knew that Transport for London was a huge client for Welit, and she knew that Amir had left some back doors open so as to hack into the system. She couldn't reprogram people without proper authorization from the 3C, but she could use a command from the decision clusters to draw people to environmental gatherings. As this command was generic, it allowed any member of the team to reprogram the drones, prompting them to attend a specific event.

Using this command, the universal Yiamas codes, and Amir's access to the lighting system used across all London transport, they were able to make sure that hundreds of thousands of people joined the vigil.

The rest was left up to the media. As people saw that the vigil was picking up pace, more and more made their way to Hyde Park. More fuel was added to the already raging fire, and millions dropped what they were doing and made the trip.

The vigil soon looked to be a historic moment, and even more people wanted to be part of it, so they abandoned their plans and began the pilgrimage. From a basement in Philadelphia, the team of three had been able to spark and fuel mass peaceful gatherings in hundreds of cities around the world. It was a celebration of what their technology could do. It was scary, but impressive. But now it was time to end it all.

She picked up the phone and made a call. "Penn Campus Police," came the answer from the other side.

CHAPTER SEVENTEEN

THE DISCHARGE

CNN got the clip first. It was a video of Bale's crumpled body lying on the pavement in New York. His legs were resting in an unnatural position, sort of behind the rest of his torso. His face, curiously, was mostly intact and had somehow rested looking upward. The video was taken from above, initially from a distance, and then zoomed in. It was clear it had been taken with a mobile phone, as it wasn't held steady for most of the duration.

But when it zoomed in, it was still for a couple of moments and you could clearly see that it was Dr. Bale, the man whom millions had mourned that day. Then, a man approached the body. The image shook but then returned to the body. The man leaned over Dr. Bale, seemingly recognizing him. Then he looked directly upwards, toward the mobile phone, the scar on his face clearly visible. On the original video, there had only been a few frames of Darko, but in the edit they had paused the frame so that his image would be visible for several seconds.

Once CNN had verified that the body shown was indeed that of Dr. Bale, Josh Cotton broke the normal program.

"We interrupt this program to bring you exclusive images of what seems to be the moment that sparked today's events. We caution you that some of these images are disturbing."

The video aired. Large parts of it had been blurred, but not the last few seconds when Darko's face came into view.

Other networks quickly picked up the video and ran with it. Within minutes, networks from all over the world were breaking their normal programming to show the moment that had sparked the most unusual of events.

***

Cecilia was pacing up and down 3C when the image playing on the 100-inch TV caught her eye. She had been hesitating to give the order, but now she knew that she could not wait any longer. Using a secure line via the internet, she made a phone call. "Do it," she told him and hung up.

***

Darko hung up and sat at the driver seat of his Tesla. He moved the car a few meters, onto the sidewalk on the lawn in front of the nanotechnology building.

***

It was a slow day for the University's Campus Police. All of the students and most of the faculty were away for the holidays. Most of the officers had also taken the day off.

Jack Stewart was on shift at the call center, watching the day's events unfold in front of him. There had been a huge march right here in Philadelphia, the city of brotherly love. It seemed like hundreds of thousands had skipped the first lunch of 2024 to go to Fairmount Park. Jack wished he could have joined them.

Then, his phone rang. The guy whose picture was now plastered all over TV had been spotted around the nanotechnology building.

He alerted the Philadelphia Police Department, and within five minutes, both PDs were approaching the building from different directions.

When they arrived, they were surprised to find a Tesla Model X parked right on the sidewalk, directly underneath the gravity-defying second-floor structure. It looked like someone had accidentally driven off the street and narrowly missed hitting the building. They proceeded with care towards the building and the car.

Then, the car bomb exploded, taking seven police officers with it.

***

Darko barely had the time to look up from his cell phone to see the blast. Hidden on an access ramp behind a brick wall next to the Moore Building of Engineering, some two blocks away, he and his companion narrowly escaped injury themselves as glass broke and debris flew all around them.

The blast blew all the glass panels from their frames. The glass itself did not break, but the entire façade tilted inwards. For a second, things went quiet. And then they heard it. An intense shrieking of metal as the materials holding the second-floor protruding rectangular cuboid folded like paper. At a painfully slow pace, this part of the building, which interestingly seemed largely intact, tilted to a curious angle and then dropped to the ground, right where the Tesla had stood just moments before.

The excruciating noise made by the collapsing metal as the building dropped to the ground was then drowned out by a sound like an 18-wheeler crashing into a wall, as the glass finally shattered.

***

John, Sandy and Amir were in John's office in the basement of the building when the bomb exploded. It was immediately clear to them that the structure of the building had suffered immense damage. But this was no ordinary basement. Built to block out even the most minor of vibrations in the middle of this large city, the entire basement formed its own independent concrete structure that had separate, deeper foundations. This meant that the force of the blast that had taken out the origami structure above, did not directly touch any part of the basement.

It wasn't that they didn't feel the blast. And they certainly heard it. They also heard the glass part of the building collapsing above their heads. But it was like they were in a capsule that protected them from the force of the destruction going on above them.

"Jesus, what have they done?" asked John, now seriously terrified.

"We need to get out of here. Now!" Amir shouted, but he remained still, frozen, not sure which way to go.

"Out there, we're dead," said Sandy, who was the only one thinking straight. "They will come in, they have to. Here we have the home field advantage, right, John?"

"Er, yes, I guess we do. But they have guns. We have nothing."

Suddenly, there was another loud noise and a cloud of dust entered the basement.

"Quick, get to the clean room," said John and he rushed down the corridor, fighting off dust as he went.

He opened a double door and stepped into the small foyer, surrounded by the giant air vents. Sandy and Amir followed. The humming sound started, and they felt themselves being pulled from all directions as bits of dust were removed from their bodies before they entered the clean room."

***

Darko and Ayman had reached the building, climbed through the rubble, and found the steps to the basement.

Debris had covered the first several steps, and they stopped at a double door blocking their way. Darko looked up and saw that part of the concrete ceiling above them had collapsed directly onto these stairs. Mindful that even more of the building could fall onto their heads, Darko and Ayman stepped on a large concrete block as they were trying to make their way down to the double door.

But the block tilted with their weight and skidded all the way towards the door, smashing it open and sending clouds of dust in the air. Ayman and Darko held on, and virtually surfed their way into the basement. The last thing they heard before they smashed to the floor and opposite wall was someone further in saying something about a "clean room."

***

They entered the clean room and Sandy was struck by the weird-looking machines. Nickel was apparently the material of choice inside the clean room and everything was super shiny.

Out of habit, John pulled on a lab coat and a surgical face mask. Sandy and Amir followed suit, not entirely sure why. They felt their ears pop as the air pressure inside the room rose to keep dust particles out.

They heard a noise from outside but the clean room was now in lockdown. So, when they saw Darko's face behind the small round window on the door they had just entered through, they weren't overly concerned. He couldn't get in.

***

Through the small round window in the door, Darko and then Ayman looked inside the clean room. Ayman saw weird machinery and people with masks and lab coats. Ayman was not particularly educated. He was street smart, and had seen a couple of movies. But he didn't know what nanotechnology was, nor did he know that this was a nanotechnology lab.

What he saw looked to him perhaps like a chemical lab. Surely some kind of sinister chemical weapon was being manufactured here. Ayman was a veteran of the Syrian war and had witnessed first-hand the effects of chemical weaponry.

Then, the air vents started humming, and as the noise grew louder, so did his panic. He was being sprayed, he was sure of it. So, the man who'd had no reservations about helping to blow up a building in the middle of Philadelphia, nor rushing into the same half-demolished building, nor climbing over debris in a murderous quest to find three people he had never met, was thrown into a state of panic by a sound not much louder than or different from that of a kitchen hood.

Without warning, he bailed. He turned and ran back down the corridor and climbed over the cement block that he had ridden into the basement just moments ago. He climbed upwards and reached the staircase, which was by now seriously damaged. As he made his way through the double doors, he felt the ground shake below. The staircase collapsed, and he went into freefall.

The drop was significant; it wasn't just the first basement that was underneath this part of the staircase. Directly underneath him was the staircase leading to a second basement. The impact itself was loud and painful, but it didn't kill him. For the second time in just a few minutes, he found himself on a concrete block, skidding down a staircase. Only, this time, he wasn't so lucky. As the block rapidly slid towards the bottom of the stairs, he lost his balance and fell forward. A small scream was all he could manage before he was crushed against the wall.

***

Darko was furious. He was all alone in a strange setting, once again locked out from where he needed to be. He tried various switches on the wall to unlock the door. He looked inside and saw Sandy, Amir and John, the three people who had earlier made sure he would never be able to show his face in public again.

A siege was not possible; rescue crews were surely just minutes away. Not really expecting it to work, he pulled out his handgun. He knew there were only three bullets left. Damn, Ayman had left with the ammunition.

Not knowing what else to do, he pointed the gun at the glass window on the door and fired once at point-blank range. The glass cracked but didn't break. *This is promising.* He fired again.

The clean room had been constructed by Allied Mechanics Inc., a boutique manufacturer who hadn't thought to use bulletproof material on the door. The second bullet hit at the exact same point as the first. A split second later, the glass gave in. Or rather, it gave out.

Rather than flying inwards, the glass exploded outwards. The air sudden difference in air pressure sent the glass flying towards Darko's face. And he was too close to react.

Darko knew what it meant to be stabbed in the face. He had endured Serbian torture during the former Yugoslavian war, and his facial scar had been caused by a burning steel knife slicing through his face like butter. His only crime back then was being a Muslim at the hands of Christians.

But the pain he felt now was even more excruciating. Literally, hundreds of small pieces of glass flew directly into his face and pierced his skin, eyes, lips, neck...

He took a fumbling step back, blinded, then knelt on the ground and fell forward, his face in his hands, his elbows hitting the ground.

***

Sandy watched in horror as the glass broke the last barrier between them and Darko. But then she heard the scream and knew that he had been seriously hurt. She had never heard Darko scream.

She knew that this was their chance. She rushed towards the door, fumbled with the switches and opened it before John and Amir could react.

John was the first to follow her as she left the clean room. Amir stood, frozen, for a fatal extra second. By the time he reached the door, Darko, still kneeling, had managed to pull his head up and had his gun in his hands. Amir made a snap decision to make a run for it, but Darko, who was partially regaining his eyesight, was well trained. He lifted his gun and fired a single shot.

The last bullet smashed Amir's ankle, and he fell head first to the ground.

John heard the shot and looked back. He saw Amir on the ground and Darko crawling towards him, a murderous look on his scarred face. John had had enough of Darko. He picked up a fire extinguisher that was lying on the floor next to him, and in a rapid movement, he crashed it over Darko's head, finishing him off.

John then turned to Amir, trying to help him up, but he was in too much pain.

"You have to get out of here," said Amir.

"No way am I leaving you behind," John replied.

"There's no time, I'll be OK."

"No, you won't, not if Cecilia has anything to do with it."

"Go, man, you have to get out of here. You have to stay free to stop her."

"Let's go, John," said Sandy, who was a few feet farther on, and thinking more clearly. They needed to get out of there before the emergency crews arrived.

John looked at her, torn. He didn't want to leave his friend behind.

He looked back to Amir, who whispered, "Go."

Reluctantly, he got up and turned to leave. Then he heard Amir speak again. Hoping he'd changed his mind, he knelt back beside him. But what Amir told him then surprised him.

With fewer regrets now, he got up, took Sandy's hand, and together they made their way through the rubble, looking for a way out of the building.

***

The most watched video clip of all time was the United Airlines Flight 175 crashing into the South Tower of the World Trade Center on September 11, 2001. It was shown for days, again and again, on literally every TV station in the world.

Several stations caught the event from different angles. When the first plane hit the North Tower, they pointed their cameras at the burning building in time to capture the second plane crashing into the South Tower. If Osama Bin Laden had planned this, it was a stroke of genius. The images shocked the world.

The first impact on the North Tower, however, was caught on tape entirely by luck, if "luck" was the right word. Jules Clément Naudet and Thomas Gédéon Naudet happened to be filming a documentary on firefighters checking for gas leaks north of the WTC. Their camera operator was filming when the plane flew over and instinctively swung the camera toward the impact. You might expect that the crash would inevitably be captured on film in the city that never sleeps, but had the Naudet brothers not been shooting on location that Tuesday morning, the world would never have seen the first crash. Just like it never saw the third plane crash into the Pentagon.

In the months and years that followed 9/11, several networks opted to keep cameras continuously filming the skylines of most major US cities. If any terrorist managed to get through the newly established strict security checks, and then managed to break into the locked cockpit of a Boeing 767 to hijack it and fly it into a skyscraper, the networks would at least have the images to run.

Of course, more than 20 years had gone by and no such event had ever occurred again. Most stations were subject to cost-cutting drives and reluctantly took down the cameras. But not WCAU, the NBC affiliate in Philadelphia. Through some clever negotiating with the University of Pennsylvania, WCAU agreed to support the University's renowned Annenberg School for Communication and, in exchange, the school allowed the station to keep a camera rolling atop Hamilton College House for free, the student dormitory where Sandy had lived for a year, also known as High Rise North.

From the twenty-fourth floor of the building, the camera had unobstructed views of Philadelphia, the two Liberty Places, the Comcast Building and the newer W Hotel. Hamilton House was close enough to get some awesome footage, if such an occasion arose, but far enough away to survive any fallout. So, even if a small nuke was detonated at the landmark City Hall, the camera would be able to capture the resulting mushroom cloud without suffering any damage. Or so thought Jason Smiles, the guy who'd set up the camera all those years ago, and who was still employed at WCAU.

The nanotechnology building was about halfway between the camera and the high-rise center of Philadelphia. And directly in the camera's line of sight. What Jason had envisaged all these years ago had finally occurred. He had the tape that no one else had.

***

Cecilia was in the dark. The last time she'd spoken to Darko had been when she informed him about the video clip of him standing over Bale's dead body. He had not called since. His phone was dead.

Wayne was worried too. It was clear that the team had broken apart. This was the type of random event that he'd been worried about, though he hadn't expected to be so close to home. Cecilia had told him about the exchange she'd had with Sandy, John and Amir at Angelo's place. While Wayne could understand why they were furious with Cecilia, for him, the end justified the means. He was pushing 60, and there would be no third chance for him to make a difference. Cecilia had pulled him out of a life of luxury and complacency, and enabled him to make a difference in the world. His loyalty to her was unconditional.

As for Frank, he would never trade the position he was in now for anything in the world. He wasn't after fame. He was there to prove to himself that he was superior to others. And he was, no doubt about it. The child prodigy who'd hacked into Google at the age of 14 was now the world's first hacker of the human brain. No one would ever find out, but that didn't matter for Frank.

***

Something caught Frank's eye on the big screen in the 3C. An explosion. Cool. Then he read the banner underneath the image: "Explosion in West Philadelphia." Instantly, he knew where it was. He drew Cecilia's and Wayne's attention to it.

The video footage showed the nanotechnology building. All three of them had been there, and instantly, they recognized the origami structure. A car drove onto the sidewalk and stopped directly beneath it. The footage had been taken from a significant distance so, while you could make out a man getting out of the car and walking, you couldn't see his face, let alone his scar. But they knew who he was.

Then the police approached and, as they got closer to the car, it exploded, sending debris and smoke all over the place. A couple of seconds passed, the smoke cleared a little, and they watched the glass structure collapse into the ground where the car had been.

"Fucking hell," said Wayne quietly, as he watched the school he'd supported with millions of dollars via Uniocom being reduced to rubble.

"Do you think they're dead?" asked Frank, after a few seconds.

Before anyone could respond, the footage showed two men climbing through the rubble and into the building. Then things went quiet for a few minutes. No one spoke. They froze in front of the screen, waiting to see what would happen next.

Then, there they were. For a couple of seconds, if that, you could just make out two people climbing out of the building. Even at this distance, you could see that they were holding hands. Even at this distance, you could see the waving blonde hair.

N.Z. KOMNINOS

CHAPTER EIGHTEEN

THE EXODUS

It was soon known who the couple exiting the building had been. John had used his fingerprint to gain access to the building. Then pictures secretly released by Cecilia and Wayne were plastered all over the newspapers and online media outlets of every country in the world. It was only a matter of time before someone saw them.

Frank furiously tried to locate them. He hacked into mobile operators to locate their phones and into credit card exchanges to see if any of their cards had been used and where. After all, it was 2024 - no one used cash anymore.

And he had a billion resources at his disposal, so to speak. But right now, he only needed the five million in the greater Philadelphia area. So, he hacked into the streets' LiFi system and reprogrammed all drones to visit www.FindJohnandSandy.com and offer any information they had. A reward was also offered. Neither Frank nor Cecilia wanted John and Sandy to fall into the hands of the police or the FBI, if they could help it.

But very few people visited the website. Frank extended the reprogramming to first the rest of the East Coast and then the rest of the continental USA. But still, nothing happened. There was a bug somewhere in the code; he just had to find it.

One night, he was looking at the screen, trying to make sense of it all, when it dawned on him.

"Shit. No!" he said loudly, catching the attention of Wayne and Cecilia, who were having a quiet conversation by the window. They approached him, apprehensive.

On his screen was the footage of Darko over Bale's dead body. Frank was furiously keying in commands on his workstation. Then, the picture of Darko broke apart on the screen.

"There is a hidden message in this video," said Frank quietly.

"A hidden message... saying what?" asked Wayne.

"It's not saying anything, Wayne. It's doing something."

For a moment there was silence.

"No! No, no, no!" was Cecilia's reaction. It was more like a cry of agony, like that of a mother who had just watched her children die.

***

More than a week had passed since they had realized what Sandy had done. She, John and Amir had hidden a de-droning sequence within the Bale-Darko video clip. When it was shown via an LED screen of any kind, it acted like the portable de-droner that they'd used on New Year's Eve at 3C.

Millions, perhaps billions of people, drones, had watched the video. The Philadelphia explosion actually increased the virality of the video clip. Darko himself had been discovered, dead in the basement of the nanotechnology building, with Amir next to him, in critical condition.

Darko's fingerprints were found at the Salisbury Hotel suite, and the broken door supported the popular theory that it had been Darko who'd pushed Bale out of the window. Then, it became known that the same man who was responsible for Bale's death had planted the bomb in Philadelphia, apparently trying to kill an Israeli businessman.

So, the video clip of Darko standing over Bale's dead body became a central part of the developing narrative forming around Bale's death and the Philadelphia bombing. It meant that the video spread like wildfire as it was the top media story all around the world. While conspiracy theories were abundant, the FBI would ultimately conclude that Darko and Ayman were radical Islamic terrorists working alone.

As for John and Sandy, their whereabouts remained a mystery. No one had seen them since that day. They hadn't left the country. They hadn't used their credit cards. They weren't carrying their phones. It was driving Cecilia crazy that they had somehow escaped, after tearing her entire project to pieces.

***

The captain's cabin was not luxurious. Indeed, nothing on this ship was. For this ship wasn't built for luxury. It was built to transport oil around the world.

John woke up, left Sandy in the cabin, and made his way to the small exercise room. A treadmill, a cycling machine, and a couple of weights were the only equipment there. They would make do with what they had.

It had only taken Sandy one call from a payphone to her childhood benefactor, Nelly Roussakis. They were lucky. One of the shipping company's tankers had been docked in Philadelphia port that day. They met Captain Michalis, who gracefully surrendered his cabin to his boss's friends.

Sandy woke up and, as she did most mornings, she went up to the bridge. She loved being up here, crossing the Atlantic on this huge vessel. The irony that fossil fuel had saved her life did not escape her.

She was more relaxed now. She believed that Cecilia had lost track of them. Through satellite TV, they knew that there were no clues as to their whereabouts. They also knew that millions – probably billions – of people had seen the hidden message. They hadn't de-droned the entire population of drones. It couldn't be done. Not all people watched TV, and even for those that did, not all of them watch it through LED screens. But it would be next to impossible for Cecilia to identify, locate, and organize the remaining drones.

It had taken Sandy just 24 hours from uncovering Cecilia's ultimate plan to finding and implementing a way to stop her cold in her tracks. She was now safe, out of sight, and with all the time in the world to make sure that Cecilia was stopped, for good this time. Sandy knew in her heart that she would never have agreed to give so much power to one person. Not even Jesus Christ had that much power, and she didn't believe in Him either.

During these past few days, cruising the vast, deep sea, Sandy had had the chance to reflect on what had happened. And for her, it all came down to this: had she given the authorization for the virus to be released under the influence of the Microbees programming, or had she been swayed by Cecilia's – and Bale's – arguments? Had she made this decision out of her own free will, or had she been forced to take it? She was convinced that it was the latter. But she needed proof. She needed to see those logs. She knew that her confrontations with Cecilia Stein were not over.

As for the planet, Sandy was sad, but hopeful. While their project had come to an abrupt stop, they had managed to light a spark. The protection of the environment had taken center stage in the minds of a billion and a half people, and they had collectively changed their daily activities to help save mother Earth. Sandy was confident that they wouldn't return to old habits now that the influence of the Microbees had been neutralized.

For a few months after being de-droned, possibly longer, Kathy, Liz and Maya had continued their lives as environmentally conscious and responsible individuals, and so would the rest of the world, Sandy hoped. Perhaps Time Magazine would be proven right. Bale was indeed the man who had lit the spark. Perhaps, a single spark was all that the world had ever needed.

As she stared out at the horizon on this bright sunny day, Sandy was hopeful and proud that their project had put humanity on the right track. And she was thankful that they had stopped before Cecilia had doomed them all.

***

It was dark in 3C now. Only Frank's screen was on. On the screen was a symbol that Frank used as a signature when he hacked into other systems. It was the mask famously used by Anonymous hackers.

Also on the screen was a loading bar. It was at 43% and moving at a painfully slow pace. "224 minutes remaining." Above the bar read, "Decrypting: Microbees 2.0."

***

THE END

ACKNOWLEDGMENTS

I would like to gratefully acknowledge Abigail Willford for helping me correct and improve this novel as well as the readers of the early drafts which include my brother Dimitris Komninos and my lifelong friends, Francesco Benincasa, Alex Haidas, Onic Palandjian, and Stephanos Velissaropoulos.

This novel would not have been made possible had it not been for the support of my wife Niki and my daughters Ellie and Marina who gave me the time and space I needed to develop my creative spark.

Finally, a big thanks to all the readers, especially to those who took the time to provide feedback. If you have not yet done so, please return to the platform where you purchased the book and submit your review. Cecilia Stein et al will be back and your feedback is the (carbon-free) fuel I need to keep going.

Cover Design by Odysseas Kontis
Cover Photo by Nathan Dumlao

Want to keep up with the latest environmental news? Join our cause: www.SingleSpark.org

ABOUT THE AUTHOR

For over 2 decades, Nicholas Z. Komninos has been involved with the management of high-tech companies. He has lived, worked and studied in the US and in the UK and has traveled to over 30 countries in all 5 continents. Educated in computer science, psychology and business administration, Mr. Komninos is inspired but also deeply concerned about the application of emerging technologies and artificial intelligence in regards to the changes they will bring to our and the future generations' lives. He regularly speaks at conferences and events about these topics, notably, at TEDx Athens in 2017. In the middle of the previous decade, he decided to express his worries via a series of near-future thrillers. Single Spark is the first novel of the series.